AF369714

Have you noticed the enigmatic green light?

That shone without any apparent reason in sight

During your last trip to Rainbow Land, so wondrous and bright

As summer faded into winter's chilly night.

Have you seen the stranger dressed so conspicuously?

Appearing in a flash of light so mysteriously

Beware, for the paradise of parrots is now in jeopardy

A precious gem is stolen, and the culprit must be caught quickly.

Have you counted the number of rainbows in the sky?

A dwindling sight that makes the Rainbow Land's future lie

In your hands, the survival of this magical place does rely

For time is running out, and it's up to you to try.

Have you noticed the armed men in the National Park?

Their drills threaten to tear the mountain apart

A riddle that, if solved, could pierce the Rainbow Land's heart

Save the rainbow world by winning this chase -

And with it also the future of the parrots race!

NORTHERN LIGHTS IN RAINBOW LAND

A Swedish winter fairy tale

Table of Contents

This work is a product of the imagination. Names, characters, places, and actions are either the product of imagination or used fictitiously. All similarities to actual persons, living or dead, as well as business establishments, events, places, or names, are entirely coincidental.

@ COPYRIGHT 2020 BY (ANDREAS ADAM)

FIRST EDITION 2023

1

HIGH IN THE FAR NORTH

It was chilly, and the morning sun had transformed the color of the cloudless sky from a reddish-orange to a soft, light blue. This was Abisko National Park, a vast wilderness spanning two hundred kilometers north of the Arctic Circle. The park was known for its spectacular Northern Lights displays, snow-capped mountains, and crystal-clear lakes. Its serene beauty was enhanced by the abundant wildlife that called it home, including wolves, reindeer, and arctic foxes. The air was crisp, and the landscape was blanketed in a thick layer of snow, creating a winter wonderland.

A dog sled had pulled up in a clearing sheltered from the wind in the park. It was the end of February, the beginning of the children's sport vacation or "sportlov" as it was called in Sweden. Two adults and two teenage girls disembarked from the dog sled and began unpacking their equipment. They had come well-prepared with warm clothing, sleeping bags, and two tents in which they would be spending the night. Sleeping in tents in the wilderness would be an adventure, but the parents hadn't planned much more than that.

Lara and Nina, the two girls, were quickly bored with the prospect of just camping. They liked to be active in their leisure time, horse riding and skiing. What the two needed could be summed up in one word: action. If they were to keep up with their friends at school, then they would need a story to tell.

"Mom," Lara wheedled, "I was the best at map-reading when I was in the Girl Scouts. You know I can handle an independent trek!"

The girls' parents eyed each other as if they were having a wordless exchange.

"Pleeease!" Nina joined in, choosing to address her father instead.

He chewed on his bottom lip. "I guess the risks are minimal… and Lara is a good map reader." He eyed the girls' mother in another silent conversation.

Lara and Nina knew it was their mom who would have the last word on the matter.

"Okay, okay!" The girl's mother laughed. "But you have to be careful. Look out for each other."

"We will," Lara said, but she could hardly be heard over Nina's squeal of excitement.

The girls began preparing for their adventure, and soon, they were ready. Lara grinned with excitement as she rushed over with a heavy backpack and carefully lifted it into the dog sled lined with reindeer fur. As she was the eldest, she had decided to drive the dog sled first. Nina had already made herself comfortable and was wrapped in a thick blanket to protect her from the bone-chilling cold. To ensure they were prepared for any unforeseen events, they had packed extra food.

Once Lara was standing on the back of the runners, the dogs started barking with excitement. She gave the command, and they surged forward. At first, steering the sled required intense concentration, but Lara soon drove the dogs with ease. Certain manoeuvres still required her full attention, though, like taking turns and avoiding trees and rocks.

The snow-white dogs harnessed to the front of sled obeyed her every command while barking loudly. Out here in the great outdoors, they were in their element. Lara and Nina were filled with joy, laughing and shrieking merrily, completely forgetting the cold and the solitude. Their destination was the highest ridge in the national park, located a few kilometres northwest of where they had arrived that morning.

Lara kept looking at the map, where she had marked the ridge and their camp with thick pencil crosses. By constantly checking her position and immediately making course corrections, she hoped to reach her destination as quickly as possible. As they traveled further into the wilderness, the scenery around them changed, and they saw snow-capped mountains in the distance. The journey was thrilling, and they felt like they were the only two people in the world.

They had only a few hours of daylight to admire the landscape. The days here were naturally brief at this time of year, the park being located so far north of the Arctic Circle. Furthermore, they planned to be back at the camp before sunset, knowing how dangerous the darkness could be in this wilderness.

For orientation, daylight played a major role. A smartphone was useless for navigating the Swedish wilderness since it could only receive GPS signals in a few places in the park. Therefore, a good map and compass were essential when planning excursions in the national park. Though Lara knew the area from a several-day hike she had taken earlier, she now had problems finding her way around just by looking at the landscape. She had traveled here in the summer months; in winter, the landscape looked completely different. The branches of the trees, when the wind hit them, made creaking sounds under the heavy snow loads they carried. Countless snow crystals refracted the light of the winter sun and sparkled like tiny diamonds.

The icy, driving wind whipped the girls non-stop in the face, but instead of pulling the hoods of their winter jackets further over their faces, they left them in place. The winter landscape surrounding them was too beautiful for them to want to restrict their view of it in any way.

In the early afternoon, the silhouette of an enormous elevation appeared in the distance. It's about time!" Exclaimed Nina with relief.

"Yes!" Nodded Lara. "To be honest, I had started to worry about whether we had gotten lost after all."

Lara extended her arm toward the mountain and pointed to a specific spot with her index finger. "Right there is the white castle," she said with a strange tone in her voice.

"Where? I don't see anything," Nina said, rubbing her eyes.

"Well, I don't see it either," Lara returned. "I can only locate it with the help of the unusually-formed mountaintop over there. That's how I know the castle is there."

"Yeah?" Nina said, intrigued.

"You can't spot the white castle with the naked eye from this distance for a good reason," Lara began to explain, her eyes fixed on a distant mountain peak. "It was built from the rock of the mountain surrounding it for security reasons - namely, to camouflage it from enemies."

Lara had taken a small pair of binoculars out of her backpack as she was speaking to Nina. She peered through them at the mountainside.

"That's crazy!" She exclaimed in amazement. "Even with binoculars, the castle remains hidden - at least at this time of year. The snow must have blurred the last visible distinction between the old masonry and the mountainside."

Lara's explanation made sense, but what the girls didn't know was that even if they had been standing directly before the castle, they still would not have seen it, for all that remained was a little of the outer wall. The once-impressive building had not existed for a long time. In the Middle Ages, it had been burned to the ground by a fire that quickly spread to every room.

Lara and Nina had witnessed the fire before they fled with a witch named Anna to another era. Therefore, they had not witnessed the fire's outcome. Time travel had its fair share of confusion. For Lara, the thought of the white castle now awakened even more memories. She had been there about two years ago with Pinky, a pink parrot, and had gone on numerous, sometimes dicey adventures. They had traveled back to the deep Middle Ages, where they had met, among others, a creepy clock monk. Thinking about the encounter gave her goosebumps. The monk had been so spooky. He had played a dangerous game with them. Luckily, they had swung things in their favor and triumphed over him.

When they came within 50 paces of the mountain massif that dominated the landscape of Abisko National Park, Lara abruptly stopped the dog sled. There had been quite a bit of fresh snow in the last few days.

The sun had barely risen, casting a pale, icy glow over the snow-covered landscape. The air was crisp and biting, and the ground crunched underfoot as Lara and Nina stepped off the dog sled.

They could feel the cold seeping through their clothing, nipping at their cheeks and noses. The peaceful serenity of the moment was broken only by a soft rustling that added a haunting melody to the serene beauty of the winter wonderland.

With a practiced hand, Lara reached into a side pocket of her backpack and pulled out a handful of treats. The dogs eagerly barked and jumped as she tossed the treats to them. Their wagging tails and excited whimpers overtook the quiet of the wilderness. The Huskies quickly gobbled up the treats and then quenched their thirst by greedily devouring the nearby snow.

Excitement bubbled in Lara's chest as she looked up at the towering mountain peak they had approached.

Its snow-capped slopes beckoned, promising a breath-taking view from the summit. Nina's camera hung around her neck, ready to capture the wonders of nature they were about to witness.

Lara quickly lifted her heavy backpack, feeling the weight on her shoulders as she prepared for the adventure ahead. She tightened the straps and adjusted her hat, making sure to shield herself from the cold wind. Nina wrapped herself in a thick blanket, her face flushed with anticipation.

Finally, they began the ascent, but they had only taken a few steps forward before they stopped in their tracks, gazing in awe at the massive structure before them. The air was nearly still, and the only sound was the occasional barking of the sled dogs. The experience was surreal, as if they were standing in a world of their own.

As they looked up at the towering peak, they couldn't help but feel small and insignificant by comparison. The mountain's sheer size and beauty filled them with a sense of wonder and humility. The snow-covered slopes rose steeply upward, with jagged ridges and craggy outcroppings stretching into the sky.

"If we climb up the slope a bit more, I'm sure we'll have a terrific view," Lara said, pointing to a large rocky outcrop a reasonable distance above them.

Before Nina could say anything in reply, Lara continued her thought: "From up there, you could shoot some amazing pictures for the photo contest. What do you think?"

Nina's eyes shone. Lara had hit the bull's eye with her remarks.

The previous summer, Nina had stumbled upon photography almost by accident. Despite her initial lack of experience, she quickly developed a natural talent for it, capturing stunning images that left others in awe.

Nina dreamed of one day becoming a famous photographer, and from that moment onwards, she began to carry her camera with her everywhere she went, determined to seize every opportunity to learn and perfect her craft. She spent countless hours honing her skills, studying light and composition, and experimenting with different techniques.

Through hard work and dedication, Nina's talent grew, and she created a website to showcase her work to a wider audience, sharing her passion for photography with the world.

In addition to the joy she gained from photography, Nina also earned some pocket money by selling her photographs. People were drawn to the beauty and emotion captured in her images, and many were eager to purchase them as gifts or to adorn their homes.

Nina had subscribed to a photography magazine the week before, eager to enter a photo contest with "unique nature photos" as its theme. The grand prize was a set of professional camera equipment, which Nina believed would help her take even better pictures. Winning the competition would also attract many curious visitors to her homepage.

However, with the deadline fast approaching, Nina had been struggling to find the perfect subject for her photo. Despite her efforts, she couldn't seem to capture a unique and breath-taking image that would impress the judges. Her frustration had been mounting in recent days, causing her mood to deteriorate.

Lara had been observing her sister's distress and finally thought she had the perfect solution.

"Let's try it!" Nina shouted with enthusiasm and hurried to the backpack they had left behind in the husky sled.

Nina strapped on her heavy backpack and returned quickly to Lara in a less-than-good mood. "Did you pack stones in this backpack?" She complained but didn't wait for an answer as she began the ascent.

The girls made slower progress than they had expected because they had to mind their steps. Numerous depressions in the ground opened into tiny crevices that cut deep into the mountain's interior. A thin layer of ice covered the rocky soil in places, making it slippery; it would be easy to slip or sprain an ankle.

Finally, the two girls reached the spot Lara had indicated, gasping for breath. Nina was relieved to put down the backpack. *Finally.*

"Whew! I can't carry this pack anymore. You're welcome to carry it down again," Nina said, her face red with exertion.

But Lara wasn't listening. All her attention was focused on the breath-taking view. Though the Northern Lights weren't visible in the sky right now, the view was far from disappointing. The natural world here in the far north of Sweden was so beautiful that she had had goosebumps since they arrived with their parents. Nina opened a zipper on the side of her backpack and removed the camera she had stowed there that morning. She started taking pictures.

Lara watched her sister and smiled. She knew from experience that when Nina was busy taking pictures, she forgot everything around her.

"Mum and Dad will be so amazed at the pictures that they will regret not coming with us on this trek!" Lara said with satisfaction.

A little later, Lara noticed the sky turning increasingly red in the distance. All of a sudden, her happiness disappeared, and a bad feeling crept into the pit of her stomach. She hurriedly bent down to the backpack, rummaged in the main compartment with one hand, and finally found what she wanted.

"How can it be so late already?" She said in horror as she looked at her rainbow clock. Time had passed faster than they had expected.

They had to make their way back to the camp as quickly as possible so as not to upset their parents because they had promised to be back by nightfall. Now Lara knew why. Darkness would make it more difficult to get their bearings.

"Hurry up! We're already late. In less than an hour, it'll be dark,"

Lara called out as she checked the time on her rainbow clock again. She reached out to show it to her sister, too, but misjudged her step and slipped on a stone covered by a thin layer of ice.

She righted herself quickly but noticed the clock was gone. She bent to pick it up but couldn't find it anywhere. It had disappeared from the face of the earth! Lara had a bad gut feeling, as she thought she knew what had happened to it.

"Oh! No! The clock must have fallen into a crevice," she whined.

Nina, who had just put her camera back in her backpack, joined her sister in combing the ground for the rainbow clock.

The clock had been a thank-you gift for saving the home of the rainbow parrots. But the clock was much more than a mere souvenir; it also had a practical use. It was the only way to travel to the magical land at the end of the rainbow and back again… and, with it, they were also able to travel through time, as crazy as that might sound to the uninitiated. It had originally been invented by an eerie monk centuries ago. With its help, he had tried to forever disrupt the home of the rainbow parrots, a parallel world that peacefully co-existed with the world of humans. But Lara and Nina had helped the rainbow parrots save their land. As a sign of thankfulness, they gifted them with this special clock. Without it, they could no longer visit their feathered friends. That would be a tragedy!

Lara unpacked her headlamps and passed one of them to Nina. With them, they were able to search the rocky ground much better. The light let them peer into the notches and crevices but wouldn't let them look deep enough to find the clock. Frustration set in, and Lara felt a sinking feeling in her stomach. It was like searching for a needle in a haystack.

"What are we going to do?" She said desperately.

"I'm afraid I don't know," Nina replied, shrugging her shoulders. "But I do know that we need to get back to camp as soon as possible."

Nina was right. If they didn't keep their promise to their parents, then it would be over for future trips of this kind. And they would need to repeat this trip if they were to locate the clock.

Nina was about to start her descent when Lara called out of the blue:

"Ha, why didn't I think of that in the first place?"

Nina stopped and turned to her questioningly.

"What?"

"I get so few opportunities to practice witchcraft in the human world, I almost forget I can do it," Lara explained her flash of inspiration. "I'll just use my levitation spell - which has gotten us out of trouble a few times. With that, I can levitate the clock back up. "

"Well, let's go!" Nina prompted her.

"Wait a minute. I need to think about how that one went," Lara replied. She hadn't used the levitation spell in a very long time.

Lara paused to gather her thoughts before finally spreading her arms and reciting the spell. She and Nina waited anxiously, but when nothing happened, she repeated the formula, this time a little louder. However, her rainbow clock still did not appear.

"Oh! No! Everything is going wrong today. Not only have I lost my clock, but I've also forgotten how to do witchcraft," Lara said sadly, letting out a loud sigh.

"That's nonsense. Maybe the clock is just stuck somewhere and can't float up to us," Nina tried to reassure her sister. Unbeknownst to her, she was not wrong.

"Do you think so?" Lara asked doubtfully.

"Yes! Let's just come back here again tomorrow," Nina suggested. "By then, I'm sure we'll have thought of another way to track down your clock."

Then, they both made their way down the mountainside with giant steps. Nina almost stumbled once but managed to regain her balance. Finally, they reached the dog sled, where the huskies were already waiting for them, barking in anticipation.

It didn't take much time to get dark.

If the girls hadn't been in such a hurry, they might have looked around again and noticed a strange, greenish, pulsating light emerging from one of the numerous apertures in the mountain, continuing unimpeded on its way to the sky, where it merged into the Northern Lights - but they didn't.

This time, it was Nina's turn to steer, and Lara took the same place as Nina on the way there. Soon, she was leading the sled just as well as her sister had done before.

They were late, but when they told their already worried parents that they had gotten a bit lost on the way back, they overlooked their children's tardiness.

Their parents had already set up two tents just a few meters apart. The girls' mom had piled up wood to make a fire while their dad had procured food. He already smelled of fish and herbs.

The tents were made of a special material, developed specifically for the cold temperatures prevailing in this area. Thus, the tents were well insulated and protected against the cold and wind.

However, it couldn't get windy here because the campground was surrounded by trees and bushes, providing ample protection.

Soon, they were sitting comfortably together on chairs, warming themselves by the crackling campfire while eating dinner. However, they couldn't see the many stars in the night sky or the intensely shining Northern Lights because of cloud cover.

Lara's mood was at rock bottom, but she didn't say a word to her parents about what had happened on the trip. There was no point anyway. Her parents knew nothing of the fantastic adventures she and Nina had undertaken with the aid of the rainbow clock.

They had to promise the rainbow parrots that they would never tell anyone about their magical homeland. For this land was only safe if it remained a secret, at least, that was the belief of Paraiso, the leader of the colorful bird race. Nevertheless, this magical world had almost come to its end once before.

Their parents did not suspect anything. Due to the weak light of the campfire, the expressions on their daughters' faces remained hidden to them. They attributed their daughters' taciturnity entirely to the strenuous day's excursion, which must have made them tired. They were yawning loudly, after all.

"You'll sleep like marmots today, I'm sure," the girls' father said, grinning.

"Let's hope so!" Lara replied, thinking of the many nocturnal animals that would make noise during the night.

"Yes, and let's also hope we won't freeze in our sleeping bags!" Added Nina.

After dinner, they wanted to observe the Northern Lights. But the heavy clouds prevented it.

"What a pity!" The girls said.

"Too bad!" Lara said, glancing at Nina. "We would have loved to see the Northern Lights. Maybe tomorrow night will work!"

"But then we'd have to add another night to our stay," her dad objected. "Besides, there's no saying we'll have more success tomorrow."

"Maybe," Nina now interjected as well. "But, according to the Northern Lights forecast that I have on my phone app, there's supposed to be a lot of activity tomorrow night."

"Oh, do you really have reception out here?" Her mother wondered.

"No, but I looked at the Northern Lights forecast for the coming days when we were at the hotel," Nina explained.

That was true, but Nina didn't remember if it wouldn't be cloudy the following day as well. But that wasn't what was on her mind. All she knew was that she and Lara needed another day to search for the rainbow clock.

"I guess there's nothing wrong with spending another night here," the girls' mother replied. "What do you think?"

"I think we'll get a good night's sleep," their father returned, glancing at his wristwatch. "Then we'll decide."

"Deal!" The girls shouted to him in chorus. They knew that, in reality, their father had already decided. Lara signalled to Nina to discuss their further action in private in their tent.

After brushing their teeth, they wished their parents a good night, and their mother gave Lara and Nina each a gentle kiss on the cheek. Then, the girls retired to their tent.

"We'll all get a good night's sleep!" Were their mother's last words. But none of them could have guessed at the time that the night would turn out quite differently.

The rainbow clock lay on the strange, greenish, shimmering stone, its protective cover shattered and its delicate inner workings exposed. It was as if the impact had triggered some kind of ancient magic, causing the clock to come to life. The hands began to spin rapidly, and the tiny gears inside the timepiece whirred and clicked as if they were alive. All the while, the stone underneath the clock emitted a low hissing noise as if it, too, had been awakened by the clock's arrival.

For a moment, nothing else happened. The forest remained silent, and the clock ticked away on the stone. But then, something strange began to occur. The glow that had once surrounded the stone began to dim, and the shimmering green hue that had once defined it began to fade. Where the clock touched the stone, the glow disappeared entirely, as if the clock was absorbing the stone's energy.

2

WEATHER DISTURBANCE

It had been two great years since Pinky, the clumsiest rainbow parrot of all, had saved the world in which he lived – which was called the land at the end of the rainbow. During those two years, nothing exciting had occurred, but Pinky didn't find that adverse. On the contrary, he was glad that he had not had to participate in more time-traveling adventures.

Oh, yes. It was pretty easy to use the rainbow clock to visit other eras. However, the results of these journeys were unpredictable, and the risk that something terrible could happen was much higher than on a typical trip. Because if you were not careful for just a moment, a lot could change. For example, the future could be altered in an undesired way when going back in time.

Pinky had faced these unpleasant consequences multiple times on his past voyages. Consequently, he had determined that time travel should be limited to only dire circumstances, like when Rainbow Land was in peril. Pinky, who had earned a reputation in his homeland for being a bit clumsy, rose at his usual time, shortly before noon. As he did every day, he made his way to the kitchen and plopped down in a chair. His eyes lit up as he saw his favorite rainbow-colored cereal bowl filled with his favorite cereal sitting on the table in front of him. He dug in with gusto, washing it down with a cup of freshly brewed rainbow tea - his daily routine.

He loved this special type of tea more than anything. Its unique taste was inseparably linked to his homeland because rainbow tea was only available here in Rainbow Land and nowhere else. A calming effect set in every time he had a cup of it because it gave him the strong feeling that everything was fine.

Pinky returned the empty cup to the table and got up, eager to practice his latest flying trick - a triple loop. The aerobatic team practiced more or less regularly for upcoming occasions, mostly anniversaries, in Rainbow Land. So, he opened the front door of his tree house to step outside. He immediately noticed something was different today because a strong, unusually icy gust of wind caught him and threw him back into his old wooden domicile. Pinky landed on his backside but remained largely unharmed. The front door had also swung shut due to the pressure of the wind.

"Whoa! What the heck was that?" he muttered aloud. He had never experienced anything like that before. Sure, it could be windy from time to time in the land at the end of the rainbow, but the wind had never seemed so cool to him.

"Maybe I'm just getting sick, and that's the reason I feel the wind is too cool?" He came up with an easy explanation, scratching his soft parrot chin. But after a while, he started to wonder if this was true.

Curious, he opened his tree house door cautiously. This time, however, he only stretched a tiny parrot claw outside, which immediately felt colder than the one remaining inside the house. There was not the slightest doubt in his mind now. He quickly closed the wooden door again, feeling a sense of unease settle in his stomach.

"Strange! Something is wrong," Pinky mused, but what? He did not know. Nor did he know what he should do next.

Then, as he often did when he needed to gather his thoughts, Pinky turned to his trusty companion - tea. He hurried back to his kitchen, where he spotted the teapot still sitting on the table, nearly a quarter full. "Perfect," he thought, filling his cup almost to the brim. But instead of savoring it, as was his usual custom, he drank it all in one go. The tea's restorative powers did not disappoint, and Pinky felt a renewed sense of clarity wash over him.

As he set down the empty cup, his eyes fell upon the kitchen cabinet, and suddenly, an idea struck him. "I've got it!" He exclaimed, the perplexed expression on his face replaced by one of excitement.

He jumped up so suddenly that he almost knocked the empty teacup in front of him off the table, but at the last moment, he was able to keep it from ending up in a pile of shards on the floor. Pinky ran to the cabinet and opened several drawers before finding what he wanted - a thermometer. The cabinet was a weathered wooden piece decorated with brightly colored feathers and shells and filled with various tools and trinkets that Pinky had collected over the years.

Pinky took the thermometer and went to the very small round kitchen window, which he opened, revealing a breath-taking view of the lush Rainbow Land forest. Then, he attached the thermometer to one of the branches close to the window. It was a delicate process, and Pinky's claws trembled slightly as he fastened it securely to the branch.

A short time later, he looked out of the window at the thermometer, which was gently rocking back and forth in the wind. The thermometer was a small glass bulb with a slender stem that indicated the temperature in Celsius.

"That's completely impossible!" He thought in amazement. For him, the temperature displayed simply had to be a measuring error. It showed a value of plus 17 degrees. That was not particularly cold, but it was incredibly unusual for the home of the rainbow parrots. Usually, the median temperature was above 25 Celsius all year round. Over his whole life, he couldn't remember the temperature ever slipping this low. And that meant something because Pinky was older than one would have suspected based on his fresh-faced appearance - 251 years old, to be exact.

"The stupid thing must be broken," he mused. "If only there was a way to find out." He walked in circles, wondering who could help him figure out if the thermometer was broken. He wouldn't get any peace until he knew.

"But of course!" He exclaimed. "Why didn't I think of him right away? Dr. Schubidou can figure this out faster than any other resident of Rainbow Land. And if the thermometer is, in fact, working, then he is the best person to consult over the cause of this severe cooling." In addition, Pinky reasoned, he could also get a health check.

Dr. Schubidou was the only doctor in Rainbow Land and the smartest of all the rainbow parrots.

But just the thought of having to go out into the cold gave Pinky goosebumps.

"I'd better put something warm on," he said and went from the kitchen into the hallway, where a huge antique closet stood. The ornate woodwork was worn with age, and many tasty woodworms had made their homes within its crevices. Pinky's mouth watered at the thought of them.

The pink bird tried to open one of the double doors but failed. "The door must be stuck somewhere," the parrot grumbled. But he did not give up so quickly. With a determined look, he mustered all his strength and jerked the handle of the hinged door until it suddenly gave way, making a loud grating noise. Pinky toppled backward, buried under an avalanche of clothes that poured out of the closet.

"I was missing this mess!" He moaned when he had finally dug his way out of the pile of laundry, groaning loudly. He now regretted that he had not tidied the closet even once so far. After rummaging through his clothes, he finally found what he had been looking for: a scarf so long that he could wrap it around himself several times. It was a gift from Lara for the 502nd anniversary of his homeland.

The scarf was a colorful patchwork of different fabrics and textures, and it would have been easy to think that it didn't belong to Pinky. But in fact, it did belong to him. He had initially been highly disappointed by the present, considering it useless since he was sure that he would never wear it - at least not in the land at the end of the rainbow, where it never got cold. But Lara had shown him a photo of her house in winter and her last skiing vacation in northern Sweden, where it was usually always icy in the winter, and Pinky had decided that one needed warm clothes.

Pinky's face immediately brightened up a bit. He remembered that Lara had invited him to visit her and her family next winter. When he arrived at his tree house, he had put the scarf in his closet and forgotten all about the invitation.

Thanks to the warming scarf, the weather didn't feel quite as chilly the next time Pinky opened his front door and stepped outside. But what he saw made him stop in his tracks. "What is that?" He thought as he looked around, not wanting to trust his sharp parrot eyes at first. From the well-filled clouds fell something that looked like flakes of cotton candy. The landscape seemed somehow beautiful, even though the colorful glow of the many rainbow shades normally present seemed to have diminished slightly.

"That must be snow. If I'm right about this, then it must, in fact, be cold," Pinky said to himself incredulously, looking at the white blanket covering the ground. The air was chilly, and he could see his breath forming a misty cloud in front of him. He remembered Lara's winter pictures and realized that this strange weather must be what she was talking about. Despite not feeling sick, Pinky thought it would be a good idea to see the doctor, who could likely explain what was happening.

Pinky tried to fly to the doctor's office but found that the scarf he was wearing was pressing on his wings, making it impossible to take off. So he began the long trek on foot. As he walked further, he discovered a thick layer of snow had already covered the ground, making his journey more challenging. The half-meter-thick snow made him feel as though fate was trying to prevent him from reaching his destination. Panting, he trudged forward.

After what seemed like hours, Pinky saw Dr. Schubidou's office in the distance. He would probably have gotten lost if he hadn't seen it at that moment. But the next surprise was already waiting there! - A long line of impatient parrots had formed in front of the entrance to the only doctor's office in Rainbow Land.

"Oh no!" Thought Pinky and sighed. He looked at the long queue and concluded that an eternity would indeed have passed by the time his turn came. He did not feel like waiting so long. As if his clumsiness wasn't bad enough, being laughed at by the other parrots didn't feel good at all. Alongside clumsiness, Pinky possessed another unfortunate trait: he had no patience at all. So he decided to give it another try in the late afternoon. When he turned around, however, he got tangled in his scarf, which partially reached the ground.

Another rainbow parrot would probably have just crashed to the ground, sustaining a minor injury. But Pinky was once again unlucky. He lived up to his reputation for being the rainbow world's clumsiest parrot.

Since the route to the practice was on a slope, Pinky, tangled in his long scarf, began to roll uncontrollably down the hill. He quickly gathered snow on his feathers, making him look like a growing snowball and further increasing his rotation. Soon, he looked like a giant snowball rapidly growing in size, heading at breakneck speed for the end of the long queue.

"Get out of the way! Get out of the way! I'm coming," screeched the now panicked pink parrot increasingly loudly because the queuing, sick parrots had not even noticed the danger rolling toward them. But the waiting parrots didn't hear him until he was almost on top of them. Finally, they paused their lively conversations and turned their heads in the direction of the coming disaster. Their faces expressed sheer horror.

But then everything happened very quickly. At the last moment, the parrots managed to jump to the side and to safety. Pinky's adventurous snowball ride only stopped when it hit the practice door. Most of the snow holding the oversized snowball together detached and fell to the ground. Pinky was fortunate in his misfortune. Except for a few bruises, he had suffered no injury.

However, he still had a strong feeling of dizziness, but it quickly subsided.

"Wow, what a time saver," Pinky thought in complete surprise. However, he couldn't help a gleeful grin as he looked at the parrots now scattered on the floor. He had almost effortlessly managed to break up the long queue in record time - His clumsiness sometimes had its advantages.

At the same time, he now had a genuine medical reason to visit the Doctor - his snowball trauma. He, therefore, didn't need to feel guilty for taking up the time of the most sought-after doctor in the country.

The practice door opened, and Dr. Schubidou's receptionist called Pinky in. Before the other birds could protest, the door had already swung closed.

The receptionist knew about the friendly relationship between Pinky and the doctor. Therefore, she did not lead Pinky to an examination room but to the doctor's break room. "Why don't you take a seat? Dr. Schubidou will be here in a minute to take a break," the receptionist said, and she disappeared again. She looked stressed.

Pinky did not wait long. A few minutes later, the only doctor in Rainbow Land entered the room. Surprised by Pinky's visit, he immediately fetched two teacups from a small cupboard. Then he filled them with fresh rainbow tea and poured hot water from the kettle. Then, like Pinky, the doctor made himself comfortable on the sofa.

"These tea leaves are particularly aromatic because they come from last year's harvest," the doctor gushed, pointing to a tea tin with a label indicating the type of tea and the year of its harvest. There was no need for a title describing the tea because there was only one type in the entire country - rainbow tea.

"The tea contains ingredients that work well for an acute cold," the doctor continued. "Unfortunately, due to the high number of parrots with colds, my tea supply is running low faster than I would like. The worst part, however, is that there is no way to replenish it. The sudden cold temperatures have destroyed almost the entire tea harvest - many tea plants have frozen to death. To state it plainly, I have a serious problem," the bird doctor explained, his expression filled with worry.

Pinky was silent, not wanting to imagine what life would be like in a country with only sick parrots.

"And you? What brings you here? Do you also have a cold?" Dr. Schubidou asked his long-time friend with concern.

"No, not really," Pinky replied. "That is, I thought I was going to be sick at first because I thought I had imagined the cold. Then, when I set out to see you have my health checked, it snowed continuously the whole time. I knew then that the reading on my thermometer must be correct. After all, it can only snow when it's freezing. However, I am no longer comfortable with these low outside temperatures. Tell me, do you know anything about the cause of this weather?"

"Unfortunately, no. I haven't had time to ponder that question yet," the doctor replied, to Pinky's disappointment.

"Well, someone will have to fill in for you," Pinky suggested. "Then you'd have time for it."

"You know that this is unfortunately not possible. There is no other doctor in the whole of Rainbow Land." The doctor replied, sounding somewhat frustrated.

"But what would happen if you suddenly got sick?" Pinky now wanted to know.

The doctor stared at Pinky somewhat despondently. He knew all too well that Pinky was right. He didn't even want to imagine what would happen if he fell victim to burnout because of his current, almost unmanageable, workload. He kept quiet, his thoughts clouded with the weight of responsibility. If only it would get a few degrees warmer, then the number of patients would drop to a tolerable level. But even then, he remained the only doctor who, if he failed, had no substitute.

Then the break room door opened a small crack, and the stressed-looking receptionist appeared, eyeing them with a reproachful look.

"Yes, yes. I'm coming," the doctor sighed. "We'll talk more later." The doctor dismissed his old friend before walking out into the hallway to resume his duties without another word.

However, what he meant by 'later' remained open, much to Pinky's chagrin. He probably knew very well that he would have to work a new overtime record today to cope with the rush of patients.

Pinky felt displaced and angry. His trip to Dr. Schubidou had failed to solve the cold problem. But, at least, he now knew that the sniffles problem was a more serious issue than it had at first seemed.

As he sat there thinking about what he should do next, Pinky unconsciously let his gaze wander around the break room. The room was bare, but his eyes rested on a bookshelf in the corner. He noticed something strange. There were no medical reference books there, but instead, books about geography, the weather, and various other subjects.

"The weather?" Thought Pinky. The realization that he might find something of use here flashed through him like a lightning bolt.

His despair lifted. He reached for the heavy book that lay on the very top of the shelf and brought it down, causing a thick layer of dust to billow up.

"The answer should be in here," he thought, and at that moment, he felt brilliant again.

Pinky carefully ensured the book was hidden from view as he left the break room unnoticed and made it to the door he had come in through. He planned to return home to absorb the contents of this book. That would, of course, take a little more time, but nowhere did he feel more comfortable than in his own home. Investing a bit more of his time was nothing compared to the opportunity presented to him to divest himself of his bad image as the clumsiest parrot in the country. He would never admit that it bothered him - but it did.

In his mind's eye, Pinky already saw himself as a celebrated hero of Rainbow Land. He imagined the surprised faces of the other rainbow parrots when he solved the problem of the cold snap. This future vision of himself made him smile.

As he left the practice area through the same door he had entered before, at least a dozen pairs of parrot eyes were waiting for him, all of them giving him nasty looks. But it didn't stop there. The rainbow parrots from the queue still resented Pinky for the snowball incident, accusing him of having intended to cause trouble. They were now armed with numerous smaller snowballs and began throwing them in his direction. Two of them landed right on his face, causing the parrots to laugh at him.

"Cowards!" Screeched Pinky angrily, but it only made things worse. The parrots continued to have fun throwing more snowballs in Pinky's direction, leaving him with no choice but to make a run for it. Though he arrived back at his tree house in record-breaking time, he was entirely out of breath. He didn't even notice that the temperature had gone down even further because of the fast sprint.

"Well, hopefully, it was worth the effort," he thought as he dropped exhausted into his favourite armchair. Then he opened the book he had brought with him and was soon deeply engrossed in the reading, which contained numerous foreign words he was unfamiliar with and found difficult to understand. Pinky sighed. He had never read anything so challenging before and found it exhausting. Nevertheless, he soon gained some idea of how rain came to be and what a low and a high-pressure area was in this context. Reading soon made him very tired, and he fell into a deep sleep.

He woke up again when his chair began to vibrate slightly, which lasted only a few seconds. Pinky believed he had only imagined it and did not think about it further. He had also become cold again and quickly made a cup of his beloved rainbow tea, wrapping himself in his cuddly pink blanket made from his old feathers. As he sat there, he picked up the weather book again, sighing.

To get the information he was looking for more quickly, he flipped forward to the table of contents. There, he came across a chapter that might explain the weather problem. He began to read and was soon so absorbed in his reading that nothing in the world could have disturbed him. When he had read the heading of the last chapter, he could no longer keep his eyes open from fatigue. His grip on the book loosened, and soon, snoring could be heard loudly in the room.

After glancing at the waiting room, Dr. Schubidou understood why his receptionist had harassed him so much. The room was bursting at the seams with sick birds, and no more room was left for them. They were spread everywhere, including the corridors, registration counters, and even the ceiling lamps of his practice.

"Stop, you can't be up there. Get off that, now!" Shouted the doctor, who had reached the end of his patience, surprising his patients. Then he took a deep breath and tried to calm down. He thought to himself, "True, this place is one big nightmare! But if I panic, I won't manage a single patient!" He stood up in front of the still-confused-looking parrots in the waiting room and apologized briefly to all present.

And so, Dr. Schubidou finally continued his work. By the end of the evening, he was more than exhausted. He felt something tickling his nose.

"Hatchoo!" Was the sound he made. It was followed up by a volley of violent sneezing. The only doctor in the country knew that he had caught a cold. Unfortunately, he had used up his tea supply, which he now urgently needed to get back on his slender parrot legs as quickly as possible.

Because on the following day, many sick parrots would surely need his help, and he needed all his strength. Then he grinned, realizing that one rainbow parrot might have more than enough rainbow tea left. He would have to pay him a visit.

3

AN UNEXPECTED THREAT

Paraiso, the leader of all the rainbow parrots, had just returned from his exhausting beauty treatment and was looking for a place to rest. He had set his sights on a beautiful, shining rainbow that was located high above the rainbow river. This spot was well-camouflaged, making it the perfect place for Paraiso to unwind. The view from up here was breath-taking, with the roar of the waterfall below adding a monotonous, soothing background noise that soon lulled the parrot chief to sleep.

But then, something unexpected happened. The rainbow slowly began to dissolve, and Paraiso, still sound asleep, fell towards the rainbow river below. It was only when he hit the water's surface with a loud splash that he woke up. He quickly dove into the cold water, which thankfully slowed his fall and prevented any injuries.

Paraiso didn't realize at that moment how lucky he was. If he had fallen into a shallower part of the river with a weaker current, he could easily have been fatally injured.

As he climbed out of the river, shivering from the cold water, he looked up and saw that the rainbow he had been sleeping on had completely disappeared. Rubbing his eyes in disbelief, he scanned the sky for any sign of his missing resting spot. But what he saw in the sky made all the alarm bells in his head go off. There were only a few rainbows left, a stark contrast to the numerous rainbows that were usually visible in the sky.

"Ha- ha- Haatchoo!" Pinky exclaimed several times as he woke up, feeling something tickling his nose. Despite being wrapped in a thick blanket, he began to feel cold.

"Oh no, I must have caught a cold on my way back from the doctor's office," Pinky reflected. Then he remembered the doctor's advice - rainbow tea was the best remedy for a cold.

He jumped up and hurried to the kitchen, but unfortunately, he found the tea tin yawningly empty. "Darn it!" He fretted. "Why didn't I realize my supplies were running low?"

He looked around the room, searching for an answer, and by chance, he glanced out of the round window of his treehouse. The setting sun blinded him, and he had to squint. However, the glowing fireball bathed everything in a magical yellow-red light, adding to the ambiance of the moment.

When he carefully opened his eyelids again, he saw that the temperature had changed significantly once again.

"This, this can't be!" Pinky stuttered. "It's as cold as my

refrigerator." He squeezed his eyes shut and rubbed his eyelids for a moment before opening them again. "No, I'm not hallucinating," he thought, growing anxious. The external thermometer showed only 9 degrees Celsius, and Pinky was startled to see that the display pointer indicated the temperature was continuing to drop. Finally, it settled at a value of 3 degrees. "Three degrees??? Whoa!" The clumsy parrot shook himself, getting goose-bumps. "The very first thing I need is some new rainbow tea," he decided, "I can't concentrate on anything for very long without it. And concentration is needed to track down the solution to the current weather puzzle."

He thought about it, realizing he had missed the weekly market where tea was sold, as it had been yesterday, on Saturday. He immediately thought of using his rainbow clock to transport himself into the past but dismissed the possibility as too dangerous. Somewhat perplexed, he looked around and saw a document hanging on the wall that read: "Honorary Citizen of the Country." "Honorary citizen," Pinky grumbled. "That doesn't do me any good now." But then he stopped as if shocked.

"But of course! Why didn't I think of that in the first place?" He wondered. He would ask the Supreme Parrot of the Land, Paraiso, for some of his delicious tea. As an honorary citizen of the colorful Rainbow World, he was entitled to a larger portion of it. Paraiso, being the chief, had the largest supply of any feathered fellow citizen of the land and always had plenty of visitors to whom he offered a steaming cup of tea as a welcome. The meetings were often long and nerve-wracking, and rainbow tea was more than appreciated.

"Yes," Pinky thought with conviction. "Paraiso just has to give me some of his tea rations." The possibility that Paraiso might know something about the cause of the present weather abnormalities strangely did not occur to Pinky at that moment.

Since he no longer had a scarf, Pinky decided to cut a hole in the middle of his square blanket, in which he had wrapped himself before beginning his not-very-exciting book reading. He then pushed his head through it and put on a wide hat that resembled a sombrero, which he found in his closet.

When he finally left his treehouse and headed for Paraiso's, he looked like he was coming from Mexico, with his blanket looking confusingly similar to a real poncho. Unlike when he wore the scarf, he was able to fly with this shawl. It had already become dark in Rainbow Land.

"I wonder if Dr. Schubidou is finally off duty?" Pinky wondered, feeling more than sorry for the doctor because of his unreasonable workload.

In the cloudless night sky, countless stars twinkled. It was even possible to observe the constellations of the large and small rainbow parrots, their bright colors standing out against the dark backdrop of the sky. But there was something else Pinky had never noticed before. A strange greenish streak of light, just as wide as a rainbow, was emblazoned above him and seemed endless, adding an eerie glow to the already mesmerizing view.

Wondered Pinky. But he immediately dismissed this thought because he had found no connection between cold weather and a mysterious streak of light in the meteorology book. Shivering from the cold, Pinky finally arrived at the highest tree house in the country. He landed right in front of its front door, which was adorned with intricate carvings of rainbows and parrots.

But he could no longer speak properly because his beak rattled uncontrollably from the cold, something that had never happened to him before. He had no choice but to draw attention to himself by hammering loudly on the door. It seemed like an eternity before he heard footsteps approaching the tree-house door. A pair of parrot eyes, well known to him, stared curiously through the round window embedded in the door for a few seconds. Then the door opened a crack with a loud squeaking sound. The formidable figure of the rainbow chief Paraiso appeared in the tree house entrance; his colorful feathers fluffed up to keep the cold at bay.

"Well, finally! One minute longer, and I would have frozen to death out here," Pinky complained, clacking his beak violently, which lent more authenticity to his statement.

"I'm sorry. I didn't recognize you right away in the dark," Paraiso apologized, looking Pinky up and down with concern. "Come in!" He bid his oddly dressed visitor, who followed him into the living room. The room was cozy and warm, with a crackling fire in the fireplace and colorful rugs adorning the wooden floor.

To Pinkie's surprise, the bird doctor was already sitting there. He had come straight here after taking care of the last sick person. He had himself, like Pinky, a cold, and he had, like Pinky, no more rainbow tea left. Pinky gratefully accepted a steaming cup of tea, its vibrant colors, and sweet aroma immediately lifting his spirits.

Paraiso was an excellent host, offering them delicious treats and engaging them in lively conversation. "So where were we just now?" The doctor pondered, scratching his forehead.

"You were complaining about the weather," Paraiso helped him.

"Yes, exactly! I stand by it. Something must happen immediately so that the temperatures rise again. Otherwise, we will not get this fast-spreading wave of colds under control," Dr. Schubidou protested, his feathers ruffled with frustration.

"Yes, and we could save this year's tea crop as well," Pinky interjected, eager to contribute to the solution.

"Unfortunately, that's not our biggest problem," Paraiso began seriously, his expression grave. "You may have noticed it too: there are fewer rainbows and.... "

"Well, that the rainbows would disappear was predictable, though, given the falling temperatures," the bird doctor interrupted him, his tone analytical and detached. "The many sick birds are the problem."

"Sorry! I'm afraid I can't quite keep up!" Asked Pinky curiously, his eyes darting between the two parrots.

"It's quite simple!" The doctor enlightened him. "In order for rainbows to form, rain is required. And with these low temperatures, it is not raining."

"Quiet! Please do not interrupt me!" Paraiso yelled angrily, his normally bright plumage turning a darker shade. He viewed being interrupted as a tremendous sign of disrespect. Pinky and the doctor winced because they also realized that they had gone too far.

"It's not at all as trivial as you think," Paraiso tried a second time, his voice calmer but no less firm. "There is a much more serious problem."

Pinky and Dr. Schubidou looked at him eagerly.

"As you probably already know," the chief began, his thoughts drifting back to the 500th birthday celebration of Rainbow Land, "there are numerous secrets in our world. These secrets are so explosive that only the acting chief of the land at the end of the rainbow knows them. They are passed down orally from one chief to the next. Therefore, only the chief knows when the time is ripe to reveal them. Now is the time to tell you one of them because our homeland is in very, very, very serious danger."

Paraiso paused again, cleared his throat once more, and stroked a crooked feather on his head with his parrot claw. Pinky and the doctor were bursting with curiosity but didn't dare interrupt him again.

"So, from the first Rainbow Chief of our land, Pizarro, the following story has been passed down," Paraiso began. "After the Rainbow Country came into being, the clockmaker monk who also lived here measured and mapped our new homeland. He was the only one to think that the land, despite its small size, was important enough to be accurately mapped. Why it was necessary, however, he did not mention. He didn't need to because, in the beginning, all the rainbow parrots trusted him blindly since he had the idea of bringing this country into being.

"When he finally finished this project, he appeared again before Pizarro to proudly hand over the new map. However, this became a minor matter for discussion, as his latest discovery took precedence."

"Discovery?" The curious doctor interrupted, unable to hold back any longer. Paraiso chastised the doctor with a disapproving look before continuing.

"Yes, he had noticed that the rainbows not only look beautiful but also serve an important function. They are," he took a deep breath before continuing, "indispensable for the stability of our world."

His listeners, the purple and pink birds, looked at him in surprise. They guessed what would come next.

"It means, in plain language, that if the rainbows disappear, which they are about to do, in the worst-case scenario, it could cause our Rainbow Land to collapse like a house of cards. It will not explode but rather implode." Paraiso brought his story to a close.

"If that's true, then this is an absolute disaster!" Said Dr. Schubidou, who immediately understood the seriousness of the situation.

"Yes, a downright frightful state of affairs," Pinky agreed with the doctor, turning pale. Paraiso simply nodded in agreement.

"Well, since you've known about the consequences all along, I'm sure you've been thinking about how we can get the situation back under control," Dr. Schubidou asked. "Am I right?"

"Yes," replied the handsome chieftain, sighing. "However, unfortunately, I have not yet been able to find an answer to this problem. The monk probably didn't expect any issues in this regard. That is why he didn't pass on any suggestions for solutions to my ancestor."

But Paraiso was wrong in his last statement. He had overlooked a crucial detail. Pinky remained silent, struggling to accept the hopeless situation they were in.

"If only we could ask someone who has an in-depth knowledge of meteorology. That someone could certainly help us!" Dr. Schubidou reflected.

Unfortunately, there were no meteorologists in the land at the end of the rainbow they could address right now. They had not needed them so far because the weather was so predictable. If it rained, everyone knew that the sun would come out again in the next few minutes, and vice versa.

Pinky suddenly remembered why he had come to Paraiso.

"I secretly borrowed your meteorology book and read through it," Pinky confessed.

"And what did you find out?" The doctor and Paraiso were eager to know.

"Uh, unfortunately, not as much as I expected to. The book is very thick and exhausting to read. All the technical terms don't make it any easier," Pinky replied.

"Get to the important part!" Paraiso urged him.

"Okay! So, in the last chapter, there was something about man-made climate change. It could be that there is something similar going on here," Pinky said, but he concealed the fact that he had only read the chapter title.

"But we can't talk about climate change yet because it only started getting cold last night. You can only determine changes in the climate when you study the weather over a long period of time," Dr. Schubidou objected.

"That's right! Besides, there are only parrots and no people in this world," Paraiso added.

"Oh yeah, and what's..." Pinky began but was then interrupted by a strong tremor. The teacups shattered, and he just managed to prevent the teapot from meeting the same fate. Although it was only momentary, the tremor was noticeable.

"Oh! No! It's starting already!" Cried Paraiso in horror.

There was another jolt. And another bigger one.

"What do you mean it's starting? What?" Asked Pinky, now also panicked.

"The beginning of the demise of our beautiful rainbow world, of course. The quakes are caused by the rainbows beginning to break. That is the beginning of the end unless we do something about it,"

Paraiso explained in a serious voice. The problem was that, at this point, he unfortunately didn't have the slightest idea what had to be done to avert this seemingly inevitable catastrophe.

The next earth tremor followed closely behind the last.

"We can't just stand here and watch all of this happen. We must act immediately," the doctor urged Paraiso.

"If we only knew what caused the weather to change, we might be able to turn things around, but we don't even have a clue where to start looking," lamented the leader of the rainbow parrots.

For a brief moment, the three parrots were as quiet as mice.

"But we already know that," Pinky exclaimed, surprising the other colorful parrots. Dr. Schubidou and Paraiso looked at Pinky, demanding a more detailed explanation.

Before Pinky could answer, there was a loud bang. All of a sudden, it had gone pitch black in the tree house. There had been a power failure because something heavy had fallen on the tree house, damaging the power line on the roof.

The only source of light came from the dim glow of the parrots' feathers. Paraiso quickly lit a candle, casting flickering shadows across the room. The air was heavy with the smell of burnt wires.

"What do we do now?" Asked Dr. Schubidou, worry etched across his face.

"We need to assess the damage and fix the power line," said Paraiso, the urgency in his voice palpable. "We can't afford to be in the dark right now."

4

IN THE MUSEUM

Shortly before midnight on a national holiday, the loud voices of the museum-goers had finally died down. The fireworks, which had lit up the sky earlier, were now a distant memory. On the Gulf of Bothnia coast, the salty and humid air began to feel cold as the drizzle turned into light sleet. The museum was located in a small town, and clouds blanketed the night sky, obscuring the stars and moon.

The night sky was so dark that the person dressed in black lying in wait on the museum roof could barely see their own hand in front of their face. They pulled their wool cap further over their face, trying to shield it from the frigid air. In scarcely more than five minutes, it would be time, the person thought as they glanced at their outrageously expensive Rolex watch for the umpteenth time.

To see the time, they had to continually press a small button on the watch case's side, which then momentarily brightened the display.

Suddenly, the lights went out in the whole museum district. It was now precisely midnight. The breeze coming from the sea carried on it the ringing of bells from a distant church clock.

"Now it's show-time," the dark silhouetted figure thought with a sinister grin.

He moved to retrieve a glass cutter from his backpack, stepped on an icy roof panel, slipped, and fell hard onto the roof. He slid several meters on the seat of his pants towards one end of the roof and almost fell off. But, he had the presence of mind to reach out and grab the rope with which he had climbed onto the roof. He was lucky. At the very last moment, he had prevented a probably life-threatening fall.

"Whew, by a hair, I wouldn't have existed anymore," he thought, noticing his heart was still pounding with fear. At that point, he swore to himself that this would be the very last mission of this kind. Then he moved back to the point where the skylight was. The man again applied the glass cutter, this time a lot more carefully, to the window. Skilfully, as if he had practiced, he cut a fist-sized piece of glass out of the window. He noticed a dull pain in his shoulder as he did so, but fortunately, it wasn't very severe. He must have suffered at least one bruise in the near fall just now. With a swift movement of his hand, he grabbed the window handle and turned it over with a cracking sound. Then, exerting all his strength, he pushed the circular window, which moved with an audible cracking sound inward. The hooded figure then pulled up the rope with which he had climbed the outer wall of the museum building. He fastened one end of it to a stable place on the roof. Finally, he lowered the other end through the open window into the interior of the old, recently renovated building.

He waited a brief moment to make sure no one had noticed him. Everything was still quiet except for the distant cries of seagulls. Their calls had a calming effect on him, and he could hear nothing else. Above all, there was no alarm or shouts from the night watchman, who was now sitting in his surveillance room, as was usual at this hour. The watchman was probably watching something trivial on TV again to avoid falling asleep. He knew this much, as he had overheard a conversation between the night watchman and the woman at the cash desk by chance during a previous visit to the museum. Despite the short preparation time, which he was not used to, he had managed to plan the raid effectively and discern what was essential. His client only wanted the raid to take place on this holiday. At first, he did not want to accept the job because of the short preparation time. But the expensive watch he now wore on his wrist had convinced him to change his mind. He could keep it if he went through with the break-in that Friday. However, he did not learn the reason for it. Nevertheless, he did not care. His greed had triumphed over reason.

He knew that he had now reached the point where he could still back out. But he had already made up his mind. He switched on his headlamp. Since the time for planning had been far too short, he had overlooked at least one crucial thing. Namely, the night watchman would also notice the power outage and would no longer be watching a movie as he had assumed. He would probably be out looking for the cause of the power outage.

The unknown man lowered himself several meters on his rope, which ended almost two meters above the ground. He had not miscalculated the length but had simply not been able to acquire a longer cord in the time available to him. Besides, he could easily bridge the last bit by jumping. Climbing up was going to be more difficult, but he would manage that, too, as he was well-trained. He landed safely with both feet on the white and black tiled floor. He looked around to get his bearings, which wasn't a problem as he had been able to look around carefully in the past few days as a museum visitor. He had even memorized the exact location of the countless surveillance cameras mounted around the building. Back home, he had carefully written down all the information he had gathered and used it as the basis for his schedule for carrying out the heist. Although the cameras were now inoperative, he thought it was safer to avoid them as much as possible. He, therefore, ran some detours. Again, he stopped briefly to listen for anyone approaching, then carefully continued with his plan.

The uninvited guest walked the last few meters purposefully, with giant steps, along a long, dark corridor to the wing where he would find the desired object. Arriving in front of the room, he stopped again. Then he risked a glance inside. In the middle of the room, there was a display case made of special glass. He took a pair of glasses out of his backpack, with which he could see the network of invisible laser beams that surrounded the display case. But the power failure had done a great job here, too. The laser beams had disappeared.

The display case contained a meteorite only a few centimeters in size, giving off a faint greenish light that, despite its unremarkable appearance, was worth far more than a diamond of the same size. Money played only a subordinate role for the collector of rare stones from the Orient, who was his client. Though this person seemed to have more than enough of them, he still wanted the unique rock at any price. At least, that's what the man he talked to had revealed to him.

The museum burglar checked his expensive watch one more time and was satisfied that he had more than enough time to carry out the theft. He grinned because he knew that by the time the watchman discovered the cause of the power outage and fixed it, he would be long gone. He listened, but everything continued to be quiet. He breathed a sigh of relief. However, he was mistaken. The night watchman had already left his surveillance room.

The thief carefully entered the room and went straight to the display case. He placed his backpack on the floor and took out a viscous black paste, which he carefully applied to the special glass in a fist-sized circle with his fingers, which were encased in black leather gloves. The glass cutter, he knew, would be ineffective here. The paste reacted with the glass, causing it to emit smoke. He had a kind of mini vacuum cleaner, which he switched on to remove the smoke. Smoke could easily trigger the fire alarm despite the power failure since regular batteries power the fire alarms.

With a suction cup, which he placed on the specially prepared glass, he pulled out a circular piece of the glass with a strong jerk. He could not help grinning with satisfaction as he did so because everything was going according to plan! He would be gone from here in half an hour at the most. The hole created was just a little wider than his arm. So that no fibers of his jacket would get caught on the glass and remain as traces later, he pulled up his coat sleeve a little way. Underneath, a hairy, sun-tanned forearm came into view. In his spare time, of which he had more than enough, he loved to sail. The new sailboat promised him after the robbery was already free for him to use and served as a makeshift home for him.

Deep in concentration, he stretched out his arm toward the stone, careful not to make contact with the sharp edges of the glass. His hand hovered over the meteorite. He could easily grasp it. He knew little about the stone, only what his client had told him: that a little girl had found it and sold it to the museum for a lot of money. He hadn't had time to learn much more about it. Nor was he supposed to, which was why his client had demanded he steal the stone on this very holiday with so little time to prepare. The thief was sweating with excitement. Carefully, he pulled his arm out of the display case.

As he did so, dense clouds over the museum dissipated, and what an observer might have thought was the Northern Lights appeared.

Meanwhile, the night watchman, Ed, or Eddy, as his closest friends called him, had reacted to the power outage immediately, using his work cell phone to inform the headquarters of the security company for which he worked.

The supervisor had instructed him to wait until he had completed a tour to determine if there was any deliberate intention behind the power failure. He picked up the heavy flashlight from the table and turned it on. After checking his service pistol, he holstered it to his belt. He had never used it during his years of service, and he fervently hoped he wouldn't have to use it now. Quietly, he moved forward, stopping at short, regular intervals to listen. He also had his service cell phone at the ready. He began to systematically search one room after another until he finally arrived at the room where the thief was.

Suddenly, he heard a noise. He stopped as if rooted to the spot and listened. "Yes, someone must be in that room over there," he thought excitedly. He broke out in a sweat of fear, his hands becoming wet. He would leave out of the police report that he had become afraid, as it was embarrassing for him. A real night watchman was never afraid, of course.

Almost silently, he freed the pistol from its holster. With the gun in his hand, he turned the next corner, the last one separating him from the room where someone had made a mess. He would find out who at any moment. Then he heard a loud bang, and a person let out a suppressed cry of pain. He pressed his back even harder against the wall along which he was creeping in shock, ready to defend himself. "Whoever is in the room at the moment must have been injured," the night watchman thought, trying to make sense of it. Gathering all his courage, he took a giant leap forward and stopped at the passage that led into the room. He cautiously risked a glance into the room, pointing the flashlight inside. But just at that moment, he was blinded by a very bright greenish flash of light that illuminated the entire room. Then, it was as dark as before. It took Ed a few seconds, which felt like minutes to him, before his eyes could see anything again.

He was well aware at that moment that he was in great danger. The unique glass of the display case that housed the meteorite was no longer intact, and the meteorite was gone. But the suspected intruder was nowhere to be seen. There was not a single soul in the room. He searched the immediate vicinity without success. He was still in shock when, with his fingers trembling, he dialed the number of the company that had faithfully contracted him for many years. Ed was so nervous that the first attempt failed. The second time, however, he finally succeeded.

"I have a burglary to report. Yes, a burglary," the night watchman whispered into the phone. But then Ed repeated himself, almost yelling into the phone from then on. "Yes, I'm completely serious. Why would I want to tell you a tall tale?" The night watchman shouted impatiently. Then he hung up.

"The most expensive meteorite in the entire museum is gone, and all I get is a rookie at headquarters who doesn't even take me seriously," Ed thought in frustration.

He couldn't just sit around until the police arrived. He had to find out as much as possible. Armed with his flashlight and his service weapon, he moved cautiously through all the rooms of the museum, elegant as a cat. That's when he spotted the rope he thought the burglar had used to enter through the roof and probably escape again.

"The thief can't have gotten far," Ed quickly regained hope as he glanced at his watch. "If I'm lucky, he's still on the roof or in the museum grounds."

Ed knew he had one last chance to catch the thief. He immediately sprinted to the kennel in the second-floor surveillance room. Due to the cold weather, the museum's guard dogs were being housed there. He fumbled with the key and let the two Dobermans out. Ed wasted no time and led them straight to the rope, where he let them sniff around. Then the dogs, now primed, charged toward the museum's main entrance. Ed followed them, panting, and opened the door. The animals ran outside, their paws clicking against the pavement.

He still believed at that moment that he had an excellent chance of catching the thief with his loot before the police arrived. But he would soon realize that the thief had already disappeared. Despite his efforts, he had not had the slightest chance. However, he would only find that out much later. The reality of what had happened was so fantastic that he would hardly believe it.

5

A RESTLESS NIGHT

Lara had woken up, not because she was cold, but because she had heard a strange crunching sound outside the tent. Due to the freezing temperature, she was reluctant to leave her warm sleeping bag. She reached for her wristwatch, which was nestled inside her wool cap, and pressed the button on its side. The display lit up briefly, revealing that it was just after midnight.

As the crunching sound grew louder, Lara realized it was the sound of footsteps approaching the tent she shared with her sister, Nina. Lara peered over at Nina's sleeping bag, but it was still and quiet. She thought her sister was likely deep asleep.

At first, Lara thought the sound might be a wild animal searching for prey. The family was in the Abisko National Park, after all, where many wild animals, including wolves and bears, roamed freely. Lara listened intently, trying to determine what was outside the tent.

The crunching sound had stopped just outside the entrance to her tent. Lara held her breath, stiff with fear. She would have liked to scream, but she didn't know whether this would only put herself and the others in unnecessary danger.

She saw a shadow growing more prominent at the tent entrance. Lara now noticed her heart beating loudly. Her hands became wet. Then something tampered with the zipper of the tent entrance and opened it with a loud whirring sound. A face appeared, and a cone of light blinded Lara, leaving her unable to see who it was.

"Hello, what are you doing?" Lara complained loudly, hoping to wake up her sister, who she assumed was in the sleeping bag next to her.

"Sorry. I thought you were sleeping," a familiar voice said.

At the tent entrance knelt Nina, who immediately directed the beam of her flashlight to the ground.

"It's okay. Just tell me why you're sneaking around in the middle of the night. You scared me to death!" Lara returned, still a little annoyed. "Didn't our parents specifically warn us about leaving the tent at night without a valid reason?"

"Yes, yes, but..." Nina defended herself.

"But what?" Probed Lara.

"Well, I suddenly woke up because it had become daylight," Nina returned, pointing upwards towards the Northern Lights.

"What do you mean, bright as daylight? You must have dreamed it," Lara said doubtfully. The Northern Lights were visible, but she thought it unlikely they would get much brighter.

"No, it was daylight," Nina stuck to her version of events. "You just didn't wake up because you probably had your sleep goggles on as usual."

"Maybe," Lara shrugged. "So, in your opinion, the Northern Lights were the cause of the brightness?"

"Maybe," replied Nina. "Anyway, the light came from the side where our parents' tent is, but by the time I stuck my head through the tent entrance, it was already dark again, so I have no idea what caused it."

Lara's brows furrowed. "Strange," she reflected. "Perhaps it was just the glow from a distant storm or... a crashed meteorite."

"Even though it went away, I still didn't feel reassured. I had a strange feeling in my stomach," Nina said. "So, I left our tent and ran over to our parents' tent. When I got there, I found that they weren't there."

"Pardon? Where else could they be?" Lara returned in amazement. "They might have gone for a walk because, like you, they couldn't sleep."

"But I was asleep," Nina corrected her. "I hope you're right because I've been waiting for them to return for a while." Nina sat down in the spot where the campfire still glowed from the night before. She threw a few logs on the embers, quickly rekindling the fire.

"What do you mean by 'a while?'" Lara asked.

"Well, I'm sure it's been half an hour," Nina replied.

"All right. You win," Lara finally conceded with a sigh. At that moment, the disturbing thought had occurred to her that her parents could have gotten lost. Lara knew she would not be able to sleep now, either. She had to find out what had happened. Surely, there was a simple, plausible explanation.

Lara left her warm sleeping bag. She put on the woolen hat that her grandmother, who lived on the Mosel, had knitted for her for Christmas last year. Then Lara slipped on her thick, purple down jacket and scrambled out of the tent.

As soon as Lara stepped outside, she was hit by the chilly night air. She zipped up her jacket and looked around. The sky was clear, and the stars were shining brightly. Looking up, she let out an awestruck, "Wow!" In addition to the countless twinkling stars, there was also an intense greenish glow emanating from a band of light across the sky.

"Insanely beautiful!" She marveled, now almost grateful to her sister for waking her up.

They trudged through the snow to their parents' tent, their breaths visible in the frigid air. The snow crunched under their boots, and the only sound that could be heard was the distant howling of a wolf.

"Maybe you're right. Mom and Dad are probably just taking a long walk to admire the night sky. I'm sure they just lost track of time," said Nina optimistically, not sounding entirely convinced.

"We're about to find out," Lara replied curtly, still looking up at the greenish shimmering Northern Lights that seemed to be pulsating in the sky.

"That's why our parents brought us here. To show us the Northern Lights," Lara thought happily, now also feeling a great sense of gratitude toward her parents for bringing them to Abisko National Park, one of the best places in mainland Europe for viewing the Northern Lights.

As they approached their parents' tent, their excitement turned to confusion and concern. They found it abandoned, just as Nina had described it. They walked around the tent to look for tracks in the snow, but they found none.

By chance, the light from Nina's flashlight grazed the upper part of the tent and stuck on a particular spot.

"For heaven's sake! What had happened to the tent?" Nina gasped, aghast.

There was a massive hole in the tent cloth, as if something sharp had cut through it. Lara and Nina stood there stunned, realizing that something was very wrong.

"Wasn't that there before?" Asked Lara, her voice trembling with fear.

"No. That is… I don't know," Nina replied, confused. "I didn't notice it, anyway."

Lara peered through the hole into the inside of the tent, and when she saw nothing dangerous there, she went to the tent entrance and pulled up the zipper to inspect the inside more closely.

"Don't keep me in suspense. Tell me what you've found," Nina urged, her eyes darting around nervously.

"There are no signs of a struggle," Lara called out from the tent, "nor traces of blood."

"Fight? Bloodstains?" Nina tried to read Lara's mind. "Good Lord! Do you think they might have been running from a bear?" Her imagination was running wild with possibilities.

"I hope not. It's a possibility, though," replied Lara anxiously, coming out of the tent again.

"After all, there is a rather large hole in a pretty sturdy tent. What else could have caused this if not a sharp object?"

As they both stood there, staring at the damaged tent and the empty surroundings, the howling of wolves seemed to grow louder and closer. The night air was thick with an eerie silence, broken only by the occasional rustle of leaves and the sound of their own breathing.

Nina couldn't help but think of the sharp teeth or claws of a wild animal, "You mean a bear or some other animal tore the tent cloth?"

"Yes, and in the process, they must have woken up and fled," Lara suggested with a worried expression.

The girls remained silent, staring at the tent. If their parents had fled from a wild animal, they were not safe either. But where were their parents? They couldn't even use their mobile phones to call the dog sled team for help.

"We have to stay together no matter what. We only have a chance if we stick together," Lara told Nina.

Nina followed Lara back to her tent. Lara slipped inside and felt around for her flashlight, which was next to her sleeping bag. Then she searched for her survival knife, which was also there. She felt a little better having it, although she did not expect it to be of much use in a fight against a bear. Finally, she crawled out of the tent again. Carefully, she pulled the zipper down and secured it with an additional lock to prevent unwanted guests from entering the tent.

She hoped that this would reduce the likelihood of encountering an intruder when they returned.

"We need to go back to our parents' tent and take another look at the snow-covered ground near the tent. If they ran away from an animal, and we assumed that it was so big that they were scared, there must be tracks to find. Then, all we have to do is follow the tracks. Unless..."

"Unless what?" Nina echoed.

"Unless it has snowed since they disappeared. Then there should be fresh snow on the sled as well."

Nina nodded, relieved to have a big sister with a plan. They carefully searched the ground with the light from their flashlights, as Lara had suggested. They walked in an ever-increasing radius around their parents' tent, staying close together.

No matter how hard they looked, they could not find a single track except for those left by their winter shoes.

"Strange," Lara commented almost in exasperation, "There's not a single footprint."

"So it snowed then?"

"I can easily tell," the older of the two returned.

They hurried over to the wooden sled. The sisters noticed a thin layer of snow on its surface. The huskies stood up, wagging their tails and yelping happily at the unexpected visit.

Suddenly, Lara remembered her cell phone, which she had left in her tent. But as the park ranger had already warned them, it was useless out here. He had noticed her uncertain expression and had given them a signal pistol to calm them down.

Lara found the signal pistols in a large box that Bob, the park guard, had told them to leave in the sled. In case of an emergency, they could find them quickly. She opened the box, and with the help of Nina's flashlight, she carefully read through the operating instructions in a plastic package on top.

Then, she stood in the middle of the clearing, far enough away from the burned-out wood fire, the tents, and the huskies, and fired three shots toward the sky. The red balls of light whizzed upwards like fireworks, visible for a while before burning up.

Their last hope was that if their parents were lost, they could find their way back with the help of the flares.

"Still, we can't wait here for them to return. We have to actively look for Mum and Dad ourselves. They might not even notice these flares, for whatever reason," Lara explained, thinking about the possibility that her parents were hiding somewhere from the animal stalking them.

"But aren't we putting ourselves in danger too? I mean, if it really is a bear, maybe we should call for help?" Suggested Nina.

"Calling for help takes too long. We'll stay in the dog sled for safety, and if a bear appears, we'll make a quick getaway," Lara replied.

Nina pondered. They would blame themselves later if they could have saved their parents but didn't try. She also suspected that they might not have much time to find their parents. The outside temperature was in the minus range, and without appropriate clothing, they could freeze to death quickly. And their parents probably hadn't had time to get dressed.

"All right, let's go," Nina finally gave in.

"We'll take the dog sled!" Decided Lara.

Nina quickly fetched a few thick blankets for the sleigh ride, and Lara found a thermos that still contained lukewarm cocoa from the night before and packed it in her backpack.

Then, Lara untied the sled dogs while Nina took a seat in the sled. Lara steered the vehicle with the dogs harnessed in front of it, circling around the tent camp, gradually increasing their radius.

But nowhere did they find any trace of their parents. Even their urgent calls went unanswered in the cold night air surrounding them.

At some point, much later, they returned to their camp tired, frozen, and frustrated. One last time, they looked in their parents' tent, which was still empty. From there, the two walked over to the campfire site.

Lara piled up a few logs and lit a fire. In the process, she remembered what had happened the night before. They had all sat on camping chairs singing together and eating the delicious fish their father had caught from an ice hole on a nearby lake, along with some tasty grilled potatoes. They had been starving after the trip to the White Mountain range.

Lara shivered and quickly fetched a log from the covered wood supply to add to the fireplace. "They'll be back, for sure!" Lara tried to encourage herself and her sister, but this had rather the opposite effect, and several thick tears rolled down Nina's cheeks. Lara's eyes also got moist.

Lara fetched two thick blankets from her tent. Then they sat down on the folding camping chairs. Lara put one of the blankets around her sister's shoulders and wrapped herself with the other one. The wood soon began to burn well and gave off enough heat.

Lara looked up at the night sky. The greenish band of light was still visible, and if it had been able to speak, it would undoubtedly have been able to give them information about what had happened here in the past few hours. But, of course, it could not.

"It's not long until dawn," Nina said, glancing at her wristwatch. It was already four o'clock in the morning.

"You go to sleep for now!" Lara suggested and, to her sister's surprise, bent over and gave her a gentle kiss on the forehead. It was like this that their mother had always comforted them, especially when she and Nina had been smaller. This time, too, it had a reassuring effect.

"Why sleep? Hadn't we better leave to get help?" Implored Nina, yawning loudly.

"No, I'm afraid it's too early for that," Lara slowed her down. "The park ranger's office doesn't open until around 8 o'clock. We'd have to wait there for more than an hour if we left right now. It's better to stay here a little longer." Lara, like Nina, was still secretly hoping for her parents to return. And to reassure Nina, she added, "Don't worry! I'll keep the campfire going in the meantime. No wild animal will venture here."

Nina was much too tired to raise any objections. For one thing, she could no longer think clearly in this state. Yawning loudly, she retreated into the tent. In her sleeping bag, which soon became snugly warm due to her body heat, she very quickly fell into a deep but restless sleep.

Lara moved closer to the warming fire and wrapped herself in her blanket as best she could. It not only prevented her body from cooling down further but also made her feel comfortably warm. However, her plan to keep the fire burning failed miserably. Exhaustion had taken over, and soon, she could no longer keep her eyes open.

As the firewood burned down, Lara felt the chill creeping back in. She woke up and fed the fire with the last available firewood. Lara looked over at the tent where her sister was sleeping and then stared into the fire as it flared up again. The desire to sleep was becoming overwhelming, but she reminded herself that her parents would be waking her soon if they found the note she had attached to their damaged tent.

Lara returned to the fire, feeding it with enough firewood to burn for at least two more hours, or so she hoped. Then, it would be time to make her way to the national park entrance to call for professional help. She looked around the camp one last time. The sled dogs at the back were quiet, too. Lara pulled up the zipper at the entrance to the tent and crawled in with Nina, slipping into her cozy sleeping bag as soon as she could. Within seconds, Lara was asleep, reliving the fresh experiences in her dreams.

Not even two hours later, Lara's alarm clock rang, startling the girls. Nina grumbled something incomprehensible, turned to the side, and fell back asleep immediately. Lara turned off the alarm with one tap, crawled to the tent entrance, and slowly pulled up the zipper. Smoke was the only thing visible at the fireplace. Lara slipped on her warm-down jacket and pulled on her lined winter boots before closing the tent entrance from the outside and going to her parents' tent. It was still empty. As the sun rose, the sky turned a golden yellow, and Lara went back to wake Nina.

"Come on, get up! We're about to hit the road!" Lara said.

"Where to?" Asked Nina, still half-asleep.

"To the park superintendent's office, of course. We'll inform the officer about what happened, and he will help us," Lara said, hoping for the best.

"All right, I'll hurry," Nina replied, nodding.

Lara quickly wrote a short message to her parents, just in case they showed up. They attached the note to their tent entrance and left some emergency provisions in the box where the signal pistol had been for protection against wild animals. Finally, they set off, riding rapidly to the office. As they arrived, they saw the park supervisor unlocking his office door and going in to make himself a cup of coffee before starting his daily work.

However, his plans were disrupted as two downright sleepy girls were already knocking on his office door, desperate for help. The pair had wholly forgotten their desire to look for Lara's lost rainbow clock today. Now, the only things on their minds were their parents.

6

A MAGICAL SOLUTION?

Because of the sudden darkness, Dr. Schubidou and Paraiso quickly lit a few candles in the tree house.

"We must find out the reason for what just happened," Paraiso demanded.

Cautiously, the three exotic birds made their way to the highest roof terrace of Rainbow Land. Their curiosity was greater than their fear of what awaited them there.

Indeed, they found the cause of the noise and the power outage: the destruction of the power line running along the roof. The line had been severed by a massive fragment of rainbow now lying on the roof. Fortunately, the roof terrace and the tree house walls seemed undamaged.

Paraiso heaved a sigh of relief.

"Unfortunately, the repair will have to wait. Fixing the power outage will take a lot of time. Time we don't have right now."

So they returned downstairs. Paraiso thought about what Pinky had just said. "Yes, now it is far more important to discern who Pinky is blaming for the chilly weather," Paraiso concluded.

"Speak up! Who do you think is to blame for the cold?" Paraiso requested, his irritation evident.

Dr. Schubidou, who usually knew almost everything, also glanced at Pinky with a look that suggested impatience. "Don't keep us waiting any longer! We don't have time for trifles. The predicament is grave."

But before Pinky could answer, the ground shook again.

"So," Pinky started in a tone as if he were the overseer of a quiz show. He relished knowing something that even the most brilliant parrots in the nation hadn't considered. "The person you're searching for resides down by the river in what was once the clock monk's cottage."

"Anna?" Paraiso guessed easily, as there was only one dwelling down by the river.

"Yes, she is the only person who lives there..." he began but was interrupted by a much more powerful earth tremor. The tree house shook again, and there was a loud crash. The rainbow piece on the roof had now fallen to the ground beside the house.

"And according to the chapter that deals with climate disasters, yes, humans are the culprits," the pink parrot finished his conjecture.

"There really could be something to it," the bird doctor admitted.

"Then what are we standing around chatting about?" Paraiso exclaimed, incensed. "We need to get to Anna immediately and find out if Pinky is right."

The parrots immediately set off, taking the shortest route to the river where Anna had established her new home, having fled from the Middle Ages to escape the king's henchmen. The shortest way was a direct flight, but it took longer than expected due to the falling snowflakes that significantly limited visibility.

"What terrible weather!" Grumbled Pinky. However, as they approached the place where they supposed Anna lived, the snowfall stopped, and the clouds in the sky cleared, revealing some pretty rainbows. Despite their wet feathers, they finally arrived at the hut by the river, Anna's home, which came into view.

"We're here!" Shouted Paraiso first, as he could see the farthest of all the rainbow parrots.

"I hope she's home," said the less optimistic doctor.

Only when they had landed did they notice an unusual structure next to the hut. This structure consisted of a semi-circular transparent dome with lights on the inside, reminding Dr. Schubidou of a vast greenhouse. From inside, every shade of green shone, with a lot of steam in between. The steam emerged from a blue strip that flowed into a small lagoon where someone was singing. Although they did not recognize who it was, the singing voice was more than familiar to them.

"Anna? Is that you?" The colorful birds enquired.

The singing stopped. "Oh, visitors! How nice!" Anna called out to them enthusiastically. She had adjusted her language style to that of Lara and Nina after living with them for a while and no longer spoke like a woman from the Middle Ages, which, of course, she was. "Yes, I'm in here. Come on in!"

"How?" Dr. Schubidou asked. "I'm afraid I don't see a door anywhere."

"There aren't any," Anna replied. "Just step through."

First Pinky, then Paraiso, and finally, the doctor stepped inside the artificially created bubble. It was warm and incredibly humid, and the trio quickly got rid of their warming clothes. Their beaks remained open in amazement.

The lagoon in which Anna sat connected on three sides with the water of the Rainbow River. One tributary brought in steaming hot water, while another contained ice-cold water. "Anna can regulate the temperature of the water inside the lagoon with a witch's spell," the doctor thought.

Anna seemed relaxed as she enjoyed the warm water that caressed her body.

"Did you create this wellness temple yourself?" Paraiso asked, his curiosity piqued.

"Yes, of course. Who else do you think would be capable of creating something like this?" Anna replied with a smile. "Do you like it?"

But Paraiso, Pinky, and Dr. Schubidou just looked at Anna in silence. They all had the same thought. Someone who could create this tropical world was undoubtedly capable of much more.

"What's wrong? Why are you silent?" Anna wondered.

"Admit it, you put a cold witch spell on our world!" demanded

Paraiso, not mincing his words.

"What? Are you out of your mind?" Replied Anna, astonished at the outrageous accusation.

"You have to admit, it's an easy assumption to make," the doctor apologized for his suspicions.

"Are you crazy?" Anna angrily chided her feathered visitors. "I would never have thought of conjuring up this wellness oasis here if the weather hadn't turned so lousy."

The birds thought about it. There was something to Anna's explanation. Maybe they were mistaken about her after all. "Can you prove that you didn't do it?" The Rainbow Chief asked Anna.

"No," Anna admitted. "But do you have any proof that it was me?"

Paraiso then explained to Anna what they had discovered and how dire the situation had become.

"That's terrible!" Anna exclaimed, dismayed.

"Yes, indeed. We must stop this disaster!" Said the feathered Chief. "Can you help us with that?"

"I can try," Anna replied. "But this will be a significantly more complex feat than creating this bubble we are standing in."

"What do you mean, try?" Wondered Pinky. "Don't you have supernatural powers?"

"Yes, but to deal with such a complex problem, I probably need spells, such as those in my witch book. And that, as you know, is no longer available to us since the last recreation of this world."

"Does that mean you could only help us if you had that book

back?" Pinky tried to understand.

"Yes," Anna replied, nodding. But then there was another earth tremor.

"I'm afraid we don't have time to get your witch book back," Paraiso chimed in. "If the disappearance of the rainbows continues at this pace, we may have to pack our bags and leave this country."

Then, they were interrupted by a loud sound that sounded like distant thunder. But the sound did not come from the distance but a colossal rainbow high above their feathered heads. Horrified, they all looked up. The rainbow had been a source of beauty and wonder in their tropical world for as long as any of them could remember. But now, it was beginning to crumble, pieces of it breaking off and piercing the transparent bubble that protected them.

Visible cracks were forming in the rainbow, and individual parts were already crumbling off. The rainbow pieces pierced the transparent shield, which burst like a soap bubble with a popping sound. They, therefore, stood unprotected in the cold again. The parrots shivered, their feathers fluffing up in an attempt to keep warm.

"Oh! No! This is the end," screeched Paraiso in panic. At this, he turned so pale that even his otherwise magnificent plumage colors appeared greyish. It dawned on him what it would mean if pieces of the giant rainbow hit them: they would all be crushed.

"Anna! For heaven's sake! Do something!" Cried the doctor, his normally steady voice shaking with fear.

Three pairs of parrot eyes were directed only at Anna. It was clear what these glances meant. Without words, they said: "For heaven's sake, do something! Now!"

But Anna did not seem to hear them. She stood there unchanged and had a strange expression on her face, staring ahead as if she were in a deep trance. None of the parrots were sure whether their cries for help had even reached her.

Then, without further warning, a prominent centerpiece burst out of the rainbow directly above them with a loud, eerie-sounding crashing noise and began to crash down on them. The rainbow parrots did not react. It was too late for them to save themselves, so they just stood rooted to the spot, rigid with fright. In a moment, they knew they would be lying crushed under a rainbow.

Then Anna recited a short but highly effective spell. The centerpiece from the rainbow rushing towards them stopped as if by magic, then hovered silently above them for a short moment and then flew back to its original place in the rainbow. It fit back into its original position like a giant puzzle piece, moving in slow motion.

The parrots looked at Anna in amazement. It was not every day that one saw a witch's spell in action. Then Anna recited a second witch's spell. The parrots observed a white veil forming around the rainbow.

"All good things come in threes!" Cried Anna with satisfaction and, with one last witch's spell, restored the transparent shell to her created tropical world. The parrots cheered, grateful to have been saved from certain destruction.

"You saved us," Paraiso shouted in relief.

"Hooray!" Cheered Pinky simultaneously and did several somersaults, slipping and falling lengthwise, as was to be expected.

From that point onwards, none of them believed Anna was to blame for the current weather situation.

"Whew! That was a close one!" Said the doctor, who was still pale around the beak. He was aware they had dodged death by a hair's breadth.

"Poppycock!" Paraiso downplayed the doctor's concern. "Anna had the situation more than under control, as you've just seen. The end of the world is not going to take place."

"Well, that feat was easier than expected," Anna now agreed with the country's leader, nipping any last doubts in the bud.

"You are still duty-bound to call an emergency meeting of the Supreme Parrot Council as possible," the doctor urged Paraiso in no uncertain terms. The Parrot Council always convened when there was important news about their world.

"Yes, yes. I'll take care of it as soon as I get back home," the country's leading parrot finally conceded after a brief hesitation. But Paraiso's priorities differed from the doctor's. "However, before I can address the Council's concerns, I must first repair the damage to my treehouse," he continued. Suddenly, his countenance brightened. "Anna, could you perhaps use your magic to fix it?"

Anna nodded in agreement, "Yes, of course, I can."

Paraiso and Anna quickly said their goodbyes to the others and departed for his home together, she riding her broom, he using his wings. Dr. Schubidou and Pinky watched as they vanished into the distance, becoming two black dots in the sky.

As dawn approached, the doctor also said his farewells, citing an early departure for work the next day. Pinky, on the other hand, was shivering with cold. He sighed with relief, knowing he could finally warm up in the lagoon's temperate waters. Without further delay, he leaped towards the water's edge, landing with an unexpected thud on a hard surface of ice. The lagoon's warm water had suddenly cooled, and the surface was frozen over.

Rubbing his aching rear end, Pinky realized that he had failed to find warmth and was now desperate for a change in the weather. Lost in thought about a possible solution, he barely noticed the breathtaking natural spectacle above him. The sky was filled with stars and a mysterious, eerie green light.

7

FIRST NOTES

Ed, the night watchman, couldn't understand how the thief had managed to slip away from him after he had caught him red-handed. It bothered him that his spotless record as a night watchman had been tarnished by this incident, and his pride had taken a hit.

The security company promptly called the police, who arrived on the scene in less than half an hour. The officers were faced with the difficult task of calming Ed down before they could start questioning him. Meanwhile, the forensics team had already begun their investigation.

Once Ed had given his account of what had happened, the officer questioning him appeared puzzled and confused.

"How did the thief manage to escape? It sounds like he was trapped," the officer inquired.

"That's what I don't understand," Ed replied honestly.

The officer then questioned another detail in Ed's statement. "Are you sure you didn't imagine the flash of light you described?"

"As sure as I'm standing here now," Ed insisted.

The officer stared at Ed for a long moment before shaking his head in disbelief. "Are you perfectly healthy?" He asked, looking concerned.

"Yes, I am," Ed replied, wondering why the officer was asking.

"I was just considering the possibility that you might have had an epileptic seizure or something similar," the officer explained, adding that people with a certain form of epilepsy often saw strange lights at the onset of a seizure.

Suddenly, the lights came back on throughout the museum. "The blackout is finally over," Ed thought, breathing a sigh of relief. Then he looked at the officer, realizing that he still owed him an answer.

"I'm in perfect health. Last week, I went to my family doctor for a check-up because I had headaches. However, these disappeared after just one massage treatment. My doctor said it was probably caused by my hours of screen time."

The officer looked at him questioningly. "I thought night watchmen spent their time patrolling?"

"Well, that's what a lot of people think, but it's not true," Ed replied to the stunned policeman, who still did not seem convinced. "Come on! I'll show you what I mean," Ed indicated with a wave of his hand that he should follow him. The men then walked upstairs to the second floor. They stopped in front of a room with a large sign on the door. On it, one could read just two words, "Surveillance Room." Ed unlocked the door with a key he had in his pocket.

"Even though this is a heavily guarded museum, I always lock up because there's material in here that only certain people are allowed to see," he explained. Ed flipped on the light switch, revealing a room filled with screens mounted on the walls. Below them was a long wall shelf, a longboard holding several VCRs.

"This is where I work most of the time," the near-retiree said. "It used to be that night watchmen were always on the go, but since technology came along, those days are over. Unfortunately," he added with a grin, "you don't get a lot of exercise as a night watchman these days." He pointed to his stomach. Then they entered the room.

"Take a seat in one of the chairs, please!" Ed requested, like an usher at a movie theatre. The policeman looked at him questioningly but complied with the night watchman's request.

Ed walked over to the many screens mounted on the wall. Two pairs of eyes gazed attentively at the screens. These screens showed various museum rooms from the video cameras' perspective. The recordings from the room where the meteorite had been were greatly important. Ed would have checked them earlier, but he had been so shocked by this theft that he had forgotten.

Ed hoped that this demonstration would not only substantiate the statements he had made but also help them gain critical new insights into the mysterious disappearance of the valuable stone. However, the demonstration turned out to be a total failure as they could not find anything important in any of the video recordings.

The most significant events had not been recorded due to the power failure.

"Well, at least we now know that the blackout was intentional," Ed tried to gloss over the failed performance.

The investigating officer remained silent. Unlike the night watchman, he would only correlate and interpret the findings much later at the police headquarters. The forensic team had already made much progress. They had found a few splashes of dried blood on the destroyed glass of the display case. According to the conclusions drawn later by the police officers, the thief must have injured himself on the glass when destroying the display case.

Upon closer inspection of the museum building, other officers discovered an unlocked skylight from which a rope extended almost to the museum's floor. Unfortunately, forensics was unable to detect any fingerprints on the string. From this, they concluded that the intruder had probably worn gloves. They, therefore, quickly surmised that the burglar had entered the building via the roof after the power had failed. However, it remained a complete mystery how the thief had left the building.

After the police team had finished their investigations and questioning, they took their leave and headed back to the police station to further evaluate the findings. The museum break-in became the main topic of the newspapers and radio news the following day, and an extra-large article with a bold headline dominated the front page of the local newspaper:

MYSTERIOUS BREAK-IN AT THE GEOLOGICAL MUSEUM. THE POLICE ARE IN THE DARK.

The police officer leading the investigation was angry when he read the article. "This is typical," he thought. "No sooner have the police started trying to solve the case than they are criticized by the newspaper people." He crumpled up the newspaper and threw it angrily into a corner of the room. He was determined to prove that the police were not incompetent; he knew that these news stories could jeopardize his chance of a promotion.

The next day, the police held a press conference to release a short initial statement of the first results of the museum break-in. However, the full report containing sensitive data could not be disclosed as it could jeopardize the ongoing investigation. The report revealed that the blood found on the display case was of blood type A and that the cause of the power failure was a short circuit in a power box attached to the museum wall.

The police investigated two possible courses of events. In one version, a large stranger entered the museum from the outside after deliberately cutting off the power, stole the stone, and somehow left the museum. However, the police considered the second scenario more plausible - that the thief had already been in the museum. This led them to suspect the night watchman, who had blood type A, which was consistent with the traces of blood on the display case. Furthermore, it was unlikely that the thief could have left the museum unnoticed.

The lead investigator believed that the night watchman had not only turned off the electricity but had also staged the intrusion himself. He was convinced that the night watchman had hidden the valuable meteorite somewhere in the museum and had taken the stolen goods out of the museum unnoticed just before the museum opened in the morning.

The police quickly found a motive for the theft - the night watchman wanted to increase his pension fund by selling the rare stone. The investigator had the night watchman come to the police station the next day under the pretext of requiring more information salient to the case. He asked Ed to sign his name to confirm the information he had put on record.

After Ed had left his rented apartment to go to the police station, two police officers in disguises were already at his door, tampering with the lock. With a few swift movements, they were able to get inside and begin their search for the stolen goods.

Meanwhile, at the police station, Ed entered the investigating officer's office and waited patiently for him to finish his urgent task. Unbeknownst to Ed, this delay was part of the officer's plan to keep him at the station as long as possible, giving his men enough time to search Ed's apartment undisturbed.

As the officer educated Ed on the importance of the investigation, his eyes fell upon the Band-Aid in Ed's hand. Curious, he asked about the injury, suspecting it could be related to the theft.

Ed quickly tried to explain it away as a gardening accident, but the officer remained skeptical, noting that it was an unusual excuse for winter. This only added to his suspicion about Ed's involvement in the theft.

Just as Ed was about to sign the protocol, the officer received a signal from his men that they had completed their search of Ed's apartment. With a sense of satisfaction, the officer quickly allowed Ed to leave the station.

Once Ed had left, the officer called his two officers over to inquire about their findings. Unfortunately, they did not find any incriminating evidence. The officer was not pleased and assigned them the task of shadowing the museum guard around the clock.

Despite his men's failure, the officer still had one more piece of evidence against Ed—his recent injury. With this in mind, he settled into his chair and continued his investigation.

Yes, he now had no doubt that Ed was the thief. He considered the case solved and had a gut instinct that it would only be a matter of time before Ed made a mistake that would lead to his conviction. He secretly looked forward to that moment, as it would secure his promotion, which had been pending for quite some time. However, until then, he had to deal with a growing pile of other unsolved cases. Sighing, he picked up the first file he saw and opened it.

Ed, on the other hand, returned to his apartment, oblivious to the fact that some objects were no longer in the same places he had left them. Still caught up in thoughts about his visit to the police station, he couldn't shake the memory of the questioning officer's disbelieving expression from his mind. Did he suspect Ed of being involved in the break-in? Or perhaps he was just frustrated…? Ed now felt a sense of sympathy for him, realizing that he was probably overworked and stressed. Thoughts of police incompetence began to haunt him, and he started to doubt whether they were capable of solving the mystery of the break-in at the museum. These doubts followed him throughout the day and even into his dreams at night, where he imagined an incompetent police force accusing him of failing in his work. He woke up in a cold sweat, desperate for a drink of water. However, when he reached for his cup, it was not in its usual place.

"I can't take this anymore," he thought resolutely. "I have to take matters into my own hands before I go crazy."

The next day, feeling exhausted, Ed made himself a strong coffee and retrieved a large notepad from his kitchen drawer. He wrote down any terms that came to mind and began to connect them, eventually producing a satisfactory result. As he did not consider himself the perpetrator, he pondered how the burglar or burglars had left the building undetected. Perhaps they were still hiding in the museum when the doors opened for the first visitors the following day and escaped at a convenient moment, undetected.

When he returned to his regular night shift the following night, he decided not to waste his time watching a movie or some exciting sporting event. Instead, after brewing himself a strong cup of coffee, he deliriously watched the videotapes from before the break-in.

At first, it seemed that watching the video recordings for hours would lead to nothing. The watchman was about to give up, feeling frustrated by the lack of progress. Several young families with children, an older gentleman in a grey suit, and a man with a Southern appearance were the only ones who had entered and left the museum that day. Despite this, he felt that he must have missed something, and his gut feeling urged him to keep searching.

Above all, he found no evidence that anyone had secretly hidden in the museum, leaving his main question unanswered for the time being. However, in the following nights on duty, he also reviewed the surveillance camera recordings, especially those of the days and weeks before the break-in, hoping to find some clues.

One night, he was about to put a tape back on the shelf when he accidentally pressed play, and a particular video sequence appeared on one of the screens. Suddenly, his facial expression brightened, for he had finally found what he had been searching for. This was the decisive clue! He believed he finally knew what the thief looked like.

Excited, he packed the videotape containing his evidence into a briefcase and ran down the stairs to the first floor with it. There, he quickly slipped his coat on. He couldn't wait to see the puzzled face of the policeman handling the case.

8

THE WEATHER STATION

Lara and Nina were in the office of the park supervisor, still in shock from the previous night's events. They were restlessly sliding back and forth in their chairs. Nina almost fell off her chair once, but Lara courageously intervened, preventing it at the very last moment. Bob felt sorry for the girls. He could see that they hadn't gotten much sleep last night.

"Would you like some warm cocoa first?" Bob tried to reassure the children.

Lara and Nina accepted his offer with thanks. Bob, therefore, left the room, only to reappear shortly after with two mugs of warm cocoa and a plate of cookies and chocolate muesli. He also gave them both a warm woolen blanket to wrap themselves in.

"I'm afraid I only have one blanket. You'll have to share it," the meteorologist apologized.

"That's fine," Lara replied. "We like to share. We're sisters."

Bob glanced at the clock hanging above the entrance to his office. He needed to get started slowly on his actual work. "Well, let's hear what's on your minds."

Lara and Nina took turns telling him with tears in their eyes about the mysterious disappearance of their parents. However, they did not mention their trip to the White Mountain massif and the disappearance of the rainbow clock because they did not consider this information relevant.

Bob listened with interest. He nodded and immediately reached for his radio on his desk once they had finished. With this, he could easily communicate with his team members in a large part of the national park. It worked like a walkie-talkie and depended on satellite signals.

He quickly called in a protection squad with motorized snowmobiles and drones with thermal cameras in their equipment. The latter was great for searching for people who had disappeared in the park. Bob knew from experience that the chances of survival for the missing couple were vanishingly small in these low temperatures. But he preferred to keep this to himself since it was important not to alarm the girls, who were freshly traumatized by the loss of their parents. A psychologist, whom Bob had also contacted, was to attend to the well-being of the children.

Then, Bob's workday began. As usual, his phone didn't stay silent for a second. Unfortunately, he no longer had time for the waiting girls. In addition to the constant ringing of Bob's telephone, the woman who worked in the other part of the building, in the tourist information office, poked her curious head through the door regularly, either to ask him something or to tell him something. Meanwhile, the two girls waited on the red sofa in the corner of Bob's office.

"If only we could do something," Lara soon whined impatiently.

"Yes, this waiting is unbearable," Nina agreed with her.

Then, they heard loud engine noises approaching outside. Lara and Nina looked out the window. It was the requested search party. A dozen people, primarily men, parked their snowmobiles just a few feet from the building. Soon, they all crowded into Bob's small office. But one important person was missing: the psychologist. A bearded man in his mid-fifties bent his muscular torso over Bob's desk and whispered the reason in his ear. Bob nodded. The psychologist was still on assignment elsewhere and would not arrive here until the morning of the next day. Bob didn't like that at all, especially since he didn't have time to deal with the two girls still sitting on the couch.

There was a knock at the door. A white-bearded, middle-aged man wearing nickel glasses came in.

"Oh, you have visitors!" The bearded man said in surprise when he saw the many men. "I don't want to be a bother. I won't stay for long! I just wanted to say hello and see what's new."

"No, no. You're not interrupting. Why don't you come in?" Bob urged him, his exasperated expression immediately brightening.

"This is Gunnar," he introduced the man to Lara and Nina. "He works at the Abisko weather station, and his job is to investigate weather phenomena here in the park."

The park supervisor quickly told him about the girls' problem and introduced the others to him as the rescue team. Then, the park supervisor took Gunnar aside and talked to him so quietly that the others could not hear what he was saying.

Bob knew that Gunnar had studied psychology for a semester or two, so he asked him to give him some tips on how best to engage the girls now.

Gunnar felt sorry for the girls. To Bob's surprise, he made a better suggestion.

"If you want, you can stay at my weather station until your parents are back," he told Lara and Nina kindly. "You'll be surprised, I'm sure. The station has several places to sleep. You'll have the best view of the Northern Lights from there; there is a large telescope."

Nina hesitated. Lara gave her a push and said, "Why not? We can't contribute much to the search anyway. Everything we know, we've already said."

"Yes, go ahead! A little distraction won't hurt. Gunnar will bring you back here tomorrow morning at the latest. Then, I will inform you about the current status of the search for your parents. I'll contact Gunnar directly with my special outdoor cell phone if we find them sooner. Do you all understand?"

"Yes, that sounds good," the girls agreed with the suggestion. It was 10 a.m. when Gunnar left the building with the sisters.

Gunnar got behind the wheel of his snowmobile and stepped on the gas while the girls let the wind blow around their noses and admired the breathtaking wilderness passing by.

Lara couldn't help but think of her long-ago trips to the land at the end of the rainbow, which, in contrast, shone with intense rainbow hues.

Around noon, the three finally reached the weather station. Housed inside a large rectangular building with a partially round dome-like roof, the weather station was inconspicuous from the outside.

"Underneath," Gunnar pointed upward to the roof dome, "Is this institute's most expensive acquisition? The telescope!"

"Wow," the sisters exclaimed, curious.

They followed the white-haired scientist inside the weather station, where he showed them to a room with two simple beds, where they left their luggage.

"I'll see you again in 10 minutes. In the meantime, you can freshen up. Then I'll start the tour of the station," Gunnar said before leaving.

Nina gave Lara a brief, irritated look. When they were alone, the words burst out of her:

"Why are we here? I want to know if they've found Mom and Dad!"

"I don't want to be here either. But we have to stay somewhere because we can't help them with the search."

"Why not?"

"Because they already know all the details," Lara repeated what had been told to her in the office, but she was no longer sure if this was the real reason she and Nina had been excluded from the search party. Perhaps the search team expected their parents to be... dead? She swallowed, trying to think of something else.

Nina sighed and gave in.

Later on, Gunnar gave them an extensive tour of the observation station, relishing the opportunity to show them everything in detail until, at the end of his private tour, he proudly presented the centerpiece of the scientific observation station to his visitors.

He led them to the dome-shaped room that housed the huge telescope.

"With this, you can study the Northern Lights, among other things. Do you know why we can watch the Northern Lights here in the north?" Gunnar asked the girls, who had taken seats in two of the many spectator seats.

"I read something about it once," Nina replied, "but I've already forgotten it, unfortunately."

Lara didn't know the answer either and just shook her curly, blonde head.

"So, the Northern Lights are created," Gunnar began to explain, "when high-energy particles from space and the sun hit the Earth's magnetic field. These particles leave the sun in a constant stream, called the solar wind."

"That sounds exciting," Lara said politely, but Nina disagreed.

"In the long run, doesn't scientific observation of the Northern Lights eventually become boring?"

"Well, we don't just look at the Northern Lights. We do a whole bunch of other things," the meteorologist replied with a smile. As he spoke, he scratched his disheveled beard. "For example, we also observe weather patterns throughout the year, and sometimes, we look at the stars."

"Who are *we*?" Wondered Nina.

"I and my work colleague, but he is currently on vacation.

Therefore, the bedroom you may now use is free. You are lucky!"

Gunnar continued, "And it's not as dull as you think, dear Nina. Last night, for example, I saw something I had never seen in my whole life. And believe me, kids, I've seen a lot of phenomena."

"What it was it?" Lara inquired curiously.

"Unlike the normal aurora borealis, the Northern Lights seemed to pulsate last night. I sent the pictures I had taken to my colleagues worldwide and asked for their help. But they could not explain this phenomenon. And that is not all! Normally, the Northern Lights eventually disappear, but this phenomenon shows no signs of going anywhere. Since its emergence, it has been present, even though its luminosity has become minimally weaker."

Gunnar sat down on a chair that was firmly connected to one end of a gigantic magnifying glass, which could be swiveled together with it.

"Look for yourself!" He urged the girls after pointing it at the object and bringing it into focus.

First, Nina looked through the magnifying glass, then Lara. Lara remembered that she and Nina had also seen a greenish light when her parents disappeared. However, she had not attached any importance to it because the Northern Lights could be seen, like so many other objects in the night sky, from different places.

"Really, a beautiful view," Lara said in amazement, but her thoughts had long since returned to the mysterious disappearance of her parents.

On the other hand, Nina found the scientist's explanations interesting, but his workplace was a bit dull since there weren't many people to talk to there. Besides, she found it nicer to look at the Northern Lights without scientific analysis. To see them through scientific eyes robbed the Northern Lights of their mystery and, with it, the feeling of being a small part of something huge. No, this was not a job she would consider in the future.

Meanwhile, the search team was on its way to the northern part of Abisko National Park, where the girls' parents had disappeared without a trace. Once they arrived, the search team found everything exactly as the girls had described it. The torn canvas tent gave rise to some speculation.

Based on the information provided by the girls, specifically the time when they had last seen their parents, the team tried to calculate the maximum distance that the couple could have walked from their tent. Using this information, they then drew a circle on a map.

"The area inside this circle," explained one of the squad leaders, "we need to search as best we can."

The team split into several smaller search parties to explore as much of the search area as possible in the shortest amount of time.

However, some members of the search team remained on the spot to investigate the campsite more closely. This investigation included, among other things, sending drones to take as many pictures as possible of last night's crime scene from high up in the air with the help of a thermal camera, among other things. Data analysis would be conducted off-site due to the few daylight hours available. Therefore, they planned to analyze the data once they had returned to Bob's office.

Finally, after several hours of searching, the search team returned to their starting point at the camp. They finished their search and made their way back to the park ranger's office. But they did not let this time go to waste and informed Bob about the state of affairs. He had just been about to call it a day, but with a loud sigh, he dropped his fat butt back into his desk chair.

It took the team several hours to analyze the images, especially the thermal images taken with the help of the drones. And what they found seemed to go in the right direction. There were indeed a few large objects in the vicinity of the camp, giving off body heat. However, in the end, all of these were identified as wild animals - a bear, a moose, and a lynx.

When Lara and Nina lay down in the cots provided by Gunnar at the weather research station in Abisko that evening, they were far from able to fall asleep, even though they were dog-tired. With Gunnar as their tour guide, they had not had time to think about anything else, not even their parents, which had likely been Gunnar's intention all along. Now, a stream of thoughts and feelings rushed over them, among them, guilt and fear. They felt guilty that they had not joined the search team. They feared that they would have to go through life on their own from now on. Perhaps they would even have to sell the house where they had spent their childhoods to have enough money to live.

"Do you think the search party has been more successful than we were when we tried to look for Mom and Dad?" Asked Nina, suppressing tears.

"Definitely," Lara replied. She tried to give Nina hope so that she could finally fall asleep. But she herself continued to doubt because she remembered what Bob had said to them that morning. Namely, that if their parents were located, he would inform Lara and Nina immediately. But he hadn't contacted them yet. That could only mean that...

At that moment, there was a knock at the door. It was Gunnar.

"Sorry to bother you two so late, but Bob just called to let me know he'd like to see us at his office at the park entrance around 9 a.m. tomorrow."

"That's all he said?" Asked Nina, almost bursting with curiosity.

"Yes," Gunnar replied. "He said someone would be there to talk to us."

Lara and Nina looked at each other. New hope sprouted in them. Did this someone mean their parents? And if so, why all this secrecy?

"What time are we supposed to be there?" Inquired Lara.

"Around 9! I will, therefore, set my alarm for 8 o'clock and then wake you up. After a short breakfast, we'll set out."

Nina was satisfied with this information for the time being, but Lara lay awake for quite a while because a constant stream of unanswered questions disturbed her thoughts. Above all, she tried to imagine what would await her and Nina the following morning. When she couldn't keep her eyes open any longer, she fell into a restless sleep, plagued by vivid dreams.

But when Gunnar woke the girls the following morning, Lara could no longer remember her dreams, as her only thoughts were of her parents.

"Rise and shine, you late risers!" Shouted Gunnar. "Breakfast has been ready for a while."

They were still tired and would have preferred to lie down for a while, but then they remembered their upcoming appointment with Bob and were eager to hear his news. In the small kitchen of the weather station, they had a simple breakfast of cereal and milk, which Gunnar had prepared.

"Unfortunately, I can't offer you pancakes. This weather station is not a 5-star hotel," the meteorologist said with a grin, noticing that this remark had also elicited smiles from the girls. But the girls had no appetite; the tension of the meeting with Bob had hit each of them in the stomach.

Shortly after breakfast, the girls were back on the snowmobile behind Gunnar, whizzing away at a fast pace towards the Abisko National Park entrance. The snowmobile bounced and jerked over the icy terrain, sending snow flying in all directions.

Shortly before 9 a.m., the meteorologist parked the vehicle in front of the Abisko National Park information office, a wooden cabin with a sign reading "Welcome to Abisko National Park" above the door. As they entered the building, the door to Bob's office opened. The park ranger had already seen them coming through his window. Bob asked to speak to Gunnar in private for the time being, which seemed strange to the sisters and only further increased their nervousness.

"Something is not right! I can feel it," Lara whispered to Nina. They had to know where they stood. Therefore, they crept on silent feet to the closed office door and pressed their ears against it to listen.

They did not understand everything the men were talking about, but they picked up three words: "Search... unfortunately... inconclusive."

Nina and Lara had heard enough. They moved away from the door and looked at each other sadly. Yes, they had both heard the same thing. Then they fell into each other's arms and hugged tightly.

Lara suddenly remembered the strange dream she had had last night, where she had met her parents and found her rainbow clock again. She had a strong feeling that the dream had been trying to reveal something to her, something about her future. Lara also had a strong sense of what they had to do next. Wildly determined, she looked Nina in the eye and whispered, "I'm not going to let this end like this. Deep down, I know that we will get our parents back. I promise you that!" Lara no longer felt comfortable remaining in the park ranger's office. "We're going home right now!" She added. "There's someone there who can help us."

When the door of Bob's office opened and Bob, Gunnar, and the psychologist who had come, especially for the children, entered the anteroom, they found no trace of the girls who had been waiting there just a moment ago. It was clear to them that there could only be one explanation: They must have overheard their conversation and run away.

9

THE HIGH COUNCIL OF PARROTS

araiso hadn't been waiting long, and as promised, he had made his most recent announcement come true. The following day, the most talented rainbow parrots in his home country had been invited to a midday meeting.

These parrots formed the highest parrot council, comprising twelve members. They had all arrived on time at a large tent that only they knew the location of. The tent was situated on a grassy field with a clear blue sky overhead. Colorful flowers bloomed in the surrounding fields despite the chilly weather. The parrots made themselves comfortable on the tent floor, sitting on bright cushions arranged in a circle. This allowed all the council members to make eye contact with every other parrot. With their vibrant plumage, they appeared like Indians on the warpath. Their leader, Paraiso, was seated on a remarkably vivid cushion, nervously plucking at his tail feathers.

As always, he was perfectly styled and looked as if he had just come from a beauty contest.

Indeed, he had a beauty session in the new spa area in his wooden domicile. When he had gone back to his house, Anna hadn`t not only fixed the power outage. No, Paraiso had persuaded her to do more for him. Like Anna, he wanted to have a big place for wellness where the daily beauty appointments should take place. And Anna didn't disappoint him. With her witchcraft, she created the home spa with the name "Fire and Ice." As the name pointed out, fire and ice were the elements that were used to get the best recreation possible. Sitting in a wood-fired sauna with a finishing ice bath was the best relaxation ritual Paraiso had ever experienced. But to get ice-cold water, ice cubes were needed. With the actual, unusual low temperatures, the generation of ice cubes was an easy thing to do. So, the climate change really had a positive effect – at least for Paraiso.

 At noon sharp, Paraiso opened the secret session with a loud clearing of his throat, instantly silencing the murmur of council members' voices. "I welcome you, the honorable members of the Supreme Rainbow Parrot Council. As we all know, this Council only meets when there is something important to discuss. That is also the case this time. The current freezing temperatures were about to make all the rainbows of our magical world disappear. But at the last moment, we were able not only to stop this process but even to reverse it."

A loud, astonished murmur filled the tent as the rainbow parrots present heard this for the first time. However, Paraiso had deliberately concealed from them the consequences that threatened a rainbow country without rainbows. He did not want to go that far and worry the council members unnecessarily. After all, the danger was over. At least, that was what he believed.

"How?" One of the parrots asked curiously.

"Very simple! With magic," Paraiso replied.

"Magic?" Another colorful bird echoed.

"Yes, Anna, the only human in our world, has magical powers similar to mine. She used to function as," Paraiso cleared his throat, searching for the appropriate word, "a sorceress and regularly performed her show in front of a large audience."

The council members listened intently, their colorful feathers rustling in the gentle breeze.

Paraiso had deliberately avoided using the term 'witch' to avoid spreading fear among the members present, which could lead to misjudgment. This, in turn, could result in the banning of the witch book from the Rainbow World. The council members whispered among themselves, but there were no awkward interjections.

"They probably think Anna once worked in a circus," Paraiso thought, breathing a sigh of relief. "We finally come to the main point of today's meeting," he announced. "Due to the significant decrease in the number of rainbows, we urgently need to change the name of our world."

Paraiso looked expectantly at the members of the High Council. "I ask for suggestions for a new name!"

Dr. Schubidou, a member of the council who had calmly followed Paraiso's introductory sentences, winced. He could not believe what he had just heard. The doctor looked again at his invitation and noted the date and time. The meeting place was only indicated by an X in case an invitation card was lost, and an unauthorized parrot found it. The Rainbow Land doctor also looked at the back of the card, which he had not done before. Today's topic of the meeting was written there. Astonished, he now read the following words:

Topic: Name change

"What was that about?" He was annoyed by Paraiso's list of priorities. "You brought us here today to find a new name for the land at the end of the rainbow because the old one was no longer suitable?"

The doctor couldn't just let that pass. He knew he had to intervene immediately but didn't know how. Then an idea came to him. "Yes, that will work!" He thought with a smile.

Shortly afterwards, a member of the High Council Of The Parrots heard a repeated "hiccuping" sound coming from the bird doctor. The doctor seemed to have caught a veritable hiccup. Nobody suspected that this hiccup was just a clever ploy and that Dr. Schubidou had produced this strange sound entirely by intention. The leading bird forgot what he had wanted to say next, and almost a dozen pairs of eyes now looked at him uncomfortably. Paraiso's face turned dark purple with embarrassment.

However, Dr. Schubidou used this moment of silence to raise his objections, which he had just briefly thought out:

"Dear members of the High Council, everything Paraiso just said is true. Yesterday, our beautiful homeland was on the brink of destruction. Only with the help of Anna were we able to avert this terrible fate just in time. It seems that the state of our world has stabilized for now. Unfortunately, we still have not found the cause of the low temperatures. Therefore, the danger still exists. We must prevent it from happening again. My urgent appeal to the Council is this: We must not rest until we have found and eliminated the cause."

Paraiso had not expected an objection at this point. He stared angrily at the doctor, considering the further action he suggested to be unnecessary.

"I hate to repeat myself, but for you, I will: The threat has been dealt with." Paraiso tried to sound friendly.

"Yes, yes. I understand that," the doctor said. "Anna is protecting us. But how long do you think this will work? What if she gets sick or wants to travel to the human world? Then, she won't be able to rush to our aid when the need arises. It is your duty as the head of the country to do everything conceivable to protect the inhabitants of this world. Everything! Do you understand?"

"I just told you that I, Paraiso, have the whole situation under my control. CONTROL. There is currently not the slightest danger," screeched the highest-ranking parrot in the country, now entirely out of his mind.

"I don't believe you! I want proof," the doctor added.

"Evidence? You have seen it with your own eyes. Anna has not only stopped the crash of the rainbow, she also turned the clock back and repaired it. That's my proof!" shouted Paraiso angrily. He didn't like the fact that the doctor kept contradicting him. It was simply disrespectful. Paraisos was convinced that he was right. The land at the end of the rainbow had been created by a magic spell. So, a magic spell could be the solution to hold the situation stable.

"Maybe you're right, and the situation will remain stable," the doctor tried again, this time in a deliberately calmer tone. "Nevertheless, I'm afraid, and that's why I want something to happen. For by a hair, we all would have perished."

"Do you have proof that the situation is unstable?"

"Well, er…no! But…," the doctor started.

"As you all can see," Paraiso interrupted him and turned to the other parrots with a smile, "the situation is under control, and we have all the time in the world to find the cause for the weather change."

"I am still not convinced!" The doctor said stubbornly. "I want to solve this riddle as soon as possible!"

The council members watched helplessly their Chief exchanging blows with the doctor. Their heads turned in one direction, then the other, as if they were watching an exciting ping-pong match. But there was no end to this argument. They did not know whom to believe.

Finally, one of the older members of the High Council interrupted the two parrots, who were bickering like fighters.

"I don't know which of them is correct. I can't decide. All I know is that I certainly don't want to lose our dearly beloved Rainbow Land."

This last sentence was enough to set an avalanche rolling. Others jumped to his side because they felt similarly. Dr. Schubidou observed them with a sense of benevolence.

What exactly should happen next? No one knew, but all except Paraiso agreed that something had to be done. But to believe that Paraiso would now give in was a mistake. He made a desperate, last attempt to go over the schedule:

"You're all right, of course," he said kindly, making all the parrots feel that he understood them perfectly. "Something is already happening, after all, or we wouldn't all be here now, would we? So I'm asking for suggestions for names for our country."

"How about 'the country that no longer exists?'" Dr. Schubidou quipped, earning a few laughs.

Paraiso turned red. He was bursting at the seams, but before he could vent his anger, an older yellow-orange parrot dared to ask the doctor a question.

"You've said you were calling for more far-reaching measures. What exactly did you have in mind?" The parrot asked.

"Well, I thought that we could, for example, entrust a team of experts to find the cause of the cooling temperatures. Only if we know the root cause can we try to eliminate it," Dr. Schubidou explained. "If the cause disappears, temperatures should return to normal."

"But that's not important right now," Paraiso snorted angrily. "What's important is for me to decide and no one else. The Council only helps with the implementation."

"I'm sorry," another bird interjected. "I see it a little differently than you do!"

Several parrots nodded in response. Paraiso realized that he had lost more ground than he could make up right away. Moreover, he now felt that his honor had been offended.

"Why don't we just vote on which course of action to take?" Again, the all-knowing doctor was getting in Paraiso's way.

"I'm sorry! I don't see any reason for that," Paraiso screeched, but it was too late.

An increasingly loud chorus of "Vote! Vote! Vote!" Filled the room.

"Okay! We'll vote," the Chief finally bowed to the pressure of the parrots present.

After a short break, the vote took place. To the surprise of the present council parrots, the result was very close. The doctor's proposal received only a narrow majority of 51 percent, but this slim majority was sufficient for the doctor's demands to be met.

Paraiso was still angry because the doctor had contradicted him, but he was also relieved since the vote could have been worse for him. The meeting of the High Council ended, dissolved by Paraiso.

Afterward, he quickly made his way back to his parrot house, a beautiful structure with rainbow-colored walls and an intricately designed roof. On it, there was a new sign on which any approaching visitor could easily read the words "FIRE & ICE" already from a big distance. Several parrots from his beauty team were already waiting impatiently for him inside. Paraiso settled in and opened a pack of warmed mud from the Rainbow River. As he sipped the deliciously warm liquid, he began to think about the first possible candidate for the required expert team. He needed someone who could handle the job with expertise and experience. Suddenly, he thought of Pinky, of all parrots, the clumsiest one in the whole country.

If Pinky didn't succeed, which was highly likely, Paraiso knew that the well-intentioned suggestion of the cheeky doctor would look like a wrong decision in retrospect. In the future, Paraiso would ensure that all decisions were made exclusively in his favor as the leader of the colorful rainbow world. He was already secretly looking forward to this scenario.

10

OWN INVESTIGATIONS

Ed's discovery electrified him; he was so excited that he immediately called the police officer investigating the meteorite theft.

"I have important news!" The night watchman proudly announced.

"Really?" The officer asked him doubtfully.

"Yes, it's better if I tell you in person!" Ed replied.

"Fine by me! But it's just before lunch, and I'm off this afternoon. It would be better if… Hello? Are you still there?" He frowned, as Ed had already hung up on him.

After stowing the videotape containing the evidence in a bag, Ed put it into one of the pockets of his winter jacket. He then grabbed his keys and headed straight for the police station.

Ed imagined the investigating officer would be grateful to him for this decisive tip. It did not occur to him that the police might think he was the thief and that the story he told was just a red herring to put them off the scent. He was so lost in thought that he almost slipped on an icy patch on the sidewalk on his way to the station.

Very soon, he was knocking on the office door of the officer in charge of the case.

"Come in!" Rumbled the man behind the desk. It was 5 minutes to noon.

The door opened, and the night watchman from the museum appeared in the doorway. The expression on the policeman's face spoke volumes.

"Well, what do you have that is so important that it can't wait until tomorrow?" He moaned.

Ed looked shocked for a moment, then he took a seat on the wooden chair at the policeman's desk, sitting directly opposite him. The officer stared at him irritably, hoping the last meeting of the day would at least be brief so as not to sacrifice any more of his valuable free time.

The police station was old and cramped, located on the outskirts of the city. The walls were lined with outdated posters and notices, and the musty scent of old papers lingered in the air.

Ed was too enthused to notice much of this, though. He shared, in a few sentences, everything he had found out. "I've brought proof!" He concluded, pulling the videotape out of his jacket pocket.

The ticking wall clock already showed 10 minutes past 12. The officer sighed softly, knowing he was about to lose yet more of his free time, as it would be difficult for him to dismiss the night watchman's claims.

He opened the desk's bottom drawer and pulled out a thick file folder containing the documents about the break-in at the museum. Then he put it on his desk. He looked into the folder and finally found where he had filed the protocol for the break-in at the museum. He quickly skimmed through it, but nowhere did he find an entry made about this suspicious visitor. He picked up an elegant blue and gold ballpoint pen and added Ed's details in handwriting.

"Let me see that!" The policeman said, gesturing towards the videotape. The officer opened another drawer, which contained a digital video camera. Much to Ed's surprise, the tape fit the camera.

"Fast forward to 9:55, please! And then to 2:32!" Ed prompted him. Sure enough, on both occasions, as Ed had claimed, a particular male came into view.

The policeman closed his eyes for a moment, seemingly lost in thought. Then he said in a skeptical tone, "Is that all you have?"

"I'm afraid I don't quite understand," Ed replied, looking confused.

"Well, even if this man entered the museum several times on a certain day before the burglary, that is far from proof that he is our thief. Isn't the collection in your museum relatively popular?" The police officer asked.

"Yes, it is, but..." Ed began, but the policeman cut him off.

"Well, this man was undoubtedly traveling as a tourist and was only in this city for a short time. He must have found the exhibits so interesting that he wanted to see everything, so he returned in the same afternoon."

"Or maybe he came by again to plan his upcoming robbery," Ed said, sticking stubbornly to his version of events.

The police officer studied the expression on the museum employee's face for a moment. He recognized Ed's determination and knew that he would not be able to brush him off with a simple remark. Therefore, he decided to take further steps to be rid of his unwanted visitor.

"If you don't believe me, then we'll have a look at the police database to see if the man has ever been convicted of a crime," he said.

Ed's face suddenly brightened. He waited patiently as the police officer typed something into the computer's keyboard in front of him. The museum employee watched as the officer opened an electronic criminal file containing a long list of criminals with criminal records. The officer then took a still image of the suspect from the surveillance video and forwarded it to his computer via an internet link. He copied the photo and entered it into the mug shot search program.

As suspected by the police officer, the image did not yield a single hit. However, neither Ed nor the investigating officer could have known that someone had deliberately deleted the file of the man in question the day before.

"There you go. Nothing!" The policeman said, trying to get rid of Ed.

But, for Ed, the man's lack of a criminal record was not definitive proof that he had been wrong in his suspicions.

Ed didn't trust the police computer to be infallible. He decided not to leave the room yet and asked, "Have they figured out the reason for the power outage?"

"Of course! The police are not entirely stupid," the policeman replied, sounding slightly offended. He had forgotten that he had wanted to end the conversation. "There was a short circuit in the electric box attached to the museum wall."

"What caused the short circuit?" Ed asked.

"According to the electric company, it was likely a coincidence," the policeman said.

"But don't they understand?" Ed interrupted him. "The thief got into the museum unnoticed via the roof only after the power went out. The surveillance cameras didn't work either, and he was able to take a rare meteorite from its display case without setting off any alarms."

"Thank you for that tutorial," the policeman retorted, sounding slightly sour. "I wasn't finished. I wanted to add that it is still possible the burglar triggered the power outage, but even if we know he did it, it still doesn't help us one bit."

"Why not?" Ed wondered.

"Because the question of how the thief was able to leave the museum without leaving the slightest trace remains unanswered," the policeman said. "Neither you, nor the museum's modern alarm system, nor the dogs have been able to get us anywhere on this. Don't you think that's strange?"

"Yes, I haven't been able to make sense of it either," Ed confessed.

"Too bad. Then we won't get anywhere today," the officer tried to end the conversation. "You'd better go home and take some time off. Why don't you relax and take a vacation?"

"But... I don't need a vacation," Ed returned, feeling irritated.

"Well, then do something else. Pursue one of your hobbies," the officer continued, his patience wearing thin. "In any case, I don't have any more time to entertain your suspicions. Other unsolved cases are waiting for me tomorrow. But now I'm finally off duty!"

The policeman pointed to a stack of files piled high on a corner of his desk. Ed wanted to say something else, but when he saw that the officer had left the room without another word, he had no choice but to leave. The wall clock showed that it was shortly before 1 p.m.

Only when Ed had made his way down to the lobby of the police station did he stop and take a few deep breaths. He finally felt better. He was relieved to have shared his findings with the officer in charge.

After a moment, doubts crept into the night watchman's mind. Perhaps the officer had been right, and he did indeed need to take a break. However, he quickly pushed these thoughts aside and focused on finding a solution to the power failure at the geological museum. As he pondered his next move, an idea struck him.

He reached into his pocket and pulled out his smartphone, quickly went online, and typed in a search term. Within seconds, he found the website of the local power company. Glancing at the homepage, he noted that the power station was still open until 4 p.m. It was now shortly after 1 p.m., which meant he had plenty of time to visit. On his way there, he stopped by a street kiosk to grab a quick bite to eat.

He soon found himself in the waiting room of the power company.

Two people were already waiting, so he took a ticket and sat down to wait. When it was finally his turn, he met with a relatively new employee who was eager to answer any questions he had.

Ed introduced himself and mentioned the break-in at the geological museum and the power failure that preceded it. The power plant employee confirmed what he had already heard from the police – it was a short circuit that had caused the outage due to an overload of the power supply. However, what had caused the overload was still unclear.

The night watchman had hoped to learn more about the circumstances surrounding the power failure, so he was disappointed by the employee's response. Just as he was about to leave, he remembered the videotape he had in his jacket pocket.

"May I show you a video recording from the museum?" He asked the employee cautiously.

Ed proceeded to give an eyewitness account of the break-in, spurring the employee to agree to view the tape. "I'll be off work soon anyway, and I don't have anything important to do here today," the employee said, glancing at the deserted waiting area of the power station.

Together, they went to a room that served as the secretary's office, where they found a laptop and video players. They quickly watched the video sequence Ed had previously shown the police officer.

"Strange!" Remarked the power plant employee. "This is the man who contacted us just a few days ago in response to a job ad."

"Are you sure?" Ed asked, making sure he had heard correctly.

"Yes, for sure. You don't forget an appearance like that very quickly," the employee replied. "He seemed very interested. I showed him around the entire power plant on my boss's instructions. He was especially interested in the power supply infrastructure of important buildings. For instance, we happened to visit the museum."

"You *happened* to visit the museum?" Ed thought sarcastically. He knew the museum visit was no coincidence.

"So, what was his name?" He asked curiously.

"Gordon. But I'm afraid I don't remember his full name," he replied, shrugging his shoulders.

Seeing Ed's disappointed expression, he added: "But perhaps the secretary who received his application folder knows more about him. Come with me, and we can ask her."

They left the room and arrived at a small office with "Secretary" written in capital letters on the door. They knocked, but no one answered.

"She must have already gone home," the new employee said, pulling a key out of his pocket and opening the door. "This is a master key. It fits most rooms," he explained with a grin.

In the back of the dimly lit room stood a large wooden desk surrounded by stacks of files and folders. The surface of the desk was cluttered with a computer, a few application folders, and an open appointment calendar. The desk belonged to a bored-looking employee, who was busy scanning through the names of the applicants in the folders.

As Ed entered the room, he approached the employee and asked, "Excuse me, have you seen Gordon's application folder?"

The employee raised his eyebrows and replied, "I'm afraid you're out of luck; the secretary has already sent Gordon's application folder back to him."

Ed's heart sank. He had been hoping to find some information about Gordon's whereabouts, but it seemed like he was too late. Nevertheless, he pressed on with his questions.

"When was the date of his interview?" Ed inquired more randomly.

"It was last Tuesday," came the reply as if shot from a pistol.

Ed thought for a moment. Tuesday was three days before the break-in at the museum.

"Do you know anything more about him? For example, where he lives?" Ed inquired.

"Unfortunately not. That is, he said he lived on a boat," the man replied.

"Boat?" Ed asked tensely.

"Yeah, he mentioned that to me anyway."

Ed's mind raced. If Gordon lived on a boat, he could be anywhere by now. But then the man on the desk remembered something:

"He told me at which marina his boat was moored so we could send his application back if his employment with us didn't pan out. I think it was somewhere on the East Coast."

"More details, please," drilled Ed.

"Sorry, I don't know any more than that," the clerk replied and then suggested contacting the secretary in charge via email.

But when the clerk sent his message, an automatically generated message came from the system. He read: "I'm on vacation for four weeks as of now!"

"She has a full four weeks of vacation. I'm afraid you'll have to wait a bit for an answer," the clerk apologized.

Ed sighed. It seemed like he was back to square one. He wondered if he would ever be able to track down Gordon and find out the truth about the museum break-in.

Ed was disappointed. He had already walked out when he realized he was missing his smartphone. "I think I left it in the office. It must have fallen out of my pocket," he said.

He returned to the room. His smartphone was resting on the chair where he had been sitting. As he pocketed it, his eyes fell on the open appointment book lying on the desk. Acting on a hunch, he stepped closer and briefly glanced at it.

On Tuesday of last week, he saw a handwritten entry. It was a Spanish name, Gordon Eduardo Vallez, and an address. Ed's heart raced with excitement. This could be the breakthrough he had been waiting for in his investigation.

"Have you found your phone?" Inquired the clerk, looking impatient.

Ed wheeled around quickly. "Uh, yeah! I did. Just now. It's under the desk. Just a minute, I have to pick it up."

The night watchman bent down and pretended to reach for his smartphone, but in reality, he took several pictures of the entry in the appointment book. Then, he hurriedly said goodbye to the man.

On the way home, Ed took his phone out of the inside pocket of his winter jacket to check whether the photographed text was legible. He smiled with relief as he examined the result. He was pleased with his visit because he had the name of the man that the surveillance cameras in the museum had recorded. He also had the address of the marina, the place where the alleged meteorite thief was likely staying at the moment.

Ed knew that the drive would take them a couple of hours in his aging pickup truck, and it was too late to start the journey today. The sun was already low on the horizon, bathing the sky in a golden-yellow, magical light. He decided that he would set off for the marina the very next day to get a closer look.

11

BACK AT HOME

After Lara and Nina learned that Bob had called off the search for their parents, they couldn't stand to be in the park superintendent's office building for another minute. They left without saying goodbye to Bob or Gunnar. Lara briefly thought about her missing rainbow clock, but she had little hope of finding it again. Instead, she came up with a better plan. The sisters hopped on the next bus to the town's train station, which shared the same name as the national park.

As they boarded the train that same afternoon, the girls couldn't help but feel the strange emptiness of leaving without their parents. Nevertheless, they felt as if they had made the right decision. They sat alone in the train compartment, staring out the window in silence. The passing landscape consisted mainly of picturesque lakes and dense forests, and the only sound was the rhythmic rattling of the train.

Eventually, Lara decided to break the silence and shared her plan to save their parents with Nina.

After she had finished, Nina asked excitedly, "So we're going to ask our neighbor, Mr. Arvidsson, if he can build us a time travel clock again, right?"

Lara nodded, "Yes, exactly. Once we have that clock, we can go back in time and stop ourselves from going to Abisko. That way, our parents won't disappear in the first place."

Nina couldn't have agreed more with Lara's brilliant plan. "That could work! It's brilliant!" She said.

They both smiled, feeling hopeful again. Mr. Arvidsson had successfully assembled a fully functional rainbow time travel clock for them twice before, and they were confident he could do it again.

The train rattled south all night until they finally arrived in the town where they lived. They had to walk for half an hour as they couldn't afford a cab. The girls didn't stop to rest when they arrived home but headed straight to their neighbor's house. They rang the doorbell, but the aging clockmaker wasn't there at the moment. "Maybe he's out shopping. Come on! We'll try again later," Lara suggested.

As they walked back home, a girl from across the street came running up to them. Lara and Nina knew her well since they often played together. "Are you looking for Mr. Arvidsson?" She asked. They both nodded, and she added, "I'm afraid you're too late. The old clockmaker is in the hospital. He was picked up by an ambulance yesterday."

"Oh no! Is he sick?" Nina asked in dismay.

"No, I think he got hurt in the fire in his garage," the girl replied.

"What do you mean?" Asked Lara, horrified. "What fire?"

"Imagine that," the girl said almost to herself, ignoring Lara's questions, "a terrible fire, right here… Several fire trucks came racing up the road and stopped right over there," the girl said, pointing to the street where they were standing.

"What happened then?" Asked Nina impatiently.

"Well, what do you think? The firefighters extinguished the fire. But it was already too late to save the garage."

Suddenly, a terrible thought came into Lara's mind. The garage had been the retired clockmaker's hobby workshop. Even if he had survived the fire, would it even be possible for him to build them a new rainbow time travel clock?

After saying their goodbyes, Lara and Nina were alone again. Nina gasped, "Oh no! What are we going to do?"

"We're sticking to our plan. We're going to ask Mr. Arvidsson for help. We need to go to the hospital right away and visit him," Lara insisted.

They went into their house and looked for some change. A short time later, they were on the bus that took them straight to the hospital's side entrance. From there, it was only a short walk to the main entrance. In the entrance hall, they inquired at the information desk about the whereabouts of their neighbor.

Mr. Arvidsson was looking out of the window when they arrived. He glanced around and was surprised to see Lara and Nina. The first thing he told them was that the doctors had confirmed that he was suffering the effects of smoke inhalation. But he continued, saying that he had been lucky, having been given extra oxygen in the ambulance.

When he heard what had happened to Lara and Nina, his face fell. "Oh, dear! That doesn't sound good at all. I'm sorry."

They hurriedly told him about their idea to change their parents' fate.

"For this, we would urgently need a new time travel clock. Could you build us one?" asked Lara.

Mr. Arvidsson only looked at her thoughtfully at first. Then, finally, he answered, "Maybe. But first, I need to tell you a little more about the fire." He cleared his throat. "Only where is the best place to start?" He pondered aloud, scratching his head.

"It's best to start at the beginning," Nina offered sagely.

"Yes, of course! How silly of me. So, on the day of the fire, I was still in my clock workshop because I was working on a friend's order. His watch no longer worked, and I was supposed to find out the reason why and fix it. But the repair turned out to be more complicated than expected and, therefore, dragged on a bit longer. I got thirsty at some point and interrupted the work."

Lara and Nina listened carefully to Mr. Arvidsson's story, trying to piece together what had happened. As he continued to talk, they began to understand the chain of events that led to the fire in his garage.

"Consequently, I walked back to my house, up the stairs to my kitchen. When I headed back to my workshop after a short coffee break, I immediately noticed something was wrong. I saw large clouds of smoke coming from my garage. I ran towards it. When I opened the garage door, smoke, and high flames rushed towards me. I grabbed the fire extinguisher located at the garage entrance, but I could not deal with the fire alone. I called loudly for help. Luckily, a neighbor heard me. He tried to help me, but we soon realized it was better to call the fire department. When the fire truck finally arrived, the street was full of onlookers. You should have seen it!

"Though I was struggling with the smoke that had enveloped the entire garage, I still managed to save a few essential things." Mr. Arvidsson looked around. Then he continued in a whisper, "Among them were my friend's watch and the translation of the clock monk's diary, which I used to build the rainbow time travel clock. But the journal was unfortunately damaged in the fire. Several pages are illegible and thus unusable. The fire department was quickly on the scene and brought the fire under control. But unfortunately, it was already too late to save my garage.

"Only then did I notice that I was getting severe headaches, dizzy spells, and bouts of coughing. Some people in the neighborhood thought it prudent to call an ambulance. So I ended up in the hospital."

"How did the fire happen in the first place?" Asked Lara, her interest piqued.

"Unfortunately, I don't know. Nor did the police who visited me here in the hospital," Mr. Arvidsson said, his voice weak. "However, it may have been caused by a lamp that had fallen over."

"A lamp?" Nina asked in amazement.

"Yes," he replied. "I still use old light bulbs in some cases. These give off heat and can be a fire risk. There's just one problem with this theory."

"What?" Wondered Lara.

"I can't for the life of me remember using such a lamp, even though the police said they found the remains of one after the fire," he explained.

"Strange!" Nina exclaimed.

Mr. Arvidsson nodded.

"Maybe it wasn't Mr. Arvidsson who caused the fire at all, but someone else," Lara thought to herself, remembering what he had told her when he made her first rainbow time travel clock, namely that the secret service was very interested in this invention and might try to get their hands on it. Lara now had a queasy feeling in the pit of her stomach.

"Can you build the clock or not?" Asked Lara again.

"The clock workshop is gone," her neighbor answered evasively. "I can continue to work in my basement, but it is far less comfortable there because the space is much smaller."

"You said earlier that the construction manual for the rainbow time travel clock is damaged," Lara reminded him.

The old clockmaker nodded.

"How badly?" Lara wanted to know, guessing that she had found his sore spot.

"That's exactly the problem," Mr. Arvidsson finally spoke up. "Only the part describing how to build a clock for the journey to Rainbow Land has been preserved. Unfortunately, I can't build a time travel clock."

"You've got to be kidding!" cried Nina, aghast.

"Are you sure?" Lara inquired. She, too, simply could not, or *would* not, believe this.

"Unfortunately, yes," her neighbor confirmed.

"That means we can't get our parents back," Lara said softly.

A prolonged silence filled the hospital room.

"Wait a minute!" Exclaimed Nina suddenly. "I have another idea. We might still be able to save them. But to do that, we urgently need to get to the land at the end of the rainbow."

Lara gave her a questioning look.

Turning to Mr. Arvidsson, Nina asked, "You said you can still build a clock to get us there?"

"Yes, that shouldn't be a problem," her neighbor replied, nodding. "It's true that some of the instructions for building the rainbow clock have been irretrievably damaged, but I still remember pretty clearly how I assembled the first clock of this kind."

"Then please do your best!" Nina urged him.

"I still don't see how this helps us save our parents," Lara interrupted.

"No? If we manage to get to the world of the rainbow parrots, we'll just borrow a rainbow clock that is fully operational and will allow us to time-travel. With it, we will return to our world and then travel back in time to talk our parents out of going to Abisko," Nina said excitedly.

"That's brilliant!" Lara exclaimed, her eyes wide with wonder. "I have to admit I hadn't thought of that possibility."

"Wait a minute," their neighbor interrupted them, holding up a hand. "I have to be released from the hospital first."

Lara and Nina exchanged disappointed glances. "And when will that be?" Lara asked, trying to remain hopeful.

"Tomorrow," the old clockmaker replied, grinning from ear to ear. "The doctor said, during his round this morning, that I could leave the hospital as early as tomorrow morning. Because my lungs are again in good working order."

"Great!" Exclaimed Lara, feeling relieved, and Nina shared her excitement.

"Tomorrow," said Mr. Arvidsson, "I will look over my old orders. A while ago, I ordered various parts from a wholesaler on the internet to build another rainbow clock. As a self-employed clockmaker, knowing what you take in and spend is the most important thing. Remember that."

The girls nodded, understanding the importance of financial management.

He continued, "I also drafted plans for a quicker to assemble, and therefore more practical, Rainbow Clock. Luckily, the plan was folded up in my wallet." Mr. Arvidsson opened the top drawer of his bedside table with one hand, rifling through it until he found a small wallet. With a broad, triumphant grin, he pulled out a sheet of paper folded several times and held it aloft. "Here it is!"

The door creaked open, and a group of medical professionals entered the room. It was time for ward rounds, and all visitors were instructed to leave. Once the medical staff had finished, Lara and Nina returned to their neighbor's room, finding him smiling.

The next day, a Sunday, Mr. Arvidsson returned home from the hospital as he had promised. Despite his exhaustion from being in the sterile, antiseptic-smelling environment for so long, he still managed to tip the cab driver generously.

Although he typically allowed himself to rest on Sundays, Mr. Arvidsson didn't let that stop him fulfilling his promise to Lara and Nina. He disappeared into his cellar, and the sound of muffled knocking could be heard later on. Most of the neighbors weren't bothered by the sounds since they were out for the day.

Unfortunately, the installation of an additional time travel unit proved to be a challenge due to a lack of written instructions. However, Mr. Arvidsson was resourceful and had the necessary spare parts to construct a Rainbow Clock. He worked obsessively through the night, emerging the next morning with thick rings under his eyes.

Nina was skeptical when she saw the result. "And you think it will work properly despite the lack of instructions?"

"I hope so. But if you have any doubts, just try it out," Mr. Arvidsson suggested, yawning.

Lara was worried. "Isn't that dangerous? What if it works differently than we thought?"

Mr. Arvidsson chuckled. "No, not at all! Either it works, or it doesn't work. There's nothing in between!"

Lara was about to voice her concerns, but Mr. Arvidsson interrupted her. "Nothing!" the old clockmaker emphasized, audibly offended. "Please try it out before you complain about my work. You can still do that. Until then, I'm going to take a nap. I'm dog-tired because I've been working all night. Good day!"

Without waiting for an answer from the girls, he turned on his heel and shuffled back to his small house.

"You know, I think he's mad at us," Nina whispered to her sister, feeling uncomfortable.

"I just wanted to make sure we wouldn't disappear too," Lara tried to justify her actions.

"So you don't have any more concerns over testing it?" Asked Nina.

"Actually, no," Lara gave in.

"So we just wait for the rainbow gate to open next. But when and where will that happen?" Nina asked.

"We'll find out in a minute," Lara replied, pressing a few buttons on the clock. The clock was an intricate piece of machinery with gears and levers; its intricate design hinted at the clockmaker's expertise. Then she said, "I have some good news and some bad news. Which one do you want to know first?"

"The good news first," Nina decided.

"The next portal to the Rainbow World will open as early as 11 a.m. the day after tomorrow," Lara said with a smile.

"That's good!" Said Nina, feeling relieved. "But what's the catch?"

"The portal will form a little further south, unfortunately, because there won't be a double rainbow here anytime soon due to the cold," Lara replied. "Not until next spring when the temperatures rise again."

"How far south?" Nina asked, feeling a twinge of worry. She wanted to know how far they had to travel.

"On the south side of the Alps. We have to travel to Italy for that, Venice to be exact," Lara replied.

"Venice?" Repeated Nina, her eyes wide with surprise.

"Yes. If we want to get our parents back in the foreseeable future, we have to get there. Because I don't feel like waiting until spring," Lara said with determination.

"Neither do I. But how are we going to get to Venice? If we take the train without an adult in tow, we might be stopped and sent home. Maybe we should ask Mr. Arvidsson to accompany us?" Nina suggested.

"No. I'd rather not. We've already upset him," Lara tried to dissuade her sister.

"You upset him, not me," Nina corrected her sister. "If I ask him nicely, I'm sure he'll help us."

Lara hesitated for a moment. Then she replied, "Yeah, maybe you're right. But I have another idea, in case our neighbor doesn't want to come with us."

"And what would that be?" Asked Nina, once again annoyed by her sister's secretiveness.

"Wait here!" Lara replied. Then she left Nina sitting alone on the sofa in the living room while she rushed up to her room on the second floor, probably to get something. A few minutes later, Lara was back again, holding a black hat in her hand.

"An old hat," Nina frowned, "so what?"

"This is not just any ordinary hat. It's an exact copy of the witch's hat that made us invisible once in the past. I got it as a gift from Anna on our last visit to Rainbow Land," Lara explained.

"So you plan to use it to make us invisible?" Nina asked in surprise. "But it's still not acceptable to travel without a valid train ticket."

"I didn't say anything about traveling without tickets. We can ask Mr. Arvidsson to help us buy the tickets online," Lara suggested.

Nina agreed, and they went over to Mr. Arvidsson's house again and pressed the doorbell. It took a while before Mr. Arvidsson opened the front door. He had already put on his pajamas, ready to take a nap.

When Mr. Arvidsson heard about their plans to travel to Venice, his sour expression immediately disappeared, and he became excited. He had dreamed of traveling to Venice since childhood but had never quite made it there. He used some money he had saved to book one of the best hotels in Venice for a whole week. He also paid for the sleeping car on the trains.

"Our journey starts today!" He exclaimed. "Tonight, around 10 p.m., our train leaves. We have just under 6 hours to pack. It's a night train that goes via Malmö to Denmark, then across Germany to Basel in Switzerland. There, we have to change trains once. If everything goes according to plan, we'll be in Venice the day after tomorrow morning."

"All done!" Mr. Arvidsson said, grinning with satisfaction as the train tickets emerged from a slot in his printer.

Relieved that their neighbor was coming along and quite excited about the trip that was about to take place, Lara and Nina walked back to their house. They packed clothing suitable for the spring-like temperatures in Venice and the summer-like ones in the land at the end of the rainbow at the same time. Nina also found a pocket-sized guidebook about Venice in the guest room. "We can read through that during the train ride," she said, beaming, and

Lara nodded in agreement.

"What about the money? We need Euros, don't we?" Nina interjected.

Lara nodded. "Yes, we have quite a bit of change in our piggy banks that we have saved up. Let's stuff our pockets with it. It's better that way anyway because Venice is supposed to be crawling with pickpockets."

Mr. Arvidsson ordered pizza for dinner and invited the two girls to join him. There was delicious spaghetti ice cream for dessert, which had curiously been invented by an Italian living in Germany.

Finally, the time had come. The doorbell rang, and the cab driver standing outside took Lara and Nina to the train station. The train was a little late, but Mr. Arvidsson assured them they had plenty of time to change trains.

After two days of train travel without significant delays, they finally arrived at their destination: Venice. Excited, they stepped off the train, but Lara and Nina had trouble getting their bearings. Thankfully, Mr. Arvidsson had memorized some important Italian terms during the train ride, which helped them find their way from the station out to the pier where the water cabs were leaving and arriving.

There, they boarded a water cab that was waiting to take them to the famous St. Mark's Square in the early hours of the morning. Nina had, of course, packed her camera and took photographs like crazy. St. Mark's Square was teeming with people, and Lara and Nina became increasingly nervous because of the numerous pickpockets.

"St. Mark's Square is one of the most famous places in the world,"

Mr. Arvidsson enthused. "Among other things, St. Mark's Basilica and the Doge's Palace are located here."

"Look at the clock up there!" Exclaimed Nina.

"Yes, that's the Clock Tower, another beauty of St. Mark's Square," her neighbor, the clock expert, returned in amazement.

"No, I mean the time. It's a quarter to 10 now," Nina replied.

"Yes, then we have plenty of time before the double rainbow will form here," Lara immediately understood what her sister was getting at.

They decided to go to the hotel where Mr. Arvidsson would leave his heavy suitcase behind the reception desk. The hotel was nearby, but on the other side of the canal, so they first had to cross the nearest bridge.

On the way to the hotel, Lara and Nina discovered a small ice cream parlor. "Come on, let's go buy some ice cream and wait until Mr. Arvidsson checks in!" Suggested Nina, who was also starting to get a little hungry.

"That's an excellent idea," Lara returned, beaming as she saw many different types of ice cream she had never tried before.

Lara and Nina sat down to enjoy their sundae in peace. Then Lara heard a tourist at the next table asking a lady with a dachshund in English what time it was. When she answered, "A quarter to eleven," Lara became attentive and looked at the rainbow clock built by Mr. Arvidsson. She had stowed it at the bottom of her backpack in fear of pickpockets.

"Oh, no!" Lara said, startled. "We need to get back to St. Mark's Square. We'll be late if we don't."

"But what about Mr. Arvidsson?" Nina objected.

"He's old and can take care of himself," Lara pulled her sister by the arm. "Come on!"

Raindrops began to fall from the grey sky, pattering against the pavement as two girls sat at a small table, their half-eaten sundaes melting under the sudden deluge. Hastily, they rose and left, unaware of the middle-aged man at the next table who followed them, his eyes fixed on their retreating figures. It was the same man they had seen on the train earlier. He had noted the name of their hotel, allowing him to lie in wait for them here.

Breathless, the girls reached St. Mark's Square, the rain coming down harder. To their surprise, the clock tower still displayed the same time as when they last checked. "There's only one explanation for this," Lara called out to her sister, her voice drowned out by the rain. "The clock has stopped."

They took refuge from the shower under a nearby awning, waiting for the rain to ease. As it gradually subsided, Lara suddenly exclaimed with alarm, "When we activate our clock, we must ensure that no one else is nearby. Otherwise, they'll accidentally travel with us to Rainbow Land." Unfortunately, the square was now crowded with tourists.

"What are we going to do?" Whined Nina, looking up as if willing the rainbows to delay. Then, another idea struck her. "Let's go inside one of the buildings around here. We might find an isolated spot there."

Lara agreed, and they quickly scanned the area. However, long lines of tourists had already formed at the entrances to the buildings, making it a poor choice. The rain had now stopped, and the first of the two rainbows had begun to appear in the sky.

Suddenly inspired, Lara shouted to Nina, "Follow me!" They made their way towards a stone bridge that spanned a small, less-frequented side channel. Overhead, the lower arch of the emerging double rainbow stretched across the sky.

As they approached the bridge, Lara pointed to a small pier where several abandoned gondolas were moored. "Look!" She exclaimed.

Nina didn't know what her sister was getting so excited about. All she could see were a few old gondolas.

"Yes, there are gondolas. So what?" she therefore replied.

The tower clock in St. Mark's Square struck 11. Now, the time had come. The gate to the land at the end of the rainbow was open.

Not ten steps away stood the man who had followed them from the café. The girls noticed him.

"Maybe he's a pickpocket!" Whispered Nina to Lara.

"It doesn't matter now. Come quickly," Lara urged her sister. She grabbed Nina's hand, and they both ran down the stone steps to where the boats were gently bobbing in the water. No one was there right now.

Their pursuer had also lost them briefly, but he was getting closer.

Lara pulled out her magic hat, pulled Nina close to her, and put it on herself so they were both invisible.

They looked up at the sky. The sun had now emerged from behind a cloud, casting a warm, golden glow over the city of Venice. As they gazed upwards, a dreamlike rainbow formed over the place where they had just been and their current location. The colors of the rainbow were so vivid; it seemed as though they were painted by the hand of a master artist.

Lara activated her new rainbow clock, a simple but sleek device. The man following the girls descended the same stone steps they had and looked around. Suddenly, he heard strange humming and buzzing noises. He listened intently and followed the sound, getting closer and closer to the girls' location.

Lara and Nina acted swiftly and jumped onto one of the gondolas to regain their distance. An invisible light gyroscope, already swirling around them, turned into an equally invisible flash of light as they jumped, opening a gateway to another world for a brief moment. The portal shimmered and pulsed with energy, creating a rippling effect in the air around it.

Fortunately, there were only a few boats on this branch of the Grand Canal, Venice's main waterway. However, a gondolier and a resident of the city noticed this light phenomenon. They crossed themselves, believing it to be a miracle.

Their pursuer continued to search the immediate vicinity for quite some time. The girls had managed to escape him, but how they had done it remained a mystery. He couldn't satisfactorily solve the question of whether they had noticed him. Frustrated but determined, he decided to stay in this beautiful lagoon city for a day or two longer. He trusted that the girls would soon show up again at the hotel where their neighbor had checked in. There, he would eavesdrop on them again and find out what had happened. The success of his mission was crucial. He could not return to his own time unless he succeeded.

12

THE BOAT OF THE SPANIARD

Ed had conducted a thorough investigation and finally discovered the harbor where the suspected museum thief's boat was docked. As he approached the sleek and expensive sailing yacht, he couldn't help but admire its beauty. The owner of such a vessel undoubtedly had ample resources and didn't need to resort to stealing a valuable meteorite.

The only sound was the gentle splashing of waves against the boats. There was no sign of anyone on board. He called out the boat owner's name several times, hesitant to make any assumptions without concrete evidence. When there was no response, he cautiously boarded the yacht.

The entrance to the vessel's interior was blocked by a locked hatch, but he managed to break it open with some effort. The darkness inside was overwhelming, but he eventually adjusted to it and used his flashlight to explore without fear of being noticed, as it was the dead of night.

The yacht was more spacious than he had anticipated, with a used coffee cup in one corner and numerous nautical charts stored next to the navigation table. In the center was a long, narrow table cluttered with various items. Upon closer inspection, the official realized he had struck gold. There were photographs on the table and not just any photos. They were images taken from inside the geological museum, some showing the surveillance cameras mounted on the walls, while others depicted the room where the meteorite had been housed.

Ed's heart raced as he studied the photos. He also found a floor plan of the museum, annotated with specific times. "He must have planned when to be in which room," he thought to himself. As he examined the items further, he discovered a hidden calendar with the day of the burglary marked with a red cross.

His breath caught in his throat. This was undeniable proof that Gordon was the culprit behind the theft of the meteorite. Overwhelmed with excitement and a touch of fear, he quickly took photographs of the evidence with his cell phone.

"But I'm not going to the police," he decided, "not yet anyway. They'd question everything again regardless." He had evidence that this man might have planned the break-in, but none that proved it beyond a shadow of a doubt. He had to find Gordon and the hiding place of the meteorite he had stolen. Had Gordon perhaps hidden the stone somewhere on his boat? Quiet as a cat, he crept up on deck to make sure Gordon hadn't come back from somewhere right at this moment, ready to surprise him. Fortunately, everything was still quiet up there. Far and wide, not a single soul was visible.

He returned to the belly of the boat and continued his search. He reached the boat's bow, where he found a door. Behind it, he discovered a small kitchen and a toilet. At that moment, a bright light illuminated the part of the yacht where he had just taken pictures.

Surprised by the sudden brightness, the night watchman took a few steps backward. In doing so, he stumbled and fell straight onto a large shelf. The shelf held a large blanket on it. Quick-witted, he slipped under the blanket. It was just large enough to hide his body. Only his shoes were peeking out.

In the next moment, the bright light vanished, and he could hear the hushed voices of two men.

"I said from the beginning that we should destroy all evidence of it on the boat. One of our people could have done it much earlier," one complained.

"Yes, you did," the second agreed and added with a grin. "I still think this action is over the top. The police will never get on Gordon's trail anyway because I have erased his criminal record. Hacking the police computer was a piece of cake thanks to our portable quantum computer."

"Still, the chief wants us to destroy all records related to the museum break-in."

"Yes, yes. We're doing it now, aren't we?" The other man gave in, somewhat annoyed. He knew there was no point in discussing it.

Ed carefully moved his head under the blanket, turning it to see the men. They now went to the table. A bright flash shot out of one man's hand. In the next moment, the documents that had just been lying around disappeared.

"This borders on magic," thought Ed. This demonstration frightened him because it made him wonder what these men were capable of.

"I think we're ready here," the man who had been in favor of destroying the evidence stated with satisfaction.

"Yes. Now, no one will think the flash of light that occurred at the museum had anything to do with Gordon's disappearance."

The men likely said more, but the person secretly eavesdropping on them fell asleep, likely due to his huddled position beneath a warm blanket.

"Oh, that was unpleasant!" Thought Ed, rubbing his aching knee the moment he woke up. He then stretched out his foot and accidentally bumped it against a half-empty water bottle. It fell to the floor, making a loud noise.

The voices of the unknown men instantly fell silent. One of them looked for the cause of the noise, taking a step toward the shelf where the large blanket lay. Ed held his breath. But then the stranger saw the broken bottle and immediately gave the all-clear.

"It was just a bottle. Nothing more!" The man resolved the tension that had built up on the boat.

"I knew it. You're already seeing ghosts," the other man replied with a laugh. "Come on. We'd better get out of here anyway. We've been here way too long."

But then the stranger who had given the all-clear saw Ed's shoe peeking out from under the blanket. Probably, his companion was right. He was seeing ghosts. Therefore, he did not voice his suspicions, afraid of making a fool of himself a second time. Wordlessly, he went back to the man in the other part of the boat.

After another flash of light, the strange visitors disappeared again - at least, that's what Ed assumed. He was a heavy-set man with a thick mustache and a tendency to sweat profusely, particularly when he was nervous. He had been a night watchman for fifteen years and had seen all sorts of strange occurrences, but nothing like this. He rubbed his eyes and peered into the darkness, wondering if he was hallucinating. But when he looked again, the figures were gone. He let out a sigh of relief and rubbed the sweat off his forehead.

Carefully creeping back to the room where he had just photographed the evidence, he found it empty. His assumption was right; the strange visitors had disappeared. But the photos were still on his cell phone, proof that the nocturnal visitors had not been a product of his imagination.

Upset, the night watchman made his way home. He kept thinking about what one of the men had said earlier on the sailing yacht, namely that the flash of light was responsible for the disappearance of the meteorite thief. He no longer thought the story he had put on record with the police was entirely far-fetched. After all, hadn't the men themselves appeared as if from nowhere after a bright flash of light? So, why shouldn't a thief vanish after one, also?

"But how do you follow up on a lead that seems like pure science fiction?" he pondered. He had no answer to that. He needed help from someone who understood light events. He immediately dismissed the idea of going to the police again. They would not only not believe him - no, they would declare him crazy. No, he needed an expert who knew about light events.

He finally reached his home, a small apartment on the third floor of a rundown building. He unlocked the front door and climbed the stairs, feeling the weariness of the night weighing on him. In his kitchen, he grabbed an energy drink from his refrigerator and sat down at his desk in his study.

He turned on his aging laptop, the fan whirring loudly as it struggled to keep up with the demands of modern software. With shaky fingers, he entered the term "green light" into a search engine. Several hits appeared, but one of them caught his eye. It was the website of the Abisko weather station, known for its expertise in studying strange light phenomena.

"Yes, if anyone can tell me about strange light phenomena, it will be these people," he thought with satisfaction, immediately jotting down the weather station's phone number on a notepad.

Next, he transferred the pictures he had taken on the boat with his cell phone to his laptop and saved them there. Then he closed the computer, ran into the kitchen, and attached his note to the refrigerator with a magnet. That way, he would remember to call there first thing in the morning.

He looked at the kitchen clock, which read almost midnight. Once again, it had become far too late, but fortunately, he had taken the next day off. Not to rest, as the arrogant police employee had suggested, but to push this mysterious case forward. The policeman's suggestion that he should take a break had both offended him and aroused his ambition. Plus, after what he had seen on the yacht, Ed knew he had to crack this case if he was ever to sleep peacefully again. "Nobody, not even the police, should mess with this thief," he thought grimly. "They don't know what they're getting themselves into."

A few minutes later, Ed was lying in bed and had turned off his bedside lamp, which the dark shadow, who had followed Ed from the harbor, had noticed.

Ed's pursuer was now standing outside, looking up at the apartment bathed in darkness. He had logged onto the Internet via a square interface housed on his arm and had been keeping close track of which pages Ed had just accessed. Therefore, he knew where Ed had planned to go next and would be there before him.

13

FAR IN THE PAST

Lara and Nina had become so dizzy from the sudden flash of light swirling around them that they had to sit down on the cold, hard floor to avoid falling and injuring themselves. But even when they sat down, the dizziness did not subside; on the contrary, it seemed to intensify. Then suddenly, their vision went black, and they passed out for a brief moment.

When they opened their eyes again, instead of the gondolas that had just been gently rocking back and forth on the side channel, they saw only a landscape covered with a thick blanket of snow. The snow seemed to stretch on for miles, with no sign of civilization in sight. Since Lara and Nina were dressed only in T-shirts and shorts, suitable for Venice's spring-like temperatures but not for the frigid tundra in which they now found themselves, they immediately began to shiver uncontrollably. Moreover, their hair was still wet from the Venice rain shower.

"Where on earth are we?" Said Nina, her teeth chattering.

"It doesn't matter for now! We need something to wear as soon as possible; I'm freezing," Lara replied, her voice desperate.

Unfortunately, Mr. Arvidsson had packed the girls' winter clothes into his roomy suitcase on the train, saying with a smile, "You won't need them for the next few days. It's pleasantly warm in Venice."

"Not only in Venice but also in the rainbow land," Lara had answered him with conviction.

"Can't you just conjure up some warm clothes for us?" Nina pleaded. "I mean, you're a trained witch!"

Lara looked at Nina in amazement. "Yes, of course! I didn't even think of that!" She exclaimed.

Lara thought hard for a moment.

"Well, get on with it!" Urged Nina. "I'll turn into an icicle if you don't."

"Shh!" Lara interrupted her. Then Lara muttered a witch's spell.

The girls had warm winter clothes on in no time.

"Well done!" Nina praised her big sister. "I'm getting a little warmer already."

They looked around again, searching for some indication of where they were. Almost everywhere was a monotonous white. Only against the background of the gray-blue sky was a faint greenish glow.

"Is that the Northern Lights up there?" Exclaimed Nina in amazement.

"Well, it's not a rainbow," Lara returned, disappointed. "If there isn't a single rainbow, then we can't possibly have gotten to the land at the end of the rainbow."

"Are you suggesting that the clock might be defective, as you feared?" Asked Nina nervously.

 "Do you have a better explanation? I'll have a bone to pick with Mr. Arvidsson when we're back in Venice," Lara replied unhappily.

"Don't keep talking; just activate the rainbow clock again!" Nina urged her sister.

Lara did as Nina wanted, but nothing happened, unfortunately. No buzzing or humming sound. Desperately, Lara pressed the button again, but with more force.

"This stupid thing doesn't work!" Cried Lara angrily, almost throwing it away from herself in frustration.

"Oh my, did the clock break the first time we used it?" Asked Nina worriedly.

"Or the battery is dead. What do I know?" Lara replied in frustration. But then she remembered something, and her face suddenly brightened up again.

"What's wrong with you? Why are you grinning so stupidly?" Nina wanted to know.

"Of course, it doesn't work. It can't," Lara returned.

"Wonderful!" Nina snapped sarcastically. "Why not?"

"The rainbow clock only works if there is also a double rainbow. That would certainly not be a problem if we were in Rainbow Land. But here, there is not even one."

Nina nodded. She suddenly had a feeling of discomfort in the pit of her stomach. She wasn't the only one who wanted to get out of here as quickly as possible.

Fortunately, a chance for their rescue came in the form of a distant dot approaching them at high speed. At first, they both thought it was a bird, but as the dot drew closer, it transformed into a person sitting on a broomstick, hurtling towards them with incredible speed.

Lara and Nina reacted quickly, shouting as loudly as they could to draw attention to themselves. The person on the broomstick turned their strange flying machine and flew directly towards the girls.

"Anna? How did you get here?" Lara exclaimed in surprise as the person on the broomstick abruptly slowed down and hovered a few meters in front of them.

"Heaven sent you!" Added Nina with relief.

"What are you doing here in the land at the end of the rainbow?" Anna wondered, hovering on her broomstick just ahead of them, a few meters above the ground.

"What? This is Rainbow Land?" Lara asked incredulously.

"Yes, it's just cooled off considerably here in the last few days," Anna replied, "but no one knows the reason why."

"That's strange," Nina said. "We also have a problem and could use some help."

"Whoa! I'm starting to get cold," Anna said. "You can tell me about your problem over a warm cup of rainbow tea. Come on, quickly climb onto my witch's broomstick. It'll take all three of us."

Lara and Nina climbed on the broomstick behind Anna, making room for the red backpack. Then, with a burst of speed, the witch's broomstick soared towards the largest treehouse in the rainbow village, which belonged to Paraiso.

The girls looked astonished. Lara was the first to find her words and asked, "I thought you were going to your house?"

"Yes, I was going to. Then, I remembered that I don't have any more tea in the house, but our Chief has an almost inexhaustible supply."

Soon, the three were standing in front of the thick door while Anna knocked.

Paraiso was visibly pleased by the girls' visit. He told them, as Anna had already done, about the bizarre weather changes that had occurred recently. Lara and Nina listened intently, their faces growing increasingly serious.

"It's bizarre about the weather, but we also have a serious problem," said Lara. "My rainbow clock fell into a crevice and disappeared, just like our parents did shortly after. We need to travel back in time to prevent their disappearance and that of the clock. That's why we're here. We thought we could borrow a clock with a time travel function. This one doesn't have that function," Lara pointed at her Rainbow Clock.

Paraiso pondered the request before an idea struck him. "Well, it's not that simple. At the moment, no one in possession of a rainbow clock is allowed to lend it to someone," Paraiso explained to the girls. "Because if we can't save this world, we'll have to leave it. And to do that, we'll need our clocks. However..."

Lara interrupted, "What?"

"However, I could make an exception, but only if you gave me something in return," Paraiso said with a sly smile. In the meantime, Paraiso had finally come to the conclusion that it would be better for him to send a rescue team that had a real chance to be successful. Because if Pinky failed, the high members of the council and the other parrots of this magic land could blame him and not the doctor for it, as it was within his responsibility to choose the members of this team.

"What kind of exchange were you thinking of?" Nina asked.

"We are currently looking for suitable participants to form a team to search for the reason for this weather change and eliminate it," Paraiso offered.

"Hmm," Nina pondered. "How many volunteers are there already?"

"Unfortunately, only one so far: Pinky," the chief fibbed because he had not yet informed Pinky about the mission.

The sisters looked into each other's eyes for a while, both having the same thought: They had no choice but to agree.

"All right!" Lara replied.

"So we have a deal then?" asked Nina.

"Yes, we have a deal. You save Rainbow Land and, in return, receive a Rainbow Time Travel Clock," Paraiso confirmed. "You and Pinky will form a rescue team. Your task is to set about finding and eliminating the cause of the cold. "

At that moment, there was another knock at the treehouse door. Pinky and Dr. Schubidou were now standing outside.

"You're right on time!" Paraiso greeted them with a big grin on his parrot face. "With me right now are Lara and Nina. They want to research the cause of the change in our climate with Pinky."

Dr. Schubidou was amazed that Paraiso had taken this decision, even if it was at the last second! Pinky looked perplexed. He wondered when he had signed up for the volunteer rescue team. For the life of him, he couldn't remember.

In the living room, where the crackling fireplace radiated a cozy warmth, Lara and Nina told the group about the mysterious disappearance of their parents and showed them a few photos. Among them was a photograph of the Northern Lights, displaying an array of green and pink hues.

"Let me see it!" Paraiso asked Nina, intrigued. She handed him the photo. "Thank you," he said shortly.

Dr. Schubidou looked at the photo for a moment, studying it intently. Suddenly, a tremendous thought came to him. "Excuse me," the doctor said excitedly. "I need to check something right away." Then he disappeared, and it took him quite a while to return.

"I'm sorry it took a little longer than I anticipated," he said, slightly out of breath. "But the measurements were important."

"What measurements are you talking about?" Paraiso asked, slightly irritated.

"Oh, I forgot to mention that I have built a new spectrometer. It is possible to examine things that are a lot larger. I used it to explore this greenish band of light that some parrots swear to be in the sky since the cold snap."

"So it's only been here since the weather changed?" wondered Nina. "Is there a connection then?"

"Yes, though I didn't realize it until now. It only occurred to me the moment you showed me your photograph of the Northern Lights," Dr. Schubidou explained.

"So, did you find anything out?" Asked Lara, almost bursting with curiosity.

"Yes, indeed. I think I have found the cause of the drop in temperature. It's this light. It's changing the weather," Dr. Schubidou replied, his voice filled with a newfound sense of urgency.

"Then you have already solved the problem? Therefore, we are no longer needed?" Lara hoped.

"Yes and no. Unfortunately, the origin of light is not in this world," the doctor explained.

"Where else could it originate from?" Lara asked incredulously.

"Well, that is indeed the truly fantastic thing. Its origin is in your world," Dr. Schubidou replied, looking at the girls with a serious expression.

"You're not serious, are you?" Asked Lara and Nina in amazement.

"I'm afraid I am. I don't have the slightest doubt about it. If you manage to find the source of the light and can turn it off, the temperatures in Rainbow Land will return to normal. "

"But how are we going to find this light source?" Lara wanted to know. But before the bird doctor could answer, Nina jumped up.

"I may have an idea!" She exclaimed. "This light looks oddly like the Northern Lights we've seen in our world. We happen to know someone familiar with these kinds of lights. We could question him. "

"That sounds like a good plan!" Exclaimed Dr. Schubidou enthusiastically.

"Great! Then we'll do it like this. Pinky, Lara, and Nina head off to this expert," Paraiso said firmly, "while Anna stays here with us to keep the last remaining rainbows stable."

Pinky looked at Lara and Nina. "Yes, with them, I dare to go on an adventure," he thought. "And if we make it, then the stupid snow will soon be a thing of the past, yay!"

Anna looked disappointed. "What a pity, I had hoped to come along. A bit of variety would certainly have done me good."

But Paraiso remained firm. "The land at the end of the rainbow needs you, Anna."

Paraiso was satisfied because he had put together a rescue team faster than expected. He considered the weather problem finally solved, and he no longer had to invest any unnecessary time in it. He wanted to devote his time mainly to his upcoming beauty treatments.

Pinky, Lara, and Nina were ready to leave the very next day.

Dr. Schubidou came to them with a unique object. "This device allows you to determine the wavelength of any light beam. I have entered the wavelength of the greenish light. If you find a light of the same wavelength, the LED indicator light will turn green; otherwise, it will turn red. Got it?"

They nodded. The doctor was always good for surprises, and his inventions were indispensable on adventures.

They first looked for a place further north than Venice to travel back to their world, but they unfortunately only found coordinates near Rome. The three activated Pinky's rainbow clock and disappeared from Rainbow Land, reappearing in the middle of a vineyard.

"I have an idea!" Exclaimed Lara. "I'll send a text message to Mr. Arvidsson because calling is possibly too expensive." "And do you think Mr. Arvidsson will help us?" asked Nina. Before she could say anything more, Lara had sent off a text, and her phone rang immediately afterwards.

"Thank God!" They heard their neighbor say on the other end of the line when Lara told him what had happened to them.

"I'll get on the next train - no, better, I'll rent a car. I'll pick you up, and we'll go to the airport," he suggested. "No, wait, that's not possible!"

"Why not?" Asked Lara.

"We can't just bring Pinky back to Sweden."

For a brief moment, there was silence on the line. Then, a thought occurred to Nina.

"Yes, we can," she said triumphantly. "Just trust me! I have a plan."

"Okay! At least tell me if there's anything else I can do," Mr Arvidsson said.

Nina thought for a brief moment. "Yes, you can book the plane tickets for Lara and me. With Pinky, I have something else in mind."

Arriving at the airport in the Italian capital, Mr. Arvidsson returned the rental car. According to him, no one had followed him from the hotel, but he was mistaken. A man had indeed trailed him but lost him prematurely in the thick traffic chaos of Rome. The stranger's mission here in Italy had failed, and he needed to hurry back to the geological museum in Sweden to investigate the Spanish thief's disappearance.

On entering the airport, Lara, Nina, Mr. Arvidsson, and Pinky checked the time-board and realized that their flight back to Stockholm would depart in just over two hours. They grabbed a quick snack at an airport café and headed to the bathroom. Pinky had made himself comfortable on Nina's shoulder. However, upon her return from the restroom, Pinky was nowhere to be found.

"Where is Pinky?" Asked Mr. Arvidsson.

"Oh, I don't know!" Replied Nina.

They passed through customs and boarded the plane, but Pinky was still missing. Lara grew curious and asked Nina about Pinky's whereabouts, but Nina remained tight-lipped.

After landing at Arlanda Airport and boarding the train to their respective destinations, they heard a familiar voice. It was Pinky, who had somehow climbed down from the hat rack. Lara noticed that her invisibility hat was still on the rack, and she realized how Nina had managed to smuggle Pinky onto the plane. She couldn't help but grin.

14

ED AND GUNNAR

The following day greeted Ed with plenty of sunshine. He had slept well and dreamed vividly, making him unsure if he had dreamed about the strange experiences from the previous day on the boat. After a long, warm shower to shake off any remaining fatigue, he indulged in his morning routine of drinking a hot cup of coffee and reading the daily newspapers on the internet, as well as checking the weather forecast for the day and the next few days.

It was then that he remembered he wanted to call the weather station in Abisko to learn more about light phenomena in the far north. Ed headed to the kitchen, where he had written down the phone number of the weather station on a sticky note that was still visible on the door of the refrigerator. He picked up his phone and dialed, and after a few rings, a man named Gunnar answered.

"How can I help you?" asked Gunnar, trying to be friendly. Providing information about the prevailing weather conditions, even over the phone, was one of his favorite duties.

"I… uh… I would like to know a little more about a certain light phenomenon here in the far north. I work at the geological museum, and I could see it from there, too," Ed explained.

"Yes, I'd be glad to help you," Gunnar replied politely. "Fire away. What exactly would you like to know?"

"This will take a little long over the phone. Could we meet at your weather station for a chat?" Ed asked.

Gunnar had hoped to handle the man's questions over the phone. The persistence of the speaker surprised him so much that he didn't have anything to counter. He had no desire for a meeting, but he answered anyway: "This must be important. Hold on. I need to check my calendar." Gunnar stood up and pretended to look at his calendar. In reality, he was trying to find one last way to wriggle out of meeting the man face-to-face. "All right, I can do it today or tomorrow around 3 p.m. What suits you better?"

Ed checked his watch. It was half past nine in the morning. "I'll be with you around 3 p.m. today," he replied.

"But please don't be late!" Gunnar wanted to add, but Ed had already hung up.

Ever punctual, Ed arrived at the door of the weather station at 3 p.m. and rang the bell. He had parked his car in the visitors' parking lot. From there, he had walked along a small path to the weather station. Gunnar, who had already seen his expected visitor from a distance via a video camera, now pressed a button to open the door. Shortly afterwards, the pair sat down at Gunnar's workstation, where Gunnar switched on several computers.

"Hello," Gunnar greeted him. "What brings you here?"

"I just want to know about a particular light phenomenon," Ed explained, recounting everything that had happened so far, beginning with the break-in at the geological museum and ending with his experience on the yacht of the suspected thief.

"That is why I am here now. I want to learn about the light phenomenon that occurred at the time of the break-in," he concluded.

Gunnar listened attentively and nodded now and then to indicate that he had understood everything.

"I thought there might be records of this natural spectacle here," Ed looked at him expectantly.

"Yes, records do exist," Gunnar replied, nodding. "Still, I don't understand where this is going."

"You will understand in a moment. Could you bring up the records from the evening of the national holiday on your computer?" Ed asked.

"Of course!" Gunnar replied, nodding. He moved the mouse to make his screensaver disappear. Then he opened a program called "Recall," and a globe appeared on the screen. Gunnar selected Sweden and zoomed in on the map section of the northern area.

"Here we are!" Declared Gunnar, showing Ed one of the many red dots on the map. The map indicated the entire Abisko National Park and extended to the east coast of Sweden, where the geological museum was located. Gunnar then selected the date from last Friday. He chose one of the weather symbols indicating the Northern Lights and pressed 'play,' rolling his desk chair back so Ed could see the screen as well.

The screen showed a vast, greenish light formation extending from Abisko National Park to the coast of the Gulf of Bothnia. In the area of the highest elevation in the park, a flashing greenish light was visible, which appeared to interact with the more extensive greenish light formation. It looked like the pulsating light source was increasing the intensity of the light formation. Then something unique happened: In the northern part of Abisko National Park and in the town where the geological museum was located, there was a rapid discharge of light. Afterwards, the intensity of the green light formation weakened.

Ed and Gunnar sat for a while after this presentation, racking their brains about what it all meant.

"Tell me, did any other people disappear that night?" Ed suddenly asked.

"Why, yes," Gunnar confirmed, nodding vigorously. "The parents of a family who were staying in the park at the time also disappeared inexplicably."

"Was the campsite at the location where one of the two light discharges occurred?" Ed inquired.

"Yes," Gunnar replied. "And the location of the other discharge was probably at the museum. When did you say the break-in at the museum took place?"

"Around midnight," Ed replied. "But the flash of bright light happened around half-past twelve. I was so startled that I neglected to look at the clock. I was also distracted, expecting the burglar to appear at any moment."

They ran the recording one more time but in a smaller time window. The intensity values on the screen changed again. The men stared at it as if spellbound, trying to make sense of what they were seeing.

"The discharges occurred at the same time!" Exclaimed Gunnar, emitting a low whistle.

"So the mysterious disappearance of these people has something to do with the discharge of this strange light," Ed concluded, razor-sharp.

"Just a moment, I have to check something!" Gunnar changed the parameters again and entered today's date and the current time. They both saw further pulsations on the ridge, recharging the Northern Lights in the sky.

"So the danger is still there," Gunnar exclaimed excitedly. "We must act immediately before more people disappear in the same way."

 "How?" Asked Ed.

"I'll explain on the way to the mountain range. Come on. We don't have much time! I'll see you right outside at the entrance, okay? I just need to get my snow bike out of the shed real quick."

Ed nodded in agreement.

Less than ten minutes later, Gunnar arrived with his vehicle. "Hop on!" He shouted. Ed quickly followed the meteorologist's instructions. As soon as he got onto the motorcycle, Gunnar accelerated suddenly, almost causing Ed to fall off. "Sorry," mumbled Gunnar. "But we're in a hurry!"

His snowmobile roared off with Ed clinging desperately to the back of Gunnar's jacket, not daring to move his head or body for fear of getting dizzy and being sick. Gunnar elaborated on his plan as they rode. "I had a visit today from the girls whose parents disappeared without a trace," he said, with a hint of concern in his voice.

Ed, now curious, asked, "Oh really? When were they here?"

"Just before you showed up. Their reason for being here seemed a bit strange to me at that time," said Gunnar, continuing his explanation. "They wanted to know if there was a light source up here that had a particular wavelength."

Ed muttered, "Yeah, so?"

"Well, they were in luck. The wavelength they described was exactly the wavelength of the pulsating greenish light that has been present in the northern part of the park for the last few days," replied Gunnar.

"I'm afraid I don't quite understand," said Ed, as he felt his neck beginning to ache.

"The girls seemed more than satisfied with my information and left immediately afterwards. They were suddenly in a hurry," said Gunnar.

"Because they had to get back to the train station?" Guessed Ed.

"No, I don't think so. I rather think that the girls wanted to go to the spot where this pulsating light emerged from the ground. Unfortunately, I didn't give it any further thought at the time because I thought this light source was harmless. If you hadn't shown up, I would still believe that. Fortunately, we now know more and may still get to the spot in time to prevent them disappearing like their parents and the museum thief," finished

Gunnar, and on the next incline, he pressed the gas pedal of his snow scooter to the floor. The engine howled, and the vehicle surged upwards.

"Help!" Shouted Ed, who could already picture himself lying injured in the snow.

"Don't worry!" The meteorologist reassured him. "I know this route like the back of my hand."

Ed did not reply, but his grip on Gunnar's coat tightened as they continued on their rapid ride. Gunnar, on the other hand, was used to this route, having traveled it many times before. He even managed to retrieve his mobile phone from the pocket of his down jacket and dial a number.

After several chimes, a man's voice answered. "Hey, Bob, it's me, Gunnar. I'm on my way with a man named Ed to the north part of the park, where we believe the girls whose parents disappeared are heading. It's the highest elevation in the park, and we think they're in grave danger. Please be ready in case we need your help."

"Yes, you can count on me as always. Don't worry," came the prompt reply. But before Bob could ask what the danger was, there was a crackle on the line, and the connection was interrupted. Gunnar refrained from calling again, needing both hands on the handlebars of his scooter.

This call was necessary because anyone who entered the national park was required to inform the park ranger beforehand due to safety regulations. Gunnar and Ed continued their journey unabated.

They approached their destination at top speed, hoping they wouldn't be too late, though Gunnar's gut feeling told him otherwise. He feared the worst.

Lara, Nina, and Pinky came to a halt with their husky sled on the same spot on the white mountain range the sisters had reached on the day of their climb. However, they had arrived much later this time, as indicated by the sun's low position on the horizon. Suddenly, the sky turned dark, and countless stars appeared, along with the Northern Lights, which seemed to merge with a greenish light beam shooting vertically out of the mountain. Lara pulled the handy photometer from Dr. Schubidou out of her backpack and turned it on. She pointed it at the pulsating light and exclaimed with joy, "Hooray, we found it!"

Nina and Pinky looked at Lara in amazement, wondering what had made her so happy.

"Don't you understand?" Lara said excitedly. "We have found the origin of the light responsible for the erratic weather in Rainbow Land."

"That may be so," Nina replied less euphorically, "but how do we turn it off?"

Lara looked at her in amazement. Nina was right. They had no idea how to turn off the light. Pinky suggested they could put one or more rocks on the spot from which the green light beam was being emitted to block it.

The three companions climbed up the mountainside more cautiously than on their first outing. As they approached the spot, Lara let out a loud whistle. They arrived at the source of the light, and Lara was stunned. "I can't believe it," she stated in amazement. "It's, it's...the place where I lost my clock. What a strange coincidence."

"I don't believe in coincidences," Nina countered. "Maybe your rainbow clock is the source of the light?"

They stopped near the source of the light, wondering what to do next. Nina picked up a loose stone from the ground, and as Pinky had suggested, she threw it towards the point at which the light beam shot up out of the mountain. The stone came to rest in the desired location, and the beam of light disappeared for a moment. But then it reappeared, and the stone had mysteriously disappeared.

"Where did it go?" wondered Nina, picking up a larger stone from the ground. She hurled it back into the opening, and the beam of light was blocked again, but as before, the strange light reappeared, and the stone had vanished without a trace. They tried something else - a piece of clothing. Nina took her scarf and placed it over the opening in the mountain, but the scarf disappeared without a trace.

Suddenly, Nina slipped, just as Lara had done the first time. Her right arm came into contact with the light beam, and she was startled. Lara and Pinky could see that her arm had disappeared where it had touched the light source.

"I think I'm going crazy. My arm is becoming transparent!" Nina exclaimed in shock.

"Pull her out quickly!" Lara sensed the danger facing her sister. An uncanny force had taken possession of the hand in which Nina had held the stone. This force was so strong that she could not resist it. Larger and larger areas of Nina became invisible. Quick-witted, Lara grabbed Nina's other hand and tried to pull her sister away from the light, but she could not stop the process.

On the contrary, she was also affected by it. Suddenly, the sisters saw themselves surrounded by a greenish light rotating around them at lightning speed. They felt dizzy. Then the light disappeared, and the two sisters and the parrot vanished.

Gunnar and Ed, who were watching through binoculars, saw the girls and their parrot vanish before their eyes. Unbeknownst to them, they were not the only ones watching. They were also being watched. Not far from them stood one of the men who had been on the museum thief's yacht. The watcher observed the two men hurrying in the direction of the mountain massif. They followed the same route as the two girls but took a detour around the beam of light emerging from the mountainside.

"Where did they disappear to?" Ed asked. "There's no crevice big enough for them to have fallen into it."

"I don't know," Gunnar returned, equally puzzled. "But I do know one thing. We need reinforcements urgently. This area needs to be sealed off from visitors. And I already know who's going to help us with that."

Gunnar tried to call the last number he had dialed, but no one answered.

"What a bummer!" The meteorologist cursed, looking at his wristwatch. "He must be off work already."

"Well, call his home number then!" Ed urged him.

"If I could, I would have done it," Gunnar narrowed his eyes. "But, I do seem to remember there was a sign on Bob's office door saying how to reach him in an emergency."

"Come on then, let's get there!" Shouted Ed immediately, although he didn't feel like getting back on the snowmobile. But they had no other choice.

Gunnar started the engine and turned on the lights. The stranger not far from them watched as the two soon disappeared from his sight.

The man waited a moment to be quite sure that he was now really alone. Then he emerged from the cover of the snow-topped bushes. He walked directly toward the mysterious beam of light and stopped short of it. He manifested a scanner out of thin air and pointed it at the beam of light. The scanner displayed a three-digit number. Then he turned it off again and put it back into a small bag he carried with him.

The man's appearance was otherworldly, with smooth, silver skin and large, black eyes that seemed to absorb the light. His arm was elongated and ended in four slender fingers that seemed to move with otherworldly grace. He wore a tight-fitting suit that hugged his body, revealing every muscle and curve.

Then, a small part of his forearm became transparent, revealing a square display. He entered the number displayed by the scanner. In a flash of bright light, the man disappeared. Only his footprints, and those of Ed and Gunnar, remained visible for a short while in the freshly fallen snow.

15

LOST

The meteorite thief, Gordon, felt a sharp pain in his right forearm as flying glass fragments from the display case had embedded themselves in his skin. In total shock, he looked at the fresh wound and noticed that the bleeding had already stopped. Looking around, he was astonished to find himself in the open. Not only had the room disappeared, but the whole museum, too. Something else was different; the snow that had been everywhere before he entered the museum had disappeared, and it was unusually mild. A fine drizzle began to fall.

"Strange!" He thought, confused, and for a moment, he doubted whether he had actually been in the museum at all. It was only then that he noticed his fingers were clutching something hard. He opened his fist and saw the mysterious, greenish, shimmering stone resting in his palm. It was his only proof that he had been in the museum.

But what had happened in the meantime? How had he arrived here? Many thoughts raced through his head. He wondered if he had had a blackout or if contact with the meteorite or the strange light he had seen had triggered a bout of amnesia. "Yes, maybe when that strange lightning bolt struck me," he reflected, "I fell and hit my head, which led to memory loss." But this explanation didn't seem very logical to him either. He had no headache, nor did he find any head injury when he hurriedly examined himself.

It was then that he realized he didn't know much about this strange meteorite. All he knew was that its value exceeded that of a diamond of the same size many times over and that it was rare. He had stolen it because he had been promised a large sum of money if he successfully completed the heist. As long as he didn't ask any questions, he would get the promised yacht as well.

So, he was satisfied with the information about the location of the special stone and the planned handover to his clients on the yacht. These clients, men in fashionable clothes, had approached him one day in a harbor bar as he was enjoying a double espresso. They knew him amazingly well, and he suspected that they were plain-clothes policemen or officials of a state institution. He was surprised when they only wanted to hire him for a job.

He reasoned, "Perhaps the meteorite is dangerous? That must be why the client demanded I go ahead with the theft as soon as possible. Because otherwise, I would have learned of the meteorite's true nature and refused the job." He no longer felt comfortable holding the meteorite.

Gordon put his black backpack on the ground, unzipped the main compartment, and took out a small rectangular metal container. He quickly placed the stone inside and closed it again. With the stolen goods securely stowed away, he looked around the broad field and saw that he was still alone.

Feeling tired, he yawned. He knew he wouldn't be able to solve the riddle of the stone right away. "Tomorrow," he told himself, "I'm sure I'll find a simple explanation." With that, he decided to go to his sailboat home. He planned to hide his booty there and get a good night's sleep.

Gordon pulled out his smartphone to try and find his way back, but the display read "No network." Suddenly, he remembered a paragraph he had read during his sailing training on "star navigation." Old sailors used the stars to navigate, and this knowledge could be used to help him find his way back to the harbor in the absence of modern technology.

He looked up at the sky, but it was cloudy, and he could only see a few stars. They wouldn't be enough to guide him. Disappointed, Gordon sighed. Then, he remembered that his new wristwatch had a built-in compass. However, when he checked the time, he was surprised to see that it had stopped.

"It must have taken most of the force of the lightning strike, leaving me virtually unharmed, so now it is broken," he thought to himself. Feeling helpless, he stood there in despair until he heard a faint sound that was familiar to him: the sound of waves.

"Yes, that was unmistakably a wave sound," he said. "The wind must have changed direction." With renewed hope, Gordon followed the sound of the waves, trusting that it would lead him back to his sailboat and the safety of the harbor.

With every step he took, the sound of the sea became louder. A light fog came out of nowhere, becoming denser with every passing second.

As he cautiously approached the harbor, he couldn't help but think about the fancy 17-meter yacht with the sonorous name "Sea Breeze." Soon, he would deliver the meteorite to his client's intermediary, and this wonderful boat would become his property. Although he had already used it as a shelter while he prepared for the break-in, he knew that owning it would feel completely different.

The cloud density decreased slightly, revealing a few stars and the greenish, shining Northern Lights through the gaps in the clouds. When the fog briefly lifted, giving him a better view of the sea, he couldn't spot the marina anywhere. Instead, his feet became wet as he reached the point where the sea met the shoreline.

"I should probably retire," he thought, considering his serious memory lapses of late and the fact that he still didn't know exactly where he was. The coastline before him didn't match his memory of it, which left him feeling even more disoriented. He sighed, feeling helpless. He knew he had to wait until the fog lifted at least a little.

Suddenly, the outline of a vast, wooden ship appeared out of nowhere. "Golly!" He exclaimed, surprised. He remembered having seen something similar somewhere before, but he couldn't figure out where or when it was. Although he was dressed too warmly for the surprisingly mild outside temperature, he started shivering. "It must be due to my tiredness," he thought, trying to shake off the feeling.

Curiously, he approached the giant wooden ship. As he drew closer, he could see the impressive bow of the boat, and he held his breath when he spotted the grim-looking figurehead. Suddenly, he remembered where he had seen this Viking ship before - in a museum. He noted with surprise that it must be a replica because it seemed to be very well preserved. The ship, along with the fog, made a ghostly impression.

As Gordon continued to approach the ship, he noticed a wooden plank lying on the ground, connecting the mainland to the ship. He hesitated for a moment before stepping onto it. The plank creaked under his feet as he entered the wooden boat. It was dead silent on the boat, and the thief felt nervous. He stopped short and listened, realizing that no one but him was out at this time of night.

Gordon scratched his head, and his thoughts wandered. He remembered last summer when tourists had virtually swamped the coast, but he couldn't recall seeing this wooden vessel. Surely, this ship would have been one of the main attractions. With an elegant leap, he landed on deck and looked around. Relieved, he exhaled when he saw no one. He heard only the soft creaking of the wooden ship rocking back and forth in the water and the distant screeching of seagulls.

Then he found a spot on the foredeck, protected from the wind, from which he had a good view of the blanket of fog. It still enveloped everything. He crouched down on the deck, in the best position to avoid the slightly chilly wind. He knew the wait would be a rather unpleasant one if he was also cold. As he sat there waiting for the fog to clear, he realized how tired he was. His eyelids felt as heavy as lead. The gentle rocking of the wooden ship and the monotonous sound of the waves soon caused him to fall into a deep sleep. Then, his head tilted slightly forward, and he began to snore loudly.

It was already daylight when he was rudely jolted out of his dreams a few hours later. Blinking, he looked into the face of a man who was missing more than a few teeth. He was wearing strange clothes and smiled wickedly as he stood in front of him, holding a wooden bucket. Without warning, the strange-looking guy emptied the bucket full of ice-cold water over his head. His first impulse was to jump up, but he realized that he could not move. Someone had tied him to the mainmast.

Then, he became aware of the other men who had gathered on deck to witness the spectacle. They all looked like Vikings. Some of them were bawling loudly in amusement. They had never seen such an oddly dressed stranger.

The very next moment, the man in front of him, still holding the bucket, was knocked aside by an even bigger guy who had been standing behind him, causing him to fall to the ground. This giant, his face marred by a long scar, reared up in front of him. He held the meteorite from the museum. He rumbled and said something in a language the thief could not understand. Nevertheless, he immediately understood what the Viking wanted to say to him. "He surely wants to know where I got the stone," thought the thief. Unfortunately, the only way to communicate his willingness to cooperate was through body language, which could mean different things in different parts of the world.

So he nodded cautiously, keeping a close eye on his counterpart's facial expressions. And when his facial expression did not become even angrier, the thief nodded again, but this time, much more clearly.

The fearsome man standing in front of him eyed him closely. Gordon nodded, fear sweat running down his forehead. Anxious seconds passed, feeling like an eternity. Suddenly, the Viking's facial muscles relaxed, and he raised a hand, saying something sternly. Two muscular Vikings immediately approached and untied the thief from the mast, leaving the shackles on his wrists in place. They grabbed him and carried him off the ship like a package. In the daylight, the area looked extremely familiar to him, but something was missing. The natural world looked the same, but the buildings of the village were absent.

The two Vikings brought the thief to a nearby place where they had tied up at least a dozen horses. One of the men grabbed the reins of a white and gray horse while the other hauled him across the horse's back like a sack of potatoes. It took quite a while for the ship's crew to follow them and take their places on the backs of the other horses. Then their leader raised his arm, and another Viking blew his horn, signaling the party to leave. The group began to move, with Gordon tied up on the horse's back, unable to do anything but wait to see where the journey was going to take him.

With nothing else to do but think, Gordon recalled the chain of events that had led him to this point. Most clearly, he remembered the flash of light that had caught him while he was stealing the meteorite. He still couldn't make sense of why all this was happening, but he knew for sure that this was no dream but the bitter reality of being held prisoner by a wild and angry horde of men. He feared that they would make short work of him if they found out that he couldn't help them. They weren't heading in the direction of the museum. Gordon figured there was only one way out of this situation. He had to escape, but he also had to get his meteorite back somehow.

Just before the sun reached its zenith, the Vikings' destination came into view: a small village. Several Viking children screamed around Gordon's horse, seeming to find him a welcome diversion. When the horses finally stopped in the center of the village, Gordon sighed, relieved that the ride was over; his back was aching. His stomach suddenly announced itself with a loud growl, as he hadn't eaten breakfast that morning, and now it was time for lunch. The air in the settlement smelled like a mixture of meat and smoke.

"It would be good to have something to eat before I make my escape," Gordon thought. Fortunately for him, the newcomers received fresh meat and plenty of barley juice at the village's fire pit in the center. They removed the shackles from his wrists but left the thin rope tightly connected to both ankles, giving him some freedom to move.

Next to Gordon sat a little boy no older than ten years. He watched Gordon curiously. Gordon returned the look. Sitting around the fire, the other Vikings paid no further attention to the thief. Then, the boy unobtrusively pushed something over to Gordon with his foot. Gordon put his foot over it quickly. In a moment when he felt he was unobserved, he tipped his foot a little to one side so that he could see what the item he had been passed was. He could not believe his eyes. It was a knife. "The boy has taken pity on me and wants to help me," he thought. "When I get the opportunity, I will free myself of my shackles."

Gordon managed to pick up the knife and hide it, though it took him two attempts to do so without being seen. As he did, the young boy he had befriended winked at him. Gordon watched as the boy drew a large triangle on the loamy ground, open at the bottom. Inside the triangle, the boy outlined several small objects that resembled double pyramids. Gordon didn't understand what the drawing meant, but he didn't dwell on it for too long. Instead, he focused on formulating an escape plan.

Lost in his thoughts, Gordon was caught off guard when his overseers pulled him up, causing him to wince in shock. They dragged him to a tent located in the center of the village compound and pushed him inside. Gordon stumbled and fell to the ground, rubbing his knee where he had hit it. He noticed that the ground was covered in animal skins instead of rugs, which was a testament to the Vikings' resourcefulness.

Gordon was left alone, with one of the guards stationed outside the tent's entrance. As time passed, he began to feel drowsy, and before he knew it, he had fallen asleep. The guard checked on him twice, and both times saw that he was asleep, but Gordon's nap had only been brief. On the guard's second visit, he was wide awake. He took out the knife he had hidden earlier and quickly cut through the shackles binding him. By the time the guard had returned to the entrance, Gordon had already cut a hole in the tent's back wall and slipped out.

"It's now or never," Gordon thought to himself, feeling the weight of the knife in his hand. Under cover of darkness, he crept toward the large tree where his captors had tied up their horses. He picked one and was about to untie it when he heard a voice behind him, speaking his language. He wheeled around and saw a man and a woman standing before him. Strangely, they were dressed in modern clothing similar to his own. Unbeknownst to him, they had traveled through time, just as he had, while vacationing with their daughters in Abisko National Park.

"Who are you? Did I just end up in a Viking movie?" Gordon asked, perplexed.

The woman remained calm and said, "I'll explain in a moment, but first, we need to leave quickly. This is a trap!"

Gordon hesitated, torn between his desire to escape and his fear of walking into a trap. The woman sensed his inner conflict and continued, "They wanted to test us to see if they could trust us because they seem to want our help. We failed, but it's not too late for you. You can still go back before anyone notices."

"Hmm," Gordon said, wondering if the woman could be right about that. "How did you get here, anyway?" He asked.

The woman shook her head, her expression sad. "We don't know!

We were camping with our daughters. When we woke up the next morning, we were in one of those tents here in the camp, but without our beloved children."

"I was struck by lightning last night. Strange things have been happening ever since," Gordon said, adding, "I can't explain it. There's only one thing I want right now, and that's to get out of here."

"We want to get back, too. Maybe we can help each other do that."

Before Gordon could reply, rapid, loud footsteps began to approach. Gordon pulled the couple aside into a bush. From there, they saw several Vikings pass by.

"You are right," Gordon whispered. "These Vikings are not to be trifled with and..." Unfortunately, one of the men had doubled back. He heard Gordon's voice and pulled the green bushes aside. He shouted something. The other men arrived just seconds later and surrounded the fugitives. The couple and Gordon had no chance to flee.

They soon found themselves back at the center of the camp. When the Viking leader with the scar learned of their escape attempt, he became angry and doubled the number of guards around the big tent. The thief and the couple looked at each other in dismay, realizing that there would now be no chance of escape. Gordon turned to the pair again.

"Tell me, do people living in this settlement talk to each other in a language I don't know? Is that some dialect?" He inquired, curious about the language spoken by the Vikings.

"Unfortunately, we don't know," the woman replied quietly, her voice tinged with disappointment, "because we haven't been here that long either."

"Too bad!" Gordon replied, realizing that the language barrier was a significant obstacle to their escape.

"Another thing that is extraordinary about all of this," the woman remarked, her eyes scanning the surroundings, "is the temperature. When we got into our sleeping bags last night, there was snow outside, and it was bitterly cold. When we awoke this morning, not only had the snow completely melted away, but it was unusually mild."

"That's true," her husband nodded in agreement. "The weather report on the radio hadn't mentioned anything at all about a sharp temperature rise."

"I'm not going crazy then!" Gordon said, relieved that he was not the only one who had made this observation.

Later, the group were ushered to their tents, where they spent the night feeling puzzled and unsettled.

Early the following day, the Vikings and their three prisoners were on horseback, heading towards their next destination. The Vikings guarded the prisoners closely, sitting on horses right next to them, their watchful eyes also scanning the terrain for signs of danger.

Gordon's muscles were very sore from the day before, so he felt every movement of the horse, no matter how small.

Around noon, a chalky-white mountain range came into view in the distance. Gordon suddenly remembered the boy who had drawn an inverted triangle in the soil. He understood that this triangle represented one of the mountains, and there was a rock inside it. Gordon still wondered why the Vikings needed him, but, at the same time, he was not eager to find out. The only thing he wanted was to get back the meteorite he had stolen and flee to his sailing boat. He could then retreat from his life as a thief and live a life of luxury. He would sail to the Caribbean and enjoy his life there, carefree, with year-round warm temperatures.

A loud shout tore him from his daydreams. The Viking leader gave the order to approach the mountain massif they were riding towards in a zigzag fashion. "He must be afraid of something or someone," Gordon reasoned.

A little later in the afternoon, they stopped for a rest at a small stream they had just crossed. Not only did the horses drink from the pure water of the stream, but some of the Vikings also caught a few fish. They consumed them raw rather than roasting them over a fire because the smoke could have been observed from a great distance away.

The horseback ride went on for an additional two hours beneath the cover of separate bunches of trees. Then they were in a gorge. The White Mountains appeared to be behind it. The closer they came to the hills, the stonier the ground became until they finally reached the foot of the mountain.

A camp came into view consisting of several tents. Numerous other Vikings were moving around. Some of them were busy carrying away stone and earth, emerging from a small opening in the ground. Others on horseback kept a close eye on the camp, their swords at the ready. They greeted the leader with the scar and his entourage. The prisoners they brought with them were eyed critically by all.

Finally, Gordon realized what the Vikings were doing: they were digging a tunnel into the mountain. The chief got down from his horse and faced his prisoners. He looked at Gordon challengingly while showing him the meteorite. Scarface pulled out a sizable double-bladed sword from its scabbard and lifted it up to let it fall down on the head of Gordon. Gordon was filled with fear. His hands became sweaty. The master thief saw his whole life pass before his eyes. He also remembered the drawing the boy had drawn. All of a sudden, everything made sense to him.

"Stop it!" Shouted Gordon and nodded to the leader, who immediately put his weapon away.

With huge steps and a satisfied grin on his face, he went back to his dwelling.

"I think they suspect there is more of this rock inside the mountain," Gordon explained to the couple. "I think they want me to help them find it."

"Have you been here before?" The man asked curiously.

"No, never," Gordon returned curtly. "But they obviously think that I've been here before and can find an easy way into the mountain."

"Oh my God! In that case, we are doomed!" The woman said with a pessimistic tone. "Out of curiosity, where did you get your stone?"

Gordon had been dreading this question, "Well, I, uh, found it," he answered evasively. "Yeah, just don't give specifics," he thought. Because that way, he could always talk his way out of it.

"Found it?" The woman inquired in astonishment.

"Yeah, I think it's a meteorite," Gordon said.

That sounded somehow understandable because so many fell from the sky every year.

"Are you a meteorite hunter?" The woman asked with interest.

"Yes, in a way! But it's just one of my many hobbies," Gordon replied. He hadn't lied about that. He was a man of diverse interests. "The Vikings seem to have a problem here. Despite driving a tunnel into the mountain and appearing to be close to their destination, they still require my help. We need to use this situation to our advantage," Gordon explained before he was interrupted by four men.

The four Vikings forcefully pushed them towards the tunnel entrance, leaving no chance for escape. Upon entering the tunnel, they were pleasantly surprised that it wasn't as dark as they had expected. Torchlight illuminated the passage at regular intervals, revealing the way ahead. The passageway extended deep into the mountain, leaving them in awe. However, as they progressed, they stumbled upon several Vikings who were not working, which piqued their curiosity.

Before they could investigate further, one of their guards brandished a giant sword and plunged it into the sidewall of the tunnel. To their shock, several stones crumbled from the wall upon impact. The Viking then attempted to pierce through the current end of the tunnel, but his sword broke instead.

"The rock is harder than the tools they use. Unless they receive assistance, the tunnel project will come to a halt," the woman said, understanding the Viking's demonstration immediately.

"You are absolutely right," Gordon nodded with a grin. "And I already have a plan to help them. But there's one thing I still don't understand. How does this Eric guy know that there's supposed to be more of that rock inside the mountain?"

"I can tell you that," the woman began. "A few days ago, a knight on a horse arrived at the Viking camp. His coat of arms bore a white castle on a red background. He brought a whole bag of these stones and gave them to their leader, Erik."

"You're kidding!" The thief said.

"No, why would I joke about that?" The woman replied, puzzled by the thief's reaction.

"Please continue with your story!"

"The man broke a branch from one of the surrounding trees, roughly stripped it of its leaves, and carved a plan of the treasure's location into the ground."

"So?"

"The treasure is inside the mountain. There is another entrance." The woman pointed to the more distant white castle higher up. "But that one is too heavily guarded.

"And how do they know the man wasn't lying?"

 "Simple. He was the brother of Eric; he spies for him at the white castle."

Gordon was visibly surprised.

Suddenly, they were interrupted by a man coming quickly toward them, yelling loudly. It was Eric, who now looked at Gordon angrily.

Gordon nodded emphatically, then gestured with his hands to convey to Eric that he needed his backpack in order to help him. The leader understood immediately, and within a few minutes, Gordon had his backpack back in his possession. As he suspected, the backpack was missing the meteorite from the museum, but there was something else in it that he needed for his plan.

Using hand signals, the meteorite thief indicated that he needed to return to the end of the tunnel they had dug to begin his work. While Eric contemplated his request, Gordon whispered something to the couple. Eric called forth his strongest Viking to prevent Gordon from escaping and stationed several guards at the entrance to the tunnel.

The meteorite thief and his muscular companion disappeared into the tunnel, but nothing happened for quite some time. Eric was just about to send more men into the tunnel to check on things when they almost collided with the thief and his guard, who were running out. In a moment, a loud bang erupted from inside the mountain, and smoke poured out of the tunnel opening.

Gordon and the couple took advantage of the moment of confusion and ran into the tunnel. Eric yelled at his men, who immediately rushed after them. Soon, Gordon and the couple had reached the point at which the tunnel had previously ended, though it was clear now that Gordon had blasted a way through.

"You did it!" The woman exclaimed in disbelief.

"Yes," Gordon replied with a smile. "It's amazing what a stick of dynamite can do."

The couple looked at him in amazement. Under normal circumstances, they surely would have asked where this man had obtained the dynamite. Gordon would have had trouble explaining the circumstances of the museum break-in and the fact that he had packed some dynamite for the job just in case. But there was no time for questions.

Just then, they heard the voices of their angry pursuers behind them.

"Faster! They'll catch up with us if we don't get moving!" Urged the frightened woman.

At that moment, Gordon activated another explosive device, and the tunnel ceiling behind them collapsed after another explosion.

"I have cut them off, so they can't follow us," Gordon said with a smile. "We are free again!"

"Out of the frying pan and into the fire," the man called out to Gordon, already fearing the worst. "I think it's good that we're rid of these wild barbarians, but how are we going to get out of the mountain now?"

Gordon looked at the woman. Then he said,

"You had said something earlier about Erik's brother that got me thinking. The valuable stones in the mountain must be accessible from the castle. So, there must be another passage leading from the castle to the treasure chamber inside the mountain. When I had set off the first blast, it was immediately clear to me that I had broken through to this passage because otherwise the explosion would have sounded different."

"You mean, if we continue to follow this corridor, we will reach not only the treasure but also the castle?" The man asked him skeptically.

"Yes," Gordon replied curtly.

"And what if you're wrong about that?" The woman said.

Gordon said nothing because they all knew the answer to this question.

Gordon was followed closely by the couple. He had switched on his flashlight, which he had brought with him to the museum. Suddenly, they reached a fork in the tunnel.

"Which is the way into the castle, and which leads to the precious stones?" Pondered Gordon aloud.

"I'm only interested in finding the way out," the other man added.

Gordon did not answer. There was a moment's silence, and then they heard the sound of running water somewhere. They walked in the direction from which the sound was coming. A few steps later, they were standing in a large, empty cavern. Gordon shone his light briefly in all directions. Then, they recognized something.

"Here we have the explanation for the water noise," Gordon said. "There's an underground river running here as far as I can see. But unfortunately, there is no way out of here and no treasure either." So they returned to the fork in the tunnel and took the other path.

Not 20 steps further, a door made of solid wood blocked their way. Their initial attempts to open it failed because it was firmly locked.

"Oh no, we're trapped!" The woman shouted desperately. To make matters worse, the beam of the flashlight chose that moment to go out.

Nothing seemed to have changed. Lara, Nina, and Pinky continued to stand on the mountain. However, they noticed that the ground was no longer frozen, and green moss was now growing on various parts of the stony terrain. The sky was also brighter, and the sunlight was now shining down on them. When they looked up the mountainside, they saw a small white castle, clearly visible to the naked eye.

"What happened, and where are we?" Asked Lara in amazement, still feeling dizzy.

"I don't know. It feels like we have time-traveled again," Pinky replied jokingly, though he was certain he hadn't activated his clock's time-travel function. Nevertheless, he checked his rainbow clock's display and was surprised to see the year 870 AD. The pink parrot could hardly believe it, but the evidence was clear. Wordlessly, he showed it to the others.

"Oh my god! Are you kidding?" Exclaimed Lara. "None of us activated our time travel clocks!"

"At least, we didn't do it consciously. If we really have been sent back in time, then the castle up there may be the first-built part of the white castle, built before the rest was constructed," Nina speculated.

"Wait a second. We will surely find out pretty soon if the display on the rainbow clock is accurate or not. I have my doubts about it. It is also possible that the green light beam damaged it, and it's now showing the wrong year. Let us start with the castle. Maybe there's someone there we can ask," Lara suggested.

"Good idea. Let's do it, then," Pinky replied, nodding in agreement.

They made their way toward the castle grounds when suddenly, a barrage of arrows flew toward them without warning.

"Duck!" Pinky shrieked in fright. Lara and Nina immediately jumped behind the nearest rock. Luckily, none of the arrows hit them. The rainbow parrot flew briefly into the air to assess the situation. "I can see armed men on the tower."

That was bad news. Not only were they in danger, but this was also further evidence that Pinky was right and they had indeed time-traveled.

The castle gate opened the next moment, and more than a dozen armed men on horses rode out. The sisters held their breath, realizing that they were the reason for the sudden activity. The men were after them.

16

TIME SLIPS AWAY

At the land at the end of the rainbow, the day had started quite well. However, this idyllic morning had been marred by an unexpected incident. A small rainbow had collapsed with a loud rumbling sound, accompanied by a moderate earthquake. Anna, who lived closest to it, had been the first to notice. She was surprised because she had protected the rainbow with a spell.

Weighed down by this bad news, she set out a little later on her witch's broom to Dr. Schubidou's house, which was the closest to hers.

"That doesn't sound good at all," he confirmed, his face worried. He thought about it for a moment, then motioned Anna to follow him to a larger room located at the very back of his medical office. In it, there was nothing but a strange device in the middle that looked like a combination of a large printer and a wind instrument.

"This is the best spectrometer I have," he explained. "I have already used it to examine the strange Northern Lights that have recently appeared in the sky. But it wasn't suitable for investigating the rainbows that are protected by spells because it was too weak to penetrate their cover. At least until today."

Anna looked at him questioningly.

"Because this morning, I made some improvements," he continued. "Now we can finally test the remaining rainbows to see if it works as intended."

"Great!" Exclaimed Anna enthusiastically.

Anna brought the doctor's strange diagnostic device into position by reciting a floating spell.

"Very nice!" Dr. Schubidou beamed. He pressed a button, and the spectrometer began to make a whirring sound. Then, a red light emanated from it and shot towards the rainbow above. After a while, they heard a beeping sound, marking the end of the measurement. A small piece of paper was printed out. Finally, he held the result in his parrot claws, shocked and speechless.

"What is it?" Anna entreated him.

"Rainbow Land's days seem numbered," Dr. Schubidou replied seriously. "That is what I already had assumed earlier, but now I finally have proof. We must fly to Paraiso immediately and tell him about this observation and what consequences it might have."

After stowing the note with the measurement result in his doctor's coat, they both set off flying, he with his wings and she on her witch's broom, to the largest treehouse in the country.

When they arrived at Paraiso's house, they could hardly believe their eyes. The structure was enclosed in a giant soap bubble that resembled the one they had seen at Anna's home. As they approached the house, several parrots stepped out of the front door and passed through the transparent shell.

"This is the beauty team!" The doctor explained, noticing Anna's puzzled look.

Anna shouted at them, "Where is Paraiso?"

"On the roof terrace in his newly-built spa area. But I don't recommend disturbing Paraiso now unless it's important," one parrot replied. "He needs to relax after his back massage."

Dr. Schubidou and Anna made their way to the terrace, where they couldn't believe their eyes. Paraiso was lying in a giant bathtub filled with pink and orange orchid blossoms.

"You can enjoy this view even better this way!" The vain chief enthused.

"But only for the next few days, not longer!" The doctor replied sharply, quickly bringing Paraiso back down to earth.

"What are you suggesting?" Paraiso asked him, annoyed.

"I'm suggesting that our world won't be here much longer," the doctor said solemnly.

Anna and the parrot doctor took turns recounting what had happened. Then, the doctor discussed the measurement results.

"These show that the rainbows continue to disintegrate despite the protection spells put on them. That means we cannot stop the process, and our world is coming to an end."

Paraiso looked at them with horror. The effect of his recent rejuvenation had just worn off.

"How much time do we have left?" He asked in dismay.

"Well, it's not clear from the measurements. I need to make a few more calculations before I can be certain," the doctor said.

"Good, do it!" Paraiso ordered. "I want the results by noon sharp tomorrow because the high council of the rainbow parrots will meet again at that time."

Dr. Schubidou nodded, swallowing nervously because he was unsure how long the calculations would take. They were somewhat complicated, so he immediately went back to his tree house to begin.

The following day at noon, Paraiso opened the next council meeting. Even Anna was there this time, not as a guest but as a witness.

First, Paraiso talked about the team of experts that had already been sent out to solve the existing temperature puzzle. Then it was Anna's turn.

The witch described the incident, which demonstrated the seriousness of the situation. She was interrupted by dismayed murmurs and nervous whispers that filled the secret meeting place.

"Using my measurements, together with a mathematical formula, I have calculated the precise time of this world's demise," said Dr. Schubidou. "The end of our world will be next week. We have no more than five days left. Even if Anna's magical powers can guarantee the stability of the land at the end of the rainbow, we must consider further options."

The wisest birds in the country stared at him, their faces blank with horror.

"Therefore, we must begin the evacuation immediately," the doctor finally added.

"That's nonsense!" Paraiso interrupted sharply. "We have to evacuate, but we don't need to rush into it. Every parrot in this country owns a fully functional rainbow clock. By activating it, its owner can leave our beloved country within a few seconds."

"I expected this answer," smiled the bird doctor. "The low temperatures ensure that the rainbows will gradually disappear. At the same time, the cold prevents new rainbows from forming since, as mentioned earlier, it is no longer raining but snowing. When the very last rainbow breaks, this world will collapse. When it comes to the rainbow clocks as a means of transportation, you have to remember they only work in the presence of a fully functional rainbow. If the rainbow vanishes or is not intact, it will not work. Therefore, we should start evacuation immediately."

This explanation made sense to everyone. The doctor looked around, and none of the parrot council members seemed to have any further questions. But then Anna, to everyone's surprise, raised her hand and stood up.

"You heard the doctor. He is right," Anna said. "I have no doubt that evacuation is the only way to proceed. But one important detail has not been mentioned yet. Let's assume for a moment that we get all the inhabitants of this country to safety. And let's assume that the team of experts Paraiso sent out is unsuccessful. This country will collapse. But what happens then? Can we ever return to our beloved country? The answer is no."

The council members looked at her, upset.

"No, because to recreate a new rainbow world, we need the witch book, which not only contains the spell to create the land but also contains the magical power necessary to do so. I, therefore, suggest that I immediately try to obtain this book."

Consternation spread. In fact, except for Anna, no one had thought the situation through - not even Dr. Schubidou. The meeting was coming to an end. Before Paraiso dissolved the meeting, however, two measures were agreed upon: First, the evacuation would begin as soon as possible for safety's sake, and second, Anna would travel to the parallel world where the humans live to retrieve the witch book.

After the meeting, all members went their separate ways. Paraiso didn't like the outcome of the secret meeting. If Anna was leaving the land of the rainbow parrots, she could not help him build an even bigger spa area in his birdhouse. But the importance of reactivating the witch book was beyond question, even for him.

Of course, the retrieval of the book involved certain risks, but those risks were acceptable if it meant the rainbow world could be saved. The witch book could have a negative effect on whoever read it. In addition, Paraiso assumed Anna would have to travel back in time again, possibly to the Middle Ages, to retrieve the book. However, Anna was anything but welcome in this era. She was the arch-enemy of the king and could easily end up in a dungeon.

"Maybe I don't have to travel back in time," Anna said to the astonishment of Dr. Schubidou when she visited him later the same day. "I just need to go to the place where the witch book ended up after the last creation process of this world."

"I'm afraid I don't understand," Dr. Schubidou replied, confused.

"The witch book did not dissolve, as everyone believes. It traveled on to a secret place," Anna explained.

"And where is that?" The doctor asked curiously.

"It is a place only I know," Anna said. She did not think it prudent to reveal her secret just yet.

The doctor nodded in understanding but said nothing.

"After that, I'll take care of retrieving the meteorite because we all know that the witch book is only complete with the meteorite stone imbedded in the front book cover. The last time I saw Lara, she mentioned to me that she had sold it to a geological museum in a little coastal town high up in the north," Anna explained.

"Finding the museum will probably be easy. But I highly doubt that the museum staff will just let you have the meteorite," Dr. Schubidou objected.

Anna tutted, wholly unimpressed. "I don't expect them to, but for a witch of my caliber, this poses no real obstacle."

Anna cast a single witch's spell and packed her travel bag in an instant. The bird doctor, who hadn't seen her practice witchcraft in a long time, stared at her in amazement. The witch noticed his puzzled expression and burst out laughing.

"This is just simple witchcraft," she explained, relishing the power that came with it. "It's something that can't be done any other way, even with the help of science."

The witch retrieved one of the many brooms from her authentic collection of witches' brooms, which looked just like the ones used in the Middle Ages.

"We will meet again in the near future!" She declared before leaving Dr. Schubidou alone in her home. Stepping out of the house, she found herself under a double rainbow and pressed a button on her rainbow clock. In an instant, she disappeared from that place and entered the parallel world of humans.

Although he had never done anything like this before, Dr. Schubidou, an all-rounder, quickly developed a perfect evacuation plan. However, the task of informing the population of the country at the end of the rainbow about it fell to the country's current chief.

The next day at noon, Paraiso planned to deliver his speech. The speech he was going to give had already been carefully written on a piece of paper by Dr. Schubidou. So, he only needed to read what was written on it. To ensure Paraiso knew what he had to say and didn't panic, Dr. Schubidou had marked the parts that were to be left out with a red pencil.

But when the rainbow parrots had gathered on the balconies of the surrounding treehouses shortly before noon, they noticed something strange. On the roof terrace, there was a kind of bathtub. In it was the leader of their country, screeching a loud song and enjoying a relaxing bath. He had moved his daily beauty session to the roof terrace so as not to be late and hadn't realized the hour of the meeting was already upon him.

Eventually, the parrot got out of the fragrant bath, a cucumber mask covering his eyes. When he removed it from his face, he became aware that all the parrot eyes in the country were on him. The only musical group in Rainbow Land, "Rainbow Dance," danced to the hot South American rhythms that the disc jockey played on the terrace of the largest treehouse in the country. "Rainbow Dance" consisted of seven dancers. The spotlights were now on the country's top parrot.

"Fellow citizens. We are gathered here today because it, uh," he faltered briefly, "my honorable duty is to inform you of an important decision made yesterday by the Rainbow Parrot Council." He cleared his throat. "I," he began, "regret to inform you that this cold wave is a danger to our country. Therefore, we have decided to evacuate the country as quickly as possible."

However, the audience didn't panic. Instead, they started laughing and wildly shrieking.

"Oh no!" Thought Dr. Schubidou, who had come late to the show because he had had a lot of sick parrots to attend to. "Everything that could have gone wrong has gone wrong. This parrot, totally unsuited for his job, had once again committed a faux pas."

When the rainbow parrots had left the town center, Paraiso explained to the doctor what had happened. Then, when he had finished, Dr. Schubidou said, "Too bad. Even if we can recreate the land at the end of the rainbow, it will be useless if we cannot save the rainbow parrots living in it. We have to figure out another plan to make them believe what you tried to explain to them."

Later, when Dr. Schubidou went to bed, he suddenly had an idea. "Brilliant!" He thought. "Early tomorrow morning, I am going to tell all the parrots I meet about the legend of the black parrot. This will work like magic!"

17

REINFORCEMENT

The snowmobile on which Gunnar and Ed were sitting was moving at breakneck speed. Ed almost fell off the bike at one point when Gunnar went into a sharp turn. In record time, they reached Bob's office. But the park employee had already finished work hours ago and had long since gone home.

Of course, the two men had not expected to find him at work at such a late hour. They had come here because this place was a hot spot for the internet and, at the same time, one of the best places to make phone calls.

Gunnar pulled his survival cell phone out of the pocket of his down jacket, which was well-insulated against the cold. After taking off his gloves, the weather expert typed in a number he knew well. The phone chimed several times before a man's voice answered."

"Whoever is disturbing me at this late hour better have a really good reason," Bob warned in a sleepy but sharp voice.

"Oh, come on, Bob. Don't get uppity!   I've got the best justification anyone could ever have. There's an emergency here!"

In a few sentences, Gunnar described what had happened in the last few hours. He told Bob about the unexpected visit from the girls, followed by Ed's discovery of the strange connection between the green light and the disappearing people. Finally, Gunnar recounted what they had witnessed at the White Mountain range. Bob listened intently, finding it hard to believe the story, but Ed kept insisting he was telling the truth.

"All right, you win!" Bob finally sighed. "I'll get in my car and come straight to you. But before I do, I'll call a friend in the military. I hope you guys haven't been lying to me because this could have embarrassing consequences for you."

Half an hour later, which seemed like an eternity to Gunnar and Ed because of the biting cold, Bob and a man with white hair and a military uniform showed up at the information office. Bob introduced the man as an old friend who had had a long career in the army and was now a respected general. The four of them settled in Bob's office.

Bob went to the small kitchen to make fresh coffee, returning shortly afterwards with a coffee pot and a bowl of cookies, which he placed on the table. Gunnar and Ed started to recount their experiences one more time, explaining the bizarre series of events that had brought them to this moment. The general listened attentively, his face growing increasingly serious as they spoke.

The highly decorated soldier made notes in a small book from time to time. When the men had reached the end of their story, he looked at them, scrutinizing them for a while.

Bob affirmed that Gunnar would never lie about such important things.

"Before I round up the infantry, I'd like some proof that this story is true," the general said, completely unemotional.

"But..." Gunnar began.

"No buts!" The general interrupted. "I'm sure you'll agree that your story sounds like an episode of The X-Files. I can't afford to risk my credibility."

Gunnar and Ed winced. Then they nodded. Gunnar thought for a moment before opening his mouth again. "Unfortunately, we don't have a video recording of what happened on the mountain range. But..."

"But... what?" The military man asked.

"Well, how about a little demonstration?" Suggested Gunnar as a last resort. He knew he was putting all his eggs in one basket, but they had no other choice. "We'll take a little trip together to the White Mountain massif. There, we will convince you of the truth of our story. You will see that this light is not a figment of our imaginations. Then, if you still think what we have been telling you is a fairy tale, we will leave you in peace."

A brief moment of silence filled the room. The general looked first at them and then at Bob. "All right," he surrendered due to the persistence of the two men. "But I'll only give you this one shot, though. If you can't convince me, I'll be gone faster than I got here. Understood?"

"Yes," answered Gunnar and Ed nearly simultaneously. Then they left Bob's office.

"I have another snowmobile parked at the back of the parking office building," Bob said to the general. The four men took seats on the two snowmobiles, and they were soon on their way to the White Mountain massif. The headlights of their vehicles and the mysterious green band of light in the sky were the only sources of light as they rode at the highest speed possible through the darkness.

Upon arriving at the White Mountain massif, they parked the two snowmobiles near the ridge where the light beam had appeared. It looked spooky, like an illuminated geyser emerging from an active underground volcano. The seasoned soldier had traveled a lot in his successful career, but he had never encountered anything like this before. They climbed up the ridge toward the light emerging from the mountain and shooting vertically toward the sky. There, they saw a large night bird accidentally get too close to the pulsating light and instantly disappear.

But the general wasn't convinced. "Maybe the bird has just hidden itself."

So Gunnar took a stone from the ground and fixed a piece of metal on it with the help of tape. Then he took his laptop and started it. "This is a tracking system. With it, we can see what will happen to this prepared stone when it will be thrown into the light."

"Are you ready?" Asked Gunnar.

"Ready!" Bob replied, holding the stone in his right hand. Then Bob threw it into the light beam, and the stone not only disappeared from their view. Also, the signal which had shown the location of the stone vanished on the laptop.

The general finally had the proof he needed to act. He reached into his pocket, took out his special field phone, and dialed a number so secret that only he knew it.

Before the sun had risen the next day, the mountainside was populated by a huge army. The general had a base camp set up where the soldiers could rest and sleep. Then, he met with the experts participating in his secret operation.

"Operation Light Beam begins today. It is top secret. Only you," he said, eyeing the bystanders with a scrutinizing glare as he took a large sip of water from the glass in front of him, "and I know about it."

Jeff, one of the experts, stepped forward. He placed a laptop on the table and flipped it open. A translucent 3D image of the White Mountain range they were on appeared on the screen, crisscrossed with thin green lines. Jeff pointed to a spot and explained, "We have to be very careful at the exit point of the light beam. We must not touch it under any circumstances because objects or living beings touching the light beam disappear. For this reason, we must drill a tunnel beside this light beam if we want to recover the mysterious light source located inside the mountain. We will drill until we have a hole that is just as deep as the light source and then drill horizontally until we are just beside it. We will lower a camera so we can have a look at it and formulate a plan to remove it with minimal risk."

"Very good," the general nodded with satisfaction. "How long will the drilling take?"

"If we have calculated the depth correctly, then it won't take longer than 72 hours," Jeff returned.

"Three days?" The general asked.

"Yes," Jeff nodded, "but unfortunately, we can't start right away because there's still one teensy problem."

"Out with it!" The general urged him.

"We don't have the drilling equipment on site yet!" Jeff returned meekly. "There is a delay as the delivery company has another urgent job to complete. But it should arrive tonight around 6 p.m. We'll try to get it in place tonight, and the drilling process can start tomorrow."

"Rejected," the general said firmly. "You will start the drilling tonight and will work without interruption, day and night."

"Why do we need to start it as soon as possible?"

"Because we have just a small time period to solve the light beam riddle. Already in 2 days, we will have to leave for a military exercise in Gotland."

However, the team of experts, led by Jeff, had their reservations.

"But, General," Jeff began, "I have the greatest respect for you. But this approach makes no sense in my eyes. We run the risk of..."

But he didn't get much further with his objection. The highly decorated 4-star general cut him off, annoyed, "Gentlemen, I do not like to repeat myself. Therefore, everything remains as I have already ordered. Make it possible, or I will find someone else to do this job!"

Jeff's face grew pale. He just nodded.

The meeting, held under the highest level of secrecy, was now over. The participants left the room, and the team of experts directed their dissatisfied glances at Jeff. But he only repeated the general's command: "We have our orders. The drilling starts tonight!"

In the meeting room, the general dropped back into his soft leather chair. Then he took a fat cigar out of the drawer in front of him, lit it, and was soon surrounded by a thick cloud of smoke. He tried to imagine what they would discover once they got to the bottom of this mysterious light phenomenon. He instinctively knew that time was of the essence; the longer the operation took, the greater the danger.

18

THE WHITE CASTLE

Lara and Nina were still hiding behind a big rock in front of the castle gate, weighing their options. The armed men on horses began searching the area, but the girls didn't give themselves up. They did everything they could to increase their slim chance of remaining undetected. With the help of Pinky, perched high in the air, they continuously changed their hiding place.

The parrot had the best overview and always flew in the direction of the rock that seemed safest to him. This tactic worked so well that the men of the castle soon believed the girls had escaped from them. However, the men high up in the watchtower of the white castle witnessed this game of hide-and-seek. Despite shouting and waving loudly, their attempts to attract the attention of the men on the ground were of no use.

The troop of horsemen was about to give up and ride back to the gate of the white castle, but then something strange happened. A bright flash of light came entirely out of the blue in the place where the sisters and Pinky had been standing just a few minutes before. A man materialized there, wearing modern clothing. Unfortunately, he had appeared at precisely the wrong moment. The troop of mounted men caught sight of him and, as strangers were usually enemies and thus unwelcome, rode in his direction, encircling him.

Lara, Nina, and Pinky cautiously looked out from behind a rock. The modern-dressed stranger's chances of defending himself against this mob were nil. However, they watched as the man stretched his arms forward and directed his palms towards his attackers. Short, glistening flashes of light shot out repeatedly from his palms, hitting the men encircling him. He cleverly evaded their attempts to grab him again and again. Instead, one after the other, the men fell off their horses until all of them lay on the ground.

"They're not... dead?" Pinky gulped at the notion.

"I haven't the faintest idea," replied Lara, horrified. "But we do know one thing for sure: we'd better not mess with him."

Then, the eerie stranger looked around very carefully before walking towards one of the men lying on the ground. In an instant, the stranger was wearing the man's clothes, and the man lying on the ground was wearing the stranger's 21st-century clothing. As if that wasn't strange enough, when the stranger turned his face to the sisters and their animal companion, they saw that his face had shifted to look like that of the man on the ground.

"Did you guys see that? That was awesome!" Exclaimed Lara excitedly, her voice quivering slightly.

Her little sister and the pink parrot nodded.

But then some pollen found its way to Pinky's nose. Unfortunately, he was allergic to certain types of grasses. He was able to suppress the irritation for a while, but then it burst out of him. He sneezed multiple times so loudly that the stranger heard it, too. He began to move closer to them.

"Oh my God! He's coming here!" Nina hissed in shock.

"We need to get out of here as soon as possible!" Lara returned, just as panicked.

"But then he'll see us," Nina hesitated.

Lara's brain was running hot. She feverishly searched for a solution.

"You guys stay here for now while I distract him," Pinky suggested confidently. "After all, I'm the one who got us into this dangerous situation."

Lara felt that they should not underestimate Pinky, even if he was quite a klutz. She remembered that he had successfully taken on the most powerful witch of the Middle Ages. But Lara had forgotten that Pinky had also been outrageously lucky.

Pinky flew like an arrow towards the man. But just before he collided with him, he dodged, passing very close to him. The man ducked. Then he raised his arms and aimed his palms towards the parrot. Pinky zipped away from him, gaining more altitude, but it was of no use. He managed to dodge the first few flashes of light from the man's palms, but then two volleys hit him on his tail feathers, setting them ablaze.

"Help! I'm on fire!" Cried Pinky loudly. By initiating a dive, he was able to put out the fire, but in the process, he also lost his balance and dropped like a stone from the sky, straight onto the head of the man he had been trying to distract. Upon impact, Pinky couldn't help but cry out in pain, "Ouch!"

The stranger grabbed Pinky with one hand, ready to wring his neck, but then he heard an angry voice:

"Stop! Don't do that! The parrot hasn't done anything to you!"

The stranger turned his head in the direction from which the voice came, and he saw a little girl come out from behind a rock only a few steps away from him and face him defiantly. She was a young girl with long brown hair and a determined look in her eyes. He hesitated, loosening his grip so that Pinky could fly free. The man's features now betrayed admiration for the brave little girl. Lara nevertheless continued to stay under cover of the rock.

Then she heard the strange man say, "I didn't want to hurt him. Honestly, I was only defending myself because he attacked me. In my era, any kind of violence is outlawed. It is only allowed to be used to protect yourself."

Nina looked skeptically at the man and then at the two men lying on the floor, whom the unknown man had knocked down.

"What about them? What did you do to them? Are they like...?"

"Dead?" The stranger replied, laughing. "No, they're just sleeping. I drugged them." Before Nina could say anything back, he asked, "By the way, where's your sister?"

Then Lara appeared and stood next to Nina. Putting her arm around her shoulders, she asked, "Who are you, and what do you want?"

"I have come from the distant future," the man replied, "to bring back something very important to us - the Stone of Power."

"The stone of power?" Asked Lara curiously.

"Yes," the man nodded. "It is dangerous. At least for those who don't know about its abilities."

"And you are aware of them?" Nina wanted to know.

Again, the mysterious stranger nodded. "Yes, in the distant future, almost every child knows the legend of the stone of power. It is said to have come to Earth a long time ago. It is said to be from an extra-terrestrial intelligence and to have come here to warn us."

Nina and Lara's eyes were like saucers.

"To warn us?" They both asked at the same time. "About what?"

"The danger that humans could destroy the planet."

"Through warfare?" Asked Nina.

"No, but we humans are the main cause of climate change. If we do nothing about it, the planet will become uninhabitable," the man explained seriously.

This explanation made sense to the listeners, especially to Pinky, who had already learned about climate change from the meteorology book. However, they still didn't understand how such a small stone could protect the whole of humanity from a massive climate catastrophe.

"And you also believe in this legend?" Lara doubted its truthfulness.

Again, the strange stranger nodded. "At first, I also thought it was just a fairy tale. But when my people and I got our hands on the stone and examined it more closely, we were able to prove that this story contains at least a kernel of truth."

"That there are aliens?" Nina wanted to know.

"No," the man returned shortly.

"You said you already had the stone and then lost it again. How and why?" Asked Lara.

"Yes, I was just coming to that," the stranger replied. "We strongly suspect that someone caused a disturbance in the space-time continuum by traveling through time, which in turn altered the course of history. As a result, the stone suddenly disappeared. My mission is to get it back as quickly as possible. For the future of the Earth is at stake."

Lara and Nina exchanged guilty glances. They believed their journeys to the Middle Ages could have led to this disturbance.

Pinky looked stressed. He had just come to the conclusion that if the Earth was in danger, it certainly was not a good idea for the Rainbow Parrot people to flee to the Amazonas after the land at the end of the rainbow had ceased to exist.

"We will, of course, be happy to help you get the stone back if the future of this planet depends on it!" Lara and Nina expressed their willingness to help.

The stranger was silent for a short moment, seeming to be thinking about their offer. Then he looked at the girls and said, "Why not! An offer of help is much appreciated, even if I don't yet know whether you can help me or not."

"Agreed!" Lara was excited about their upcoming collaboration.

"I'm in as well," Nina added.

"And so am I, of course," Pinky chimed in.

"What makes you think you'll find the stone here in the past?" Asked Lara.

"It's a long story," said the man from the future.

"We love stories," the girls immediately prompted him.

"All right," he replied, pausing for a moment to think. "Well, the best place to start is with me. I'm not allowed to tell you my real name for security reasons. Just call me Tom. I'm an employee of an insurance company that insures nearly everything you can imagine. But we recently closed perhaps the biggest deal in our company's history: an insurance policy on our planet - the Earth."

"Pardon? Are you kidding?" Asked Lara incredulously. She knew from her parents that you could buy insurance for houses, cars, and people, but for the whole Earth? She simply couldn't imagine that. Pinky thought this insurance was a good idea if what the man from the future was telling them was true. He would propose the idea of insurance for their constantly threatened homeland to Paraiso as soon as possible.

The insurance officer from the future, Tom, could see clear traces of doubt on the faces of his listeners.

"What I have told you is true!" He insisted. "The annual amount paid to us by all the governments of the world for maintaining the treaty is a staggering $300 trillion."

Lara and Nina rolled their eyes. That seemed like an incredible amount of money. They couldn't even imagine it because they didn't know how many zeros there were after the number three.

"And what does your company do in return for all that money?" The girls wanted to know.

"We save the world," the man replied, his eyes shining with determination. "The Earth underwent major man-made climate change. Many islands and vast coastal areas were flooded due to rising water levels in the world's oceans. Other areas suffered from prolonged droughts that destroyed crops, resulting in increased world hunger. This process seemed unstoppable."

"Until you got the stone of power?" Lara guessed, trying to follow the story.

"Yes," he nodded. "To save the world, we needed the necessary power. Also, we needed an artificial intelligence that could solve this problem and..."

"The stone part makes sense, but the AI does not," Lara interrupted.

"I was just getting to that," he replied, smiling. "Humans have learned to react to acute dangers. For example, our ancestors had to react when attacked by dangerous animals. But dealing with an insidious, far-reaching danger is something we have not yet learned to do. Think of the frogs!"

"What frogs?" Lara asked, intrigued.

"There was a frog experiment in the 20th century. Scientists took a frog and put it in a pot, slowly heating the water until it boiled."

"And then what happened?" Pinky yawned, finding the story dull.

"The frog was cooked because at no time did it feel the need to jump out of the cooking pot. In a way, our behavior is similar to that of frogs."

"That's why you needed an artificial intelligence?" Lara asked, finally understanding.

"Exactly," he replied. "But it wasn't enough. We needed the power to go beyond the legal jurisdiction of individual countries. For years, indeed, for decades, countries discussed the already ongoing climate crisis, but nothing much came of it. And then, suddenly, it was too late."

His listeners were silent, captivated by the story.

"The climate catastrophe had already begun long before you were born, but then it suddenly picked up speed. The whole world watched impotently as the climate abruptly tipped. Irreversible damage occurred, resulting in further accelerating climate change."

"Let me guess," the parrot interrupted. "That wasn't the end of the line."

"You've hit the nail on the head," he agreed. "We were on the verge of having to leave Earth. The world organization created our company. And we delivered.

"But then the Stone of Power suddenly disappeared. There could have been no break-in into the vault system where the stone was kept, so we consulted our AI about the disappearance. The AI arrived at only one plausible answer, that of time travel."

"And then you located the Stone of Power in the past?" Lara asked, her eyes wide.

"That's right. That's why we hired someone to travel back and retrieve it. But something went wrong in the process. This person, as well as the stone, has inexplicably disappeared."

"And you are here to find it?" Nina asked.

"You guessed it right! My mission is to retrieve the stone. The trail leads here."

"What kind of a lead are you talking about?" Nina inquired.

"I'll get to that in a minute. At first, we didn't know where to look for the meteorite. Then, fortunately, fate came to our rescue. The night watchman employed by the geological museum, who himself wants to solve the mystery of the theft, crossed our path in the last few days. I followed him and finally got to this mountain via the Abisko weather station," he pointed to the mountain on which the white castle was perched.

"So you saw us disappear?" Nina asked, her eyes narrowing.

"Yes, I saw you guys," the insurance clerk admitted.

"You were talking about a museum," Lara asked.

"Yes, the geological museum!" Tom replied.

"You're looking for the meteorite I sold to the museum a little over a year ago?" stated Lara in amazement.

Lara felt unwell. Tom was trying to retrieve the meteorite that the rainbow parrots would need to recreate their magic land. Therefore, a deal to help him with that seemed like a bad idea. On the other hand, if Tom found the meteorite, perhaps they could try to grab it before him.

"What a coincidence that you found us," Nina said.

"Not quite," Tom replied. "We've been researching, and all the leads have led here, and--"

A light suddenly came on for Lara. She realized Tom had also gone to her neighbor's house and set fire to his garage. She voiced her suspicion immediately.

"Yes, but that was just an unfortunate accident," Tom said, nodding. "I was looking for clues that indicated that someone had time-traveled. While searching the garage, I accidentally knocked over an old light bulb, which ignited some papers lying around. By the time I noticed, it was already too late. Then your neighbor came, and soon after, the fire department. He was only slightly injured, and his insurance will pay in full for the damage done."

"What about the thief who disappeared? Why did you think he would turn up here?" Lara asked.

"In the past? Well, the night watchman noticed a strange light, the same kind of light I found at the place where you disappeared next. And now you are here, and he might be here. I have to find out. But tell me one thing. What were you doing at the mountain?"

"Err, well, we read about this light in the museum and in newspapers," Lara lied, getting slightly red in the face. "Our parents disappeared also, and we were looking for them. We thought they could have vanished the same way."

Tom eyed her for a moment, but he was satisfied with her answer. Lara was relieved. She hadn't had to tell him anything about Pinky's homeland. Besides, it wasn't logical to assume her parents might be here because they hadn't had contact with the light as far as she knew.

"How can this stone be so powerful?" Asked Nina.

Tom cleared his throat and started to explain, "The stone is a kind of storage medium. Like a computer chip, it has information stored in it. The information the stone contains can only be accessed using an invention created in my era. This information is the key to--"

Tom was suddenly interrupted. Another squad of armed men was coming towards them. But they didn't need to hide, as the men just assumed that Tom, who had taken on the appearance of a soldier, had simply hunted down the dangerous stranger who had fallen several of their men.

"Well done. I'm sure you'll get a medal for bravery," the knights said with admiration.

"Yeah, maybe. But let's go back to the castle before more of those dangerous guys show up," Tom said. Then he saw that everyone was looking at the girls and the parrot. "I found these children and their parrot. They were separated from their parents when they ran away from the stranger, unfortunately."

"That was a super excuse the insurance clerk came up with on the spur of the moment," Lara thought.

So they entered the white building without further incident.

Once inside the castle, Lara and Nina recognized their surroundings. There was no doubt about it. This was the part of the white castle that had been erected first. The castle was majestic, with high walls and large towers. The interior was equally impressive, with ornate decorations and luxurious furnishings.

The knights in the castle greeted the travelers from the future in a friendly manner. They handed them water and freshly grilled meat. Then the girls looked around the castle grounds a bit more closely while their new ally, who was now a celebrated hero, remained indoors.

When the girls reached the basement, Pinky suddenly disappeared. They frantically searched for him until they found themselves standing in front of the entrance to a secret passage, which they knew very well from previous adventures. The passage was pitch black, and there was no trace of Pinky. Suddenly, a grim-looking guard appeared, blocking their way.

"You'd better go back up," the man said.

"Why is that?" Asked Lara.

"Because this area of the castle is haunted," the guard replied. He had made up the story to deter the girls from exploring the basement and getting hurt.

Suddenly, they heard a wailing sound that grew louder and turned into an eerie howling. The girls were startled for a moment but then looked at each other and winked briefly. They knew all too well who was responsible for the howling sound. Meanwhile, the guard ran out of the basement in a panic. Lara and Nina laughed.

"Pinky, come out of there now!" Shouted Lara into the hallway.

"Lara? Is that you?"

"Yes!"

"Thank the parrot god!" exclaimed Pinky. "I got lost down here for a minute and shouted loudly, trying to get someone's attention."

"We guessed that!" The girls confirmed, grinning at Pinky as he suddenly appeared from a dark corner in front of them.

"I've had enough for today," Pinky sighed.

"Me too. I'm tired," Nina said.

Together, they went back to where the insurance employee from the future was being celebrated vigorously. However, Lara, Nina, and Pinky decided to turn in for the night.

The next day, the girls told Tom about the secret passage. He found the information interesting but not important enough to help them solve their actual problems. However, Tom had also learned a few things from his conversations with the revelers last night. One of them had voiced a rumor that a group of armed Vikings had set up a small camp at the other end of the mountain - probably to dig a hole. Whether these Vikings existed and what they were up to remained unclear.

"Maybe they're looking for the treasure chamber," Pinky said spontaneously. The girls were dumbfounded at first but then exclaimed excitedly, "Yes, that's it! That must be it!"

Tom's thoughts drifted for a moment, and then he said, "Unfortunately, we haven't found a hot lead yet regarding the meteorite thief or your parents. We must rely on our gut feeling and follow what we have."

"Nobody, not even the Vikings, is stupid enough to just dig a hole for no purpose," Lara explained astutely. "They must have done it for a reason. It's probably the same reason why there are soldiers walking around in the basement guarding it, and the passage is deliberately left unlit. No one is supposed to find the passage because it leads deep into the mountain to a cavern. As Pinky has already mentioned, there is something valuable hidden there. The Vikings have found out about it from someone, and now they want it. So, they dug a hole, trying to get to the other end of the secret passage."

This utterance of Lara's was enough to arouse their curiosity, and they decided to look around the cellar vault that very day. They took a few torches with them, but they did not need to chase away the guard this time because Tom was welcome everywhere and was, therefore, allowed to look around undisturbed. They entered the secret passage unhindered but soon came across a wooden door that, surprisingly, nobody had locked. They continued walking and suddenly heard voices. Two strong Vikings stood in their way and shouted something incomprehensible to them.

"Oh my, I can't understand a word they're saying!" Whined Lara.

"But nor can they understand us," Tom said. "I have an idea."

Tom whispered to Lara and Nina what he was going to do.

"That's an excellent idea!" Said Lara.

Tom hit one of the two Vikings with his fist and knocked him down. Then he put his palms on the body. At that moment, an energy exchange seemed to occur between the two bodies. The Viking lying unconscious on the ground suddenly looked like Tom, and vice versa. The other Viking saw the stranger lying on the ground. He realized his friend standing next to him had probably apprehended the stranger. He was even more surprised to see his friend's hands on the shoulders of two young Viking girls.

"So, now we can continue to look around here undisturbed," Tom said with satisfaction as they walked out of sight of the Viking man.

"Wow!" Exclaimed Lara and Nina, impressed with their new looks.

They continued walking and suddenly found themselves among several Vikings walking around. None of them suspected them. Their camouflage was perfect. As Lara had thought, the Vikings had broken through to the other half of the secret passage. But that did not interest them. They turned around and suddenly found themselves in a large cave. It was the cave where Anna held her masses in the Middle Ages. But they were not alone. There were many Vikings in the cave. They were in the process of carving another tunnel into the grotto wall. This tunnel would serve as a way to steal the precious items that were located in the cavern and transport them outside.

Even though they did not see any of these items, Tom thought it right to prevent the burglary. He believed that this robbery would not have happened had it not been for his trip to the past. Tom told his friends to get behind him. Then he raised his arms and knocked down all the Vikings in the large cavern with flashes of light emanating from his palms. Among them was Erik, their leader. Tom's energy seemed to be limited. This was likely the reason his outer appearance began to flicker until he transformed back into himself.

19

PLAN B

Anna suddenly became visible again, standing under a giant rainbow that appeared to be hovering in the air. She looked around and realized she was in the middle of a vast carnival procession in Cologne, Germany. Despite being dressed as a real witch from the Middle Ages, which was her usual attire even when she had moved to the land at the end of the rainbow, Anna didn't stand out at all amidst the crowd. People assumed that her sudden appearance was a simple trick, but they didn't have time to think about it or ask her any questions.

Anna took out her rainbow clock, which she had modified to allow her to bridge great distances in the shortest possible time. She pressed a button on the clock and selected her next destination, which was the town where the geological museum was located in

Sweden.

Anna left the procession and walked to the large square next to Cologne Cathedral. Then, she turned right into a side street and made sure that no one was around. "Perfect," she thought to herself before pressing the button on her rainbow clock. In just a second, she emerged in front of the geological museum in Sweden, ready to travel three months back in time.

Anna sighed with relief as she looked around and found lots of signs indicating the way to the museum. She got off her broom and strode through the entrance into a small anteroom where the ticket office was located. Few visitors were present at that time of day in the middle of the week, so she was able to purchase a ticket quickly.

The lady at the cash desk stared at Anna through her nickel glasses for a few seconds before she asked, "Have you come from a dress-up party?"

Anna blushed, feeling a little embarrassed that she had forgotten to change into something inconspicuous. "Yes, a dress-up party," she replied with a smile. "I would like to buy an admission ticket for the museum."

The woman handed Anna a ticket and a detailed folding map of the museum rooms. "With this, you're guaranteed not to get lost," the woman said and wished her a lot of fun on her tour.

The map proved to be very practical, and Anna quickly found a shortcut to the wing where the meteorite collection was housed. She soon found the room where the green meteorite she was searching for was supposed to be, but she found its entrance sealed with several yellow adhesive strips. A sign read, "No entry! Police investigation in progress."

At that moment, a museum employee, whose name tag introduced him as 'Ed,' happened to walk past Anna.

"Hello, maybe you can help me. I would like to see the meteorite collection. I am especially interested in a certain green meteorite," Anna said in her sweetest voice, pointing at a picture of the stone in the museum flyer. She thought it was better not to tell Ed she knew anything about the rare stone the museum had bought about a year ago.

"Oh, I'm sorry you had to come all this way," Ed replied. "Unfortunately, this stone has been stolen."

"Excuse me? Stolen? When?" Anna asked, horrified because it seemed that she had arrived too late.

"Yes, there was a break-in here last week," he explained. "Didn't you hear about it? It was even in the newspaper."

"Unfortunately, no!" Anna answered, shaking her head.

"It happened when I was on my night shift. The thief got away from me in an inexplicable way. I could swear he was in the room where the meteorite was, but then he wasn't."

"How did you know he was in the room?" Anna asked him.

"Because I heard him screaming," Ed answered.

"Maybe he was a ghost?" Anna joked.

"No, I don't think so. The police found blood. The intruder must have hurt himself on the glass case which protected the meteorite."

"Ouch, that is strange!" Anna commented.

"But that's not all! Last night, another strange thing happened. A small family was vacationing in Abisko National Park. The parents vanished mysteriously, leaving the two daughters behind," Ed continued, his voice hushed with disbelief.

Anna feigned surprise, but in truth, she had already heard rumors of strange happenings in the area. Eager to know more, she leaned in closer as Ed recounted the story, ending with the tale of the two sisters who vanished after touching a greenish light emanating from a white mountain.

"And you have seen it with your own eyes?" Anna asked, scrutinizing Ed's expression for any hint of deception.

"I swear that is the truth," he replied solemnly.

Now convinced of the veracity of Ed's tale, Anna's heart raced with excitement. Could this strange light be the source of the climate change wreaking havoc in the parrot's world?

"What happened next?" Anna asked eagerly, her fiery red hair casting a vibrant glow in the dimly lit room.

"We've called in reinforcements," replied Ed, his tone laced with apprehension.

"Of what kind of reinforcements?" Anna pressed, her curiosity piqued.

"The military is there now and has cordoned off the area due to the danger. No one has to be afraid of the light any longer," Ed reassured her, hoping to calm her nerves.

Despite his attempts at reassurance, Anna felt a sense of urgency gnawing at her. She needed to investigate the source of the strange light and determine if it was linked to the meteorite theft or the climate crisis in the parrot's world. If it was linked to the theft, she would have the first hint to find the meteorite, which was essential for her witch book to recreate Rainbow Land. If the light was the cause for the cold weather in the parrot's new home, she could hopefully destroy it before this parallel world would cease to exist. In any case, she had the chance to help the rainbow parrots.

With a quick goodbye to the bewildered nightwatchman, Anna darted away, her mind racing with thoughts of time travel and adventure.

20

RESISTANCE

Contrary to Jeff's expectations, the heavy drill rig ordered by the General did not arrive at its deployment site on the White Mountain range until much later in the evening. He had briefed all senior soldiers on the project late that morning. They were responsible for its implementation and, in turn, drew up plans that they passed on to their subordinates. Thanks to Jeff's careful calculations, the heavy drill rig was moved into position without incident. The site where the drill rig stood was well-illuminated with flood lights, ensuring visibility even in the dark of night.

At about 10 p.m., late in the evening, the drilling began on the general's orders. There were enough soldiers on-site to work in shifts. The drilling produced a loud noise, and the men entrusted with the task wore hearing protectors to shield their ears. Jeff informed the general of the drilling's start time; he was extremely satisfied. He lay down in his heated tent, where his cot was, shortly after.

The drill worked tirelessly throughout the night, but regular breaks were still necessary to cool it and reduce its wear. The drill was extraordinarily hard-wearing. There was a layer of diamond on the outside of the drill bit and a special alloy on the inside. After 11 p.m. the next day, the drill's tip had almost reached the depth where the light source was. There was only a little more than a meter to go. Here, the composition of the rock changed. It shimmered green and was harder than the previous layers of rock. The diamond-coated drill, which had cut through the overlying rock like butter, heated up dramatically and broke with a loud bursting sound.

"Stop! Stop the drilling immediately!" Shouted the soldier in charge of the process, who had just been fighting fatigue but was suddenly wide awake again. He had heard an odd sound through his headphones. When he noticed that the drill's temperature had risen to several thousand degrees, it was already too late to prevent the disaster. The soldiers transported the very expensive drill up from the borehole, and at the sight of it, Jeff was speechless because all that was left of it was a pile of scrap metal.

"This is a disaster! You can forget about that promotion you were promised," Jeff told the soldier in charge of the drilling exercise. He could well imagine how the General would react to this.

"How could this happen?" The general raged as Jeff told him this horror story.

"The drill must have run hot. I guess the cooling system couldn't keep up with the working speed you ordered and..." Jeff allowed himself a slight dig against his supervisor, whose work attitude he did not like at all.

"Are you implying that I, and not you, am to blame for the broken drill?" The highly decorated general hissed.

"Well...uh no," Jeff stammered.

"Good. So how long did you say it will take you to find a replacement for the drill?" he asked angrily.

Jeff didn't answer at first. He was thinking about how he could break the bad news to the general gently. "Sir, I'm afraid that you won't like the answer," he finally began, somewhat meekly.

"Man, speak plainly! That's an order!" the general barked.

"All right, General. You asked for it," Jeff replied, but this time with a bit more emphasis in his voice. "The drill is shot. Even if we had a replacement drill here on-site, it wouldn't get us an inch further. That's because the rock layer we hit is way too hard."

"Well, then get a new, harder drill as quickly as possible," the general urged him, snorting with rage. "No matter what it costs!"

"I'm sorry, General. I'm afraid that's not going to work," Jeff sighed.

"Excuse me? I don't understand," his superior returned, more than irritated. No one had ever dared to contradict him before. This man in front of him had already done it several times today.

"The drill has been destroyed, though it was manufactured with the most resistant material we know: diamond!" Jeff explained. "It broke because the stone layer it reached was even harder."

There was a long pause. The General finally understood, but he needed a moment to digest the implications of this answer. They seemed to be facing an insoluble problem.

"What exactly is this impenetrable layer of rock made of?" The general asked. One could see that his brain was running at full speed, and he was frantically searching for a solution. This trait had brought him here. It had been instrumental in his career so far. He never gave up. Never! No matter how hopeless a situation seemed.

"Unknown. Unclassifiable. This rock doesn't seem to exist anywhere else in the world," Jeff explained.

"Pardon? What does that mean?" The general asked in amazement.

"It's simple. It's not from this world," Jeff replied. "We suspect it's a meteorite that crashed to Earth a long time ago."

The general let out a whistle of surprise. This news came entirely out of the blue. The rock was unique and must, therefore, be very valuable. Perhaps this would go some way towards countering the immense costs this military operation had already racked up.

"Our mission here still has only one goal: to recover and examine this mysterious light source. Are you and your team looking into a way to reach our goal?" The general pushed.

"Well, there is another option. But I warn you, you might not like this solution, as it may be a little dangerous," Jeff said hesitantly.

"Spit it out already!" The general railed at him, somewhat annoyed, for his patience was at an end.

"Blasting," Jeff returned curtly.

"Are you crazy?" Returned the general. "Won't we destroy the light source, which we want to recover and then examine?"

Jeff swallowed nervously, then replied softly, "I told you it was risky. I'm sorry! There is no other option. It's our only plan B."

After Jeff left, the four-star general sat silently at his desk for a while, staring ahead. For the first time in his career, he had the uneasy feeling that he was dealing with something he couldn't handle. The atmosphere in the room was tense, and he could feel the weight of responsibility on his shoulders. The thought of destroying the unique and valuable light source was unbearable, but he couldn't let his mission fail.

21

REUNITED

"Oh no, we're trapped!" The couple cried in horror. However, Gordon was a master of his trade and had a lock pick in his luggage. The lock turned out to be quite simple to pick. Once they were through the door, he locked it again, thinking they were safe.

However, the party's relief was short-lived. At the end of the corridor, they came across a cellar vault with guards from the white castle inside. One of the guards noticed them and called for reinforcements. The group heard the guards' footsteps rushing towards them and knew they had to hurry back the way they had come to avoid getting caught. Fortunately, Gordon was able to open the door again and lock it from the other side. They stopped and listened, relieved that the Vikings had not yet arrived. But their relief was short-lived as they heard the guards on the other side of the door shortly.

"Get the key! Quick!" Someone shouted.

"We don't have much time. We have to get out of here fast," Gordon urged.

The woman suggested, "Yes, we need to go back to the cave. There, we may be able to hide from both the people from the castle and the Vikings. Then we'll wait for the right moment and disappear."

Without hesitating, they ran back to the big cave as fast as they could, knowing that the Vikings were trying to break through into the existing underground passage system. They could hear the Vikings' voices growing louder and clearer as they ran.

Gordon shone his flashlight in all directions but did not see an exit. Instead, there was only an underground river running through the cave. They knew that it was the riskiest possibility, as they did not know how it flowed, and it could be entirely underwater in another section of the cave system.

Suddenly, Gordon recognized an almost vertically rising cave wall, and in it, he saw depressions in familiar places. "There's a staircase carved into the rock. We have to climb it!" He urged the couple.

"What?" The man was about to protest, but at that moment, more men entered the cave, loudly roaring Vikings.

Gordon immediately switched off his flashlight, and the three climbed the stone steps quietly and as quickly as possible. They knew that if the Vikings discovered them, they would not get another chance to escape.

After climbing the staircase, the couple and Gordon found themselves in a recess. They could see the whole cave filling with Vikings, and their scar-faced leader was also there. The leader took out the meteorite stone that he had taken from Gordon and ordered his men to drive another tunnel into the wall on one side.

The cave alcove turned out to be a trap for the time travelers. Cautiously, they groped their way into the darkness, avoiding the Vikings. Gordon didn't dare turn on his flashlight. He wanted to avoid being discovered by the Vikings in the cave. Then, they spotted a faint light on the other side of the alcove.

At that moment, a Viking with two children entered the large cave. He suddenly raised both arms and shot lightning at the many Vikings around him. Although they outnumbered him, they didn't stand a chance. Soon, they were all lying on the ground. At that moment, the Viking's face changed, and he resumed his original form. The children also transformed.

Gordon could not believe his eyes. The man who had hired him to steal the meteorite was here. He knew he had to help him and the couple.

Gordon quickly descended the stone steps carved into the rock wall and called out to Tom. The couple climbed down after him. The two children, Lara and Nina, immediately recognized them and bolted towards them.

Tom looked at Gordon in amazement. Gordon took a few steps toward him and quickly whispered what had happened to him. "So, this Viking here is called Eric, and he is their leader," Gordon said as he pointed to the Viking leader lying on the ground. "He has taken the meteorite from me that you asked me to steal from the museum."

Gordon turned his head toward the cave alcove where the man and woman were eagerly speaking to the two girls. It looked like a happy family reunion. He was relieved that they were preoccupied and wouldn't hear what he had to say to his client.

"When I tried to get the stone from the display case, suddenly, a green light shone through the skylights into the museum and hit me. After that, the museum disappeared, and I couldn't find my way back to my boat. Instead, I ran into these Vikings who whisked me away here."

Tom's expression showed that he was happy to have finally found Gordon. But at the same time, he was worried about the stone. He walked over to Erik, who was still lying unconscious on the cave floor. Attached to his robe was a small leather bag. He lifted it, opened it, and looked at its contents with satisfaction. He couldn't help but smile. Finally, he had gotten what he wanted.

"Do you mind if I ask you a question?" Gordon said. "Why did you want me to steal that stone?"

Tom answered honestly, "It is necessary for the fulfilment of my role as an insurance clerk, and it plays a pivotal role in the fate of the world."

"But why this stone exactly?" Gordon pressed. "Take a good look around! The whole cave wall seems to consist of it."

Tom looked around and then let out a surprised whistle. All the cave walls emitted a faint greenish light. He took a few steps toward the cave wall closest to him and examined it more closely to determine whether Gordon's statement was true.

"You are indeed right!" Tom replied, hardly able to believe it. "Yes, in that case, I'll have to confiscate that rock, too."

"You mean you're going to seize the whole mountain?" Gordon

asked, puzzled because he had doubts that this insurance company was allowed to do that.

"No, just this rock," Tom clarified. "I'm going to transport it to my future."

Gordon just stared uncomprehendingly at the man from the future. In his opinion, this would undoubtedly take some time and be considerably expensive. On the other hand, it was none of his business.

But for Tom, the question-and-answer session was over. He now had something more important in mind. Out of nowhere, he materialized a strange little device.

"How on earth did you do that? Was that a magic trick?" Gordon asked, rubbing his eyes in amazement. "And what is that, anyway? I've never seen anything like that in my entire life."

"With this," Tom explained, holding up the device, "I can set up a temporary transport tunnel that I can use to send all sorts of things through time."

Gordon pondered the possibility that his client had made a bad joke to put a stop to his annoying questioning. He watched with fascination as Tom demonstrated how the device worked.

At the same time, the family reunion between Lara, Nina, and their parents was taking place. The children's parents had been more than surprised to see them. "Lara!" "Nina!" They had exclaimed. "What on earth are you doing here?"

The joy of being reunited was great. Everyone chattered rapidly, talking over one another in an effort to fill each other in on the details of the past few days. Above all, Lara and Nina were eager to solve the mystery of how their parents had traveled to the past without having been at the geological museum or the White Mountain massif, either of the places where the green light had been seen. It was then that Nina noticed something; her mom was wearing Nina's great-grandmother's ring, which Anna had returned to the family some time ago. Nina blinked rapidly. Unless she was mistaken, the ring was emitting a greenish hue. But, perhaps her eyes were playing tricks on her, or maybe the polished surface of the ring was simply reflecting the green meteorite rock in the walls.

"Mom!" Lara exclaimed, making the same observation as her sister. "Let me see your ring for a second."

Her mom slid the ring off her finger and stepped towards her daughter, but her foot slid on the uneven rock surface. The ring clattered to the ground, bouncing off the rocks. Whenever it touched the ground, Lara noticed a faint green glow. "That's weird," she said, raising her eyebrows.

She picked up the ring and ran her fingers over its polished surface before giving it back to her mother. "It seemed to interact with the rock." She frowned, turning to her sister. "I have a theory on how our parents managed to time-travel. I think the stone in Mom's ring is made of meteorite rock!"

Tom believed that the mission he and the girls had embarked on was a success. He pressed a button on the peculiar apparatus he held in his hand.

"We need to get behind that rock!" He urgently instructed his companions.

Without questioning him, they quickly scurried behind an enormous boulder on the cave floor. They were just in time because something strange happened the next moment. The device began beeping, and a tiny hatch on the top of it opened up, revealing a bracket that extended, holding a scanner at the end of it. The scanner emitted a reddish light beam and began scanning the cave walls.

Finally, the scanner finished its job. Tom then typed in the following four digits: 2354.

"Wow!" Exclaimed Lara, marveling at the display on the device. It reminded her of her lost rainbow clock.

Tom glanced briefly at Lara but then focused his attention back to the task at hand. "All right," he said. "Let's get this over with!"

"What do you mean?" Gordon asked in disbelief.

"The rock transport, of course," replied Tom. "We have to leave this cave system immediately! Come on!"

"Not so fast!" Nina interjected, trying to stall for time as she couldn't locate Pinky. "What's going to happen to the mountain if you remove the rock all at once?"

"It's simple," explained Tom. "If the rock that makes up the cave walls disappears, then the whole mountain collapses."

Everyone looked at him in horror.

"If tons of rock were to fall on the light source inside the mountain, it would no longer be able to emit a signal," Lara thought. "That would be equivalent to inactivating the light source. The climate catastrophe in the land of the rainbow parrots would end."

"That's why we have to get out of here," continued Tom. "But don't worry. I've set the timer for half an hour."

"Where's Pinky?" Lara asked, realizing the bird was missing. Unfortunately, no one had an answer.

Suddenly, Pinky flew over and landed on Lara's shoulder, relieved to have found his way back to the group.

"I think I found the source of the light!" He whispered excitedly in Lara's ear. "At the end of the alcove where your parents and Gordon were hiding just now, you can see a relatively bright greenish light. I looked closer and could see your rainbow clock there. I tried to retrieve it, but unfortunately, it seems to have fused with the surrounding rock. So, I couldn't take it with me."

Lara was surprised to hear that her rainbow clock was emitting a light beam. The light source was the suspected cause for the weather change in the Rainbow Land, as well as for the non-voluntary time travels of different people.

"Too bad," Lara whispered back, surprising Pinky. "But Tom has activated a timer. The mountain is going to implode in half an hour when the meteorite rock is transported away to his era. We don't have time to recover the rainbow clock now." She explained the urgency of their situation.

Pinky hopped from one leg to the other and flew over to Nina to land on her shoulder. He couldn't believe they wouldn't have time to deactivate the rainbow clock, which was causing the cold weather in Rainbow Land and could lead to its destruction. However, he understood that they all had to get out of the cave as soon as possible.

Pinky looked at his rainbow clock and compared the time with the remaining time on the readout of Tom's device. There were only 15 minutes left before the mountain would collapse in on itself. It was possible the implosion of the mountain would deactivate the rainbow clock, but he couldn't be certain that this was the case. If the implosion didn't deactivate the clock, then there might be no time to get the watch in time to save Rainbow Land.

Pinky knew it was risky, but he decided to try to retrieve the rainbow clock on his own. "Lara and Nina, I have to say goodbye to you. Our journey together ends here," he said, stifling a sob. "I don't know if I will survive this, but if not, I give you my rainbow clock to use in the future. In exchange, I need a normal watch to track the time."

Nina nodded and gave Pinky the watch she had received from her grandma as a birthday present. Lara whispered something into Pinky's ear and fastened something around one of his legs.

"Please wait at least half an hour after the implosion of the mountain. Assuming I'm still alive, I will go to the biggest tree that can be seen from the entrance of the secret passage. Then we can travel back to our future together."

Pinky disappeared, making his way back to the small hole and squeezing through it. "Yes!" He exclaimed when he caught sight of the greenish pulsating light source. It was Lara's clock, glowing with heat and symbiotically fused with the surrounding greenish shimmering rock.

Glancing in horror and disbelief at the watch Nina had given him, he realized there were only eight minutes left until the implosion of the mountain, and he still didn't know what to do.

He only had one chance, in his opinion. He had to destroy the clock.

Pinky was looking around. He caught sight of a stone that he could throw at the rainbow clock. But there was one problem. The rock was too heavy for a parrot like him to lift.

Just 4 minutes left!

Pinky looked at the rainbow clock in horror and despair. He couldn't turn out the source of the light.

Gordon and Tom made their way outside, and the cool, fresh air hit their faces as they stepped into the open. They looked like a small family as they walked together, side by side. Tom still seemed to be in a hurry, and he spoke quickly. "Thank you for your help, but you have to excuse me now. I have to be in the future before the rock gets there to make sure it doesn't fall into the wrong hands."

"Wait, what about me?" Gordon asked. "The fact that I ended up here is all your fault! Could you please take me back to my boat?"

Tom thought about it for a moment. He wanted to leave Gordon here in the past, but it was clear that Gordon hadn't done anything wrong. The fact that he had ended up in the past was not Gordon's fault, and Tom and his partner had removed all evidence that could link him to the theft from the sailboat. Gordon's presence would continue to remain a secret.

"Well, I'll let you out on the way," Tom said. "But then you'll have to manage on your own."

"Agreed!" Gordon replied, more than satisfied.

Then, with a sudden flash of light that blinded everyone, Tom and Gordon disappeared. The girls and their parents standing nearby couldn't believe their eyes, but the girls had a strong suspicion of what had just happened.

"What a pity!" Lara thought, disappointed. "Couldn't Tom have at least waited a little longer before leaving? I still had a few important questions for him. He hadn't yet told us what kind of information the stone contained or how to make sense of it."

22

THE SECRET CHAMBER

Anna had taken the next train from the town where the geological museum was located to the tiny village of Abisko. From there, she took a bus right to the entrance of the national park, where the tourist office was located. She had prepared by bringing appropriate clothing and equipment for a trekking tour. Anna had even turned her witch's broom into a walking stick for the journey.

Fortunately, Ed had warned her about the military presence in the area. Anna didn't want to risk being detected by the military's radar while sitting on her witches' broom. As she arrived at the tourist information office, a large sign greeted her, informing visitors that they must register their stay in the national park in advance. Anna entered the small office and was lucky enough to find herself first in the queue. A young woman handed her a free folding map of the National Park's hiking trails. She explained to Anna that the area around the White Mountains was currently closed off for security reasons due to military maneuvers. Anna took note of this information. It was important to know how closely she could approach the area without being caught.

"You want to spend a whole week wandering around the park?" The lady wondered, looking at Anna scrutinizingly through her nickel glasses that sat too low on the bridge of her nose. When Anna

 nodded but said nothing more, the lady continued, "Well, that's what I call brave. Have you ever done anything like this before, or is this your first tour of this kind?"

"I know the area relatively well," Anna returned evasively. "After all, I used to live near here."

After promising to stay on her planned route, Anna finally set off. She hiked for several hours until she approached the restricted military area highlighted on the map. At first, Anna ignored the signs warning of the danger in the area. The symbols on the signs were obscure, featuring skulls and other strange markings. However, as she approached a barbed-wire fence and a barrier, Anna encountered a jeep belonging to the Swedish military. Two soldiers were sitting inside, and they immediately noticed Anna's presence.

"Stop! You're not allowed to go any further!" One of the soldiers shouted at Anna. "This is a restricted military area."

"Oh, I'm sorry! I must have gotten lost," Anna said innocently. "Perhaps you would be so kind as to show me how to get back on the right path?"

Without waiting for an answer, Anna took out her folded trail map and handed it to the two soldiers with an innocent smile on her face. The soldiers hesitated for a brief moment but then accepted it since they did not consider Anna dangerous. They stood close together as they bent their heads over the map, which was precisely what Anna had intended. Suddenly, the men sneezed and fainted.

Anna smiled with satisfaction. She knew the sleeping spell with which she had treated the map and its effects all too well. She also knew that this substance would cause the soldiers to experience short-term memory loss, which was exceedingly convenient since they would not remember her when they awoke.

"You can't keep a good witch down," Anna thought as she climbed over the barrier. Now she was in the forbidden zone! After casting a witch's spell, she found herself wearing a military uniform.

Anna cautiously approached the White Mountain Massif. Protected by the trees, she looked around carefully to make sure she didn't run into any of the military men. Soon, the mountain was less than 200 meters away. Then the trees stopped, and Anna stood at the edge of a clearing. Haphazardly erected buildings belonging to the Swedish army filled the clearing. The entrance to the underground passage system that led to the large cave in the mountain's interior was visible. Behind it, Anna could see the imposing mountain wall. The clearing was teeming with soldiers.

"The military has not yet discovered the secret entrance to the grotto," Anna said with a satisfied smile, looking through her binoculars. She saw the reason why the military had come here. At a particular spot on the mountain, a pulsating greenish beam of light shot up into the sky. But that was not all Anna saw. Directly above this opening was a massive steel construction, next to which were many soldiers. By contrast, the entrance to the secret passage was empty. She looked at her rainbow clock; it was shortly after 4 p.m. Darkness would fall soon. She knew it was time to act.

The sun was sinking against a background that was turning a glowing red. It had become quieter. Most of the soldiers had gone over to the large barracks, and the smell of food wafted through the air. Instantly, Anna's stomach growled. But she ignored it. It was time to take advantage of this opportune moment.

She stepped out of the shelter of the trees and crept to the spot in the clearing. Carefully looking around again to make sure that no one was approaching her, she finally came close to the long-forgotten entrance to the secret passage. The entrance was difficult to find. Lots of snow covered the ground, and it was dark. Anna sighed. She had no choice but to search for the metal ring with a flashlight. She used her walking stick to create a small flashlight. The place seemed to be empty. Only the sound of men's voices in the food shack could be heard in the distance.

Finally, she found the metal ring and pulled on it. With a loud scraping noise, an opening appeared on the floor. Anna didn't hesitate for a second, climbing down the stone steps. But just at that moment, purely by chance, two soldiers came out of the barracks and approached the entrance to the passage.

"I see a light!" One of the soldiers exclaimed.

Anna winced, quickly turning off her flashlight. But the men continued to approach the secret entrance, discovering the opening in the ground. Suddenly, Anna found herself standing in the light of a flashlight.

"I wasn't going crazy! There is someone down there!" The soldier shouted, pointing the flashlight at Anna.

Although a woman in uniform was quite normal in the Swedish army, long hair was strictly forbidden. Anna's long locks identified her as an intruder.

"If the woman was really a part of the army, then her long hair would have been noticed immediately," the soldier thought to himself. The only explanation was that she was a spy.

"Who are you? What are you doing here? Freeze! Any resistance is futile!" thundered the other soldier.

But Anna did not even consider following this order. She descended the stairs as fast as she could and found herself in an underground passage. She ran as fast as she could, her footsteps echoing in the darkness until she reached the place where she could hear the sound of rushing water. Here, there was a narrow passage that led to a great cave where, in the Middle Ages, a secret order of witches used to gather on the nights of the full moon. The narrow passage was not easy to find, but Anna had no problem locating it. She was pretty sure, once she arrived in the big cave, that she had shaken off her pursuers for the time being.

Meanwhile, one of the two soldiers had made his way back to the surface to report the incident to his superiors. The report eventually landed with the general.

"What are you saying? Did someone spot an unknown person in a hole in the ground? A secret passage?" The general roared at his subordinate. "What's the meaning of this?"

"General, Sir, we don't know that yet. But I've already sent a dozen soldiers after the woman to take her into custody," Jeff replied agitatedly.

"Good. Report back as soon as you know more! Dismissed!" The general barked.

In the cave, Anna switched on her flashlight, illuminating a golden throne that had remained unchanged over the centuries. She stepped closer to it and murmured a familiar floating spell. Immediately, the heavy stone structure rose and hovered several meters in the air, revealing an opening in the ground below it. Anna disappeared into the opening just as the throne settled back onto the ground above the portal.

Anna continued walking through another narrow corridor. The air was musty, and algae growth covered the walls. The plants thrived in the high humidity that prevailed in the underground passage. Eventually, she reached a place where giant black spiders had built numerous spider webs.

"I'm sorry, dear ones!" Anna said loudly. "I'm afraid I'm going to have to move your artwork out of the way." With a witch's spell, all the webs and the spiders vanished. The spiders fled into the numerous narrow crevices. Anna ran on and came to a room at the end of the passage. The area was empty except for sconces attached to the walls, which were covered with spider webs. Anna conjured several torches and hastily placed them in the sconces, lighting them with magical fire. No sooner had the torches been lit and then the room was no longer empty. Wooden shelves filled with a variety of ancient books appeared.

A smile crossed Anna's face. "Yes," she thought, relieved. "My invisible witch library still exists."

The witch books contained far more knowledge than her main witch book alone. The knowledge in all these books formed the basis of her power. Within their pages were secret recipes for reversing aging, herbs that could be used for magic drinks, and much more.

Joyfully, she randomly grabbed a book from the shelves, freeing it from a thick layer of dust to find out what kind of book it was. One book slipped from her grasp, fell to the floor, and remained unfolded upside down. When she picked it up again, the book's contents drew her attention. The pages were well-worn and faded, and a minor, green-tinted glyph was visible, written upon it in thick blood-red wax.

"Well, this is great," Anna giggled with excitement. "A genuinely great spell!" Although she found it fascinating, she nevertheless put the book back in its place on the shelf.

Anna hadn't come here to browse through all of these old books. She was here for one reason only: to get back the witch book that had disappeared during the last re-creation of Rainbow Land. If she wasn't mistaken, it had to have landed somewhere in this room.

Anna had put a protective spell on this book so that no one else but herself could consult it. But she had been afraid that the power of the magic could have diminished over time. However, the meteorite that was needed to bring it back to life was still missing, and she decided to take care of it later.

No matter how hard she searched, Anna did not find the book. She took off her golden necklace, a cross, turned it into a pendant that was supposed to represent a book, and magnetized it. With the pendant, she could track down the master witch book she was looking for. She reached a wall where there was only an empty bookcase. The pendant was suddenly so attracted to a place on this shelf that it jumped out of Anna's hand. The pendant landed on the shelf, and a book appeared in its place. It was the witch book.

Anna tucked the book under her arm and started to retreat. But as she approached the gold throne again, she heard muffled voices. "Oh no!" She thought, keeping as quiet as possible. "The soldiers have discovered the cave. I need to find another way out."

Anna walked back to the invisible library again, a little slower.

Nowhere was there a second exit. She couldn't use the witch book to fix this problem either, as the last page would remain blank until the meteorite was attached to the front cover. At that moment, someone moved the golden throne aside. Anna could hear several voices but did not understand what was being said. The soldiers were on their way. That meant that if she did not come up with a plan soon, they would probably capture her.

Anna returned to the library and started frantically looking through the titles of all the witchcraft books to find a way out of her seemingly hopeless situation.

Suddenly, Anna heard a squeaking noise. She anxiously pointed her flashlight in the direction from which the noise had come. "Oh, just a mouse," Anna calmed down again and had to grin. "Can you believe it?" She told the mouse. "Me, the most powerful witch of all time, trapped like a church mouse in my library."

"What an irony of fate," she continued to think. "I narrowly escaped the fate of being walled in, but now I face a similar fate."

She was about to go on searching for her main witch book, but out of the corner of her eye, she all at once noticed a strange green light where she had just spotted the rodent. "Strange!" Anna thought. Then, a thought flashed through her mind, and a broad smile appeared on her face. "Yes, it must be the same green light emanating from the mountain. There must be a connection from this cave to the light source."

The only problem was that she was not as small as a mouse. She needed a witch's spell that would either make her small or a witch's spell that would make the already existing opening in the rock even larger.

All of a sudden, an idea came to Anna's mind. She began searching her library for a particular book that she had almost forgotten existed. She finally found it and opened it with shaky hands. Anna almost let the book slip out of her grasp when she heard voices dangerously close to her whereabouts.

"I must find the right spell, which I know is in this book before it is too late," she thought as she frantically searched for the spell. The voices approached even closer. She knew she only had a few seconds left to escape before the soldiers would spot her. Suddenly, she found the spell she needed, and in a whisper, she began reciting it hastily:

All forms – death or alive

can be changed by magic

easily – like you dance jive

I don't want to be big like a house

But small like a mouse!

In a flash, Anna shrank down to the size of a mouse, and the shelves in the library loomed like skyscrapers around her. She quickly shrank the witch's book down as well, replaced the cobwebs and spiders with a final spell, and turned off her flashlight. Just in time, too, the soldiers' flashlights soon illuminated the entire area.

"Sorry guys, you're too late!" Anna thought with a grin on her face as she slipped away unnoticed. "Never mess with a witch!" She entered the opening that the mouse had used before, feeling a twinge of fear even though she was a witch. The narrow opening led to a wider shaft, and Anna peered down into it. The greenish light blinded her, and she had to squeeze her eyes shut, dropping her flashlight, which bounced off a rock and disappeared into the depths.

Just as she opened her eyes again, a hideous mouse pushed her, and she fell directly into the beam of light, disappearing into the unknown.

All of a sudden, Pinky felt something fall on him. His first thought was that it was a tiny stone. But then he saw what it really was - Anna in miniature form.

"Anna?" He shouted in astonishment. "Is that really you?"

"Yes, it's me!" Anna replied, just as amazed as the parrot.

"Unfortunately, we don't have time for explanations right now. The whole mountain will implode in two minutes. You must help me shut off this rainbow clock immediately. It seems to be the source of the light that is damaging Rainbow Land," Pinky shrieked desperately. Anna stared at him in disbelief. She had come here from a doomed world and now didn't feel safe here either.

"Please do something! NOW!" Pinky said anxiously.

Finally, Anna responded and tried all the witch spells that came to mind, but none of them had the desired effect. Without the magical stone on the front cover, no appropriate spell showed up on the last empty page.

The last 60 seconds were running out.

"We have to get out of here. Now!" Pinky exclaimed.

Anna looked up. It was a long way up to the mountain's surface if they wanted to climb it. Unfortunately, she had also lost her witch's broom.

Then, all of a sudden, she knew what she had to do: make use of the new function of her rainbow clock.

The last 10 seconds were on. It was too dark for Anna to see the clock, so she had to find the correct button from memory. She had only one chance to do so. She heard her heart pounding. Her hands became sweaty, which didn't make the task any easier. It was their last chance to get out of this rabbit hole.

Just as Anna found the button and pressed it, their time was up.

First, however, Lara's rainbow clock exploded, becoming non-functional forever.

After that, a time tunnel opened, and all the meteorite rocks were transported into the distant future. The last thing to collapse was the whole mountain, as predicted. Tons of heavy rock crashed to the ground, crumbling and compacting the layers beneath - the great cave no longer existed.

The military team set out to investigate the source of the light beams emanating from the gap in the rock. Equipped with a telescopic camera fitted with special photo sensors, they were able to penetrate the source. It turned out that the rainbow time travel clock was partially fused with the meteorite rock, making it more difficult than expected to separate the clock from the greenish shimmering rock with which it seemed to be symbiotic. Nevertheless, it was necessary to separate the clock from the stone if they wished to examine it further.

The team's last attempt at recovery was also the riskiest. They hoped to separate the clock from the rock with a well-regulated explosive charge. However, everything turned out differently than expected. The clock heated up and exploded before the general and his men could recover it. As a result, the light disappeared, making it more difficult to find the source of it. But it was at least as bad that the precious meteorite stone had disappeared mysteriously. The general's plan to compensate for the expensive military mission by selling the meteorite stone has failed. The general would likely have difficulty explaining the big expenditure.

23

IMPLOSION

The next morning, Dr. Schubidou continued to be very enthusiastic about his idea. It was a normal workday for him, just like any other day, and he saw many patients throughout the day. He acted as if he had stumbled upon the idea by chance, but in reality, he had carefully planned out every detail. As he saw each of his patients, he shared a story with them, hoping to sow the seeds of fear in their minds.

"Have you ever heard the legend of the black parrot?" He asked each of them. "It is said that on several nights, the black parrot appears. He is said to carry the soul of the clockmaker monk, who is planning a revenge campaign against the rainbow parrots."

Most of the parrots laughed, thinking it was just a legend they had never heard of before. But Dr. Schubidou went one step further and said, "They say that if you meet him, you have only one chance to escape."

By the time the sick birds left Dr. Schubidou's office, they had already forgotten the story. However, the doctor had other plans in motion. After finishing his workday, he changed into a black robe and picked up a strange device. With that, he headed towards the center of town.

In the center of the rainbow village, there were only a few rainbow parrots left wandering around; most were inside their tree houses where it was warmer. Suddenly, a loud whimper was heard, and many curious pairs of rainbow parrot eyes appeared in the windows of the tree houses. What they saw gave them a good scare. Outside, the huge shadow of a parrot could be seen. "I'm here to get you!" said an eerie voice. The very next moment, this figure had disappeared, but the feathered observers were not at peace. Some of them remembered what the doctor had said earlier, while others who were not ill learned about the legend quickly the next morning and what they had to do to escape.

Those who didn't believe the story went to the doctor, only to be told, "You have to activate the rainbow clock and flee to your old home in the Amazon. Only then will the haunting come to an end."

The final part of the doctor's plan was already underway. Posters were put up everywhere, clearly showing the coordinates of the old home of the rainbow parrots. Many of the parrots decided to leave for the old world before the beginning of the following night, hoping to escape the eerie figure that haunted their village.

The evacuation process was nearly complete; only Paraiso and the staff of his beauty salon were still in the rainbow world. He had fallen asleep during a beauty treatment. When a loud cracking sound had echoed through the air, followed by several smaller cracks, he hadn't noticed it. Even when all of the remaining rainbows collapsed at once, triggering a massive earthquake that damaged most of the rainbow bird houses, he still was not roused. The spa staff had reacted quickly, activating their rainbow clocks at the very last moment to vacate Rainbow Land.

It was only then that Paraiso woke up. He liberated himself from his rainbow tea face mask and looked around, astonished that he was all alone in his luxury spa.

It took just a few seconds for him to realize what had happened. Standing on the highest roof terrace of this magical land, he saw that there wasn't a single rainbow left.

"Without a single rainbow, I cannot flee from here!" Paraiso thought. Desperately, he looked around. He wasn't the kind of character to give up easily. He had to find a solution. When Rainbow Land imploded, this version would certainly be the last one. He knew very well that without him, Paraiso, recreating the land at the end of the rainbow was impossible!

Paraiso's next thought was that he wouldn't be able to survive this Armageddon. "Maybe I can figure out another way to save myself," he thought, "I just have to go deep into my mind and find it." So he began to meditate, stubbornly repeating the following sentence like a mantra: "I must survive! I must survive..."

But he couldn't switch off. He remained far too tense for that. Somewhere in the farthest corner of his brain, he unearthed a faint memory, something that was part of the secret knowledge passed down from one Rainbow Chief to the next. Unfortunately, he could not make head nor tail of this long-buried knowledge. He sighed, and his knees began to hurt from the cold. "Ouch!" He cried.

Desperate, he closed his eyes again and was about to give up. At that moment, his memories became clearer. If what his ancestors had told him was true, he was the only parrot who did not need a rainbow or a rainbow clock to travel to the other world because the rainbow color pattern was mirrored in his feathers. He needed only himself to travel. However, he had never verified the truth of these stories. If they turned out to be wrong, he, Paraiso, would soon be history. Without him, there would be no land at the end of the rainbow.

Then, all at once, without any warning, it happened. The outer shell of the land at the end of the rainbow rushed toward him like a balloon suddenly deflating. Paraiso had finally managed to drift off into a deep meditative state. He perceived himself as seen from the outside, shining brighter than all the rainbows of his homeland. He saw the luminous colors of his plumage spread out beyond his body and begin to whirl around him faster and faster. Then something flashed through his being before there was only darkness - the land at the end of the rainbow had ceased to exist!

24

EXPLOSION

Meanwhile, Lara, Nina, and their parents stood at a safe distance from the towering White Mountain Massif, taking shelter under the highest tree, which Pinky had carefully described to them. Lara's conscience weighed heavily on her.

"We should have helped Pinky," she said in a somber tone.

The four were bracing themselves, expecting an explosion, but they did not know how powerful it would be. Tension ran high, and they followed the countdown intently. Finally, the last few seconds passed, and two different explosions boomed in the distance. The ground beneath their feet shook violently.

"An earthquake!" Cried Lara and Nina, frightened. They watched as the mountain rose, lowered, and collapsed, shrinking by several meters. They waited for Pinky to appear, but he did not show up. None of them wanted to voice their fears, but they all thought the same thing - he probably did not make it.

They stared at the mountain, distraught, hoping against hope that Pinky had made it out in time. In their misery, none of them questioned the fact that they had heard not one but two explosions. Had they taken the time to absorb this fact, then they might have come to realize Lara's rainbow clock had been the source of the first explosion, but they would not have guessed the terrible reason behind the clock's destruction: its connection to the land at the end of the rainbow. When the land of the Rainbow Parrots finally succumbed to its fate, the implosion sent a shockwave through Lara's rainbow clock, causing it to implode, too.

Meanwhile, at the white castle, the earthquake had caused significant damage; one of the walls had completely collapsed. It was so severely damaged that it would be easy for possible attackers to enter unimpeded. The inhabitants of the castle, remembering the group of Vikings they had seen a few days ago, sent out two dozen well-armed men to look for them. The knights soon found their horse tracks and ambushed the Vikings, who had come to recover what they viewed to be the greatest treasure in the history of the Vikings and to transport it away on horseback. The knights lay in wait behind rocks and eventually put the Vikings to flight.

Forty-five minutes after the explosion, Pinky had still not shown up.

"He probably did not survive," Nina said, voicing the fears that everyone had. Lara and Nina had tears on their faces.

Then they saw guards from the castle, and they realized they had to leave. Lara's father spoke up, "All right. Let's get out of here and back home! Luckily, we've found each other again."

"We have to stand close together for it to work," Lara explained, and all four of them hugged. Then she pressed the activation button on Pinky's rainbow clock. The clock hummed and buzzed, rotating like a top before emitting a bright flash of light.

The guards from the castle noticed the strange bright light, but they were too late to apprehend the time-travelers because they had already left this space and time and were on their way back to 2022. They were finally going home.

"What happened?" One of the military personnel, standing beside the steel construction, asked irritably.

"Hm, I think there was a little earthquake," his friend replied.

Anna, still in miniature form, looked up at their faces that seemed to be more than 100 meters away and thought, "They are not giants; I am still tiny!"

Anna and Pinky managed to move away from the two men unnoticed. Then, once they were far enough away not to be heard, Pinky asked, "How did you do that? One moment, we were inside the mountain, and then we were here. We must have moved at the speed of light."

"Not quite," Anna grinned. "I just used a powerful spell that can move people from one place to another. It is called teleportation. But the spell can only work through an object."

Pinky was speechless. He stared at Anna, hoping to find a sign that she was joking, but he wasn't successful. "Which object did you choose?" He asked after a while.

"My rainbow clock," Anna replied, looking proud. "It is now the first rainbow clock to enable time travel, travel to the land at the end of the rainbow, and teleportation."

"Wow!"

"Yes. Nevertheless, the reason for the climate change in our homeland has hopefully come to an end now," Anna frowned. "What are we going to do next?"

"Return to Rainbow Land, of course," answered Pinky immediately.

Anna nodded, satisfied, looking at the witch's book she held in her hands, thinking, "At least there is no need to find the meteorite now." But unfortunately, she was entirely wrong.

25

THE HEARING

When the time travelers manifested themselves again at the White Mountain massif, it was bitterly cold, and snow could be seen in the moonlight. They could hear a nearby humming engine noise.

"We made it!" The little family cheered, but they had rejoiced too soon. The next moment, they were standing in the spotlight of a military helicopter circling above them. "Freeze. Any resistance is futile," blared from the helicopter's loudspeaker. Before they could respond, they were surrounded by soldiers rushing toward them, who then took them into custody.

The soldiers escorted them to a makeshift military camp in front of the mountain massif. Lara looked around several times, taking in the scene. The mountain massif was still as small as it had been after the explosions more than a thousand years ago. Most importantly, there was no greenish pulsating light emanating from the mountain. Men in uniforms were running around everywhere. Lara, Nina, and their parents were taken to a sizable prefabricated building. Inside, people were walking around and sitting behind computer screens. In the company of two soldiers, they finally reached a room. One of the soldiers knocked at the door.

"Come in!" Shouted a male voice. Entering the room, the family members saw a man with grey hair and sharp features sitting in a swivel chair. "Let me introduce myself. My name is Jeffrey Andersson. I am a highly decorated 4-star general of the Swedish Army. I earned my stars through undertaking numerous, sometimes very dangerous, missions abroad."

At that moment, the door opened, and a man the sisters instantly recognized entered the room. It was Gunnar. The girls were surprised at first, but then it became clear to them why he was here. Gunnar was an expert in weather phenomena like the Northern Lights, and the green light coming out of the mountain must have seemed to be something similar. No wonder that they had come across Gunnar, the only specialist of this kind at the moment in this part of Sweden.

"You know each other?" The general asked in surprise when he noticed the look on Gunnar's and the girls' faces.

"Those are the missing girls I told you about," Gunnar confirmed, nodding.

"And the adults?" The general asked, addressing the girls. "Are those your parents?"

Lara and Nina nodded.

"Well, then, please tell us what has happened to you!" The grey-haired man urged them.

They now had little choice but to reveal something of their adventure. Lara hesitated, thinking about what Gunnar might have told the general. Gunnar had indeed informed the general about their missing parents. Lara decided to stay as near as possible to the truth.

"We came here because we suspected that the greenish light emanating from this mountain might have had something to do with the disappearance of our parents," Lara explained. "We read in the newspaper about a similar occurrence at a geological museum where the same kind of light was observed. Having arrived at the mountain, we climbed towards the source of the light. However, we tripped and fell into a crevice, which led us to a large cave. As we walked further into the cave, we heard familiar voices and eventually found our missing parents." Lara stopped speaking, realizing she had almost revealed the existence of her secret rainbow clock to the senior military officer, which could potentially put Rainbow Land in danger.

"Go on, tell us what happened," the general urged.

"That was all. When we came out of the cave, we could no longer see the green light, but we didn't care anymore. We had found what we were looking for - our parents. On our way down the slope, we were caught by your men," Lara said, leaving out anything related to her rainbow clock.

"And why has it taken so long for you to get out of the mountain?"

"We got lost in the natural underground tunnel system. It took us a while to find our way out!"

"Did you come into contact with the light?" The general asked curiously.

"No," Lara replied, shaking her head.

The general turned to the parents. "Is it true what your daughters have just reported? Did it really happen that way?"

"Yes, it is true. We were reunited with our daughters in the cave," the girls' father confirmed.

Suddenly, there was a knock on the office door, and Jeff, the leader of the drilling team, entered, wanting to speak urgently with the general. The general excused himself, and Jeff showed him a transparent container as large as a shoebox containing a metal structure fused to a fist-sized lump of rock.

"That's the object that emitted the light," Jeff explained. "Or rather, what's left of it."

"Are you kidding?" The general replied, disappointed.

"Unfortunately not. But we're not quite sure if this fusion was the result of the dynamite we used. We think it may not be."

"I'm afraid I don't quite follow you," the general responded.

"Though the object is completely destroyed, we could still find out some things about it, like the material it is made from - a combination of a metal alloy and stone. We at first assumed this fusing of metal and stone was a result of the dynamite we used to extract it, but here comes the unbelievable part: it seems that this object had been melted with the stone like this for a very long time."

The general had a sudden bad feeling as if he had an inkling of what was about to come.

"I am talking about several hundred years. There is no possibility of error. We have examined it a second and even a third time and have always come to the same conclusion," Jeff continued.

The general felt dizzy and had to sit down immediately. "Is that all you've found out?" he asked in a desperate voice.

"Yes, more or less. I'm sorry!" Jeff replied.

The highly decorated general tried to compose himself before turning back to the little family and saying, "Where were we?" He tried to continue the conversation, but before anyone could answer, he remembered, "Oh, yes. You told me about what you experienced."

The general's gaze swung back and forth between the parents and children and Gunnar. The girls' story just didn't add up. The general had seen the light cause dead and living objects to disappear. If this had happened to the girls, it would have been nice to know how they made it back. It would help him to solve the mystery of the mysterious light. The discovery of this light was a miracle as big as finding the fountain of youth.

He had expected much more from this tale, at least something to justify his stay here and the enormous expenses racked up. Maybe something surprising about the unusually hard stone in the depths of the mountain? The military leader sighed to himself as Lara began to nod her head firmly.

"That is right. That's exactly how it happened." Then, she expertly changed the subject. "What I'd like to know is why you are here."

Nina looked at her as if to say, "Can't we just go home?"

The general cleared his throat, wondering whether he was allowed to tell the girls and their parents anything at all and, if so, what he should reveal. After all, the secret project had failed and was therefore over, so hiding its findings was likely unnecessary. He decided to share what he had found out so far.

"After being informed by Gunnar that you had suddenly disappeared off the face of the earth at the point where the green light emerged from the mountain, I declared the area around the white mountain massif a restricted military zone. We examined the light more closely and found that it had some amazing abilities. It can make objects and living beings invisible."

"Really?" The girls said in false wonderment.

"We started and tried to drill to the light source, but the drill bit ran hot and broke off," the general explained. "So, we blasted our way through. Unfortunately, this may have damaged the light source because we only managed to recover a large piece of corroded metal. And when I say damaged, I mean it. Our experts examined it in detail and were able to find out very little about it. However..."

"What?" The girls immediately inquired. They had to know how much these people had found out about Lara's clock if they were to keep the land at the end of the rainbow a secret.

"The fascinating part began…" the high-ranking soldier continued, dragging out his remarks without taking his eyes off the girls sitting opposite him, "…with the analysis."

"What did you find out?" Asked Nina, joining the conversation.

"You don't know the answer?" The general asked suspiciously.

Lara looked away furtively. She knew the general suspected she and Nina knew more about the mysterious green light than they had told him.

"No," the girls replied.

The general heaved a loud sigh. His interrogation was having little success.

"The recovered device was mostly destroyed, but it appeared to have exploded a long time ago, not recently," the general explained.

"But what happened next?" Lara asked. "Could you find out more about the strange object that might have been the light source?"

"Unfortunately, no," the general admitted. "According to our experts, repairing it is impossible because something destroyed its essential components. It would only be possible with a construction manual, but we don't have one."

"Too bad," Lara fibbed, relieved that the land at the end of the rainbow's secret remained intact.

"But we had made another discovery inside the mountain before that," he continued. "We found strange glowing rocks in a cave that we wanted to investigate."

"And…?" Nina asked eagerly.

"Well, that's where the problem lies," the general replied, looking visibly embarrassed. "Someone managed to steal the rocks from right under our noses, even though we had the entire mountain guarded permanently."

"Someone stole them?" The girls' father said.

"Yes," the general confirmed. "There were more rocks in the cave, and we wanted to take some for examination."

He watched the girls and their parents carefully. They appeared to be wide-eyed with surprise.

"And then what happened?" Lara asked curiously.

"Well, this part is hard to believe," the general said. "The cave disappeared as if by magic, along with the mysteriously glowing rocks."

His listeners held their breath, and tension filled the room.

"These strange occurrences can be attributed to only one thing," the general said, taking a deep puff from his cigar, "the existence of aliens."

The room fell silent as everyone tried to process what they had just heard. The general's statement was met with looks of disbelief.

"Pardon? Could you please repeat that one more time?" Lara's father finally spoke up.

"You mean this place is something like the Swedish Area 51?" Gunnar asked incredulously.

The general's facial expression left no doubt that he meant what he had just said.

"So, they have nothing more than a few, well, let's say, very far-fetched theories," Lara thought to herself, stifling a smile.

"Can we finally go home?" Nina asked wearily.

"Not yet!" The general replied sternly, looking at the time travelers. "What I have just told you falls under the heading of military secrecy. If any of it gets out to the public, each of you will face severe punishment."

At the last sentence, the listeners gulped, knowing that possessing military secrets came with a great deal of responsibility.

26

THE NEW CREATION

Canaima Lagoon, South America, ancient home of the rainbow parrots.

It smelled like scorched earth, the acrid odor of destruction permeating the air. The once-lush rainforest had been reduced to smoldering ruins by a sea of flames, extinguished only by the onset of the rainy season.

"This is a disaster!" Grumbled the doctor, staring in disbelief at the still-steaming remains of the forest.

This part of the rainforest had recently been densely populated with numerous animal species, all of whom had lost their habitat. Even the former enemies of the Rainbow People must have fled to another place, as the devastation was too great to survive.

With their enemies gone, this could have been an opportunity for the Rainbow Parrots to re-establish their life here, but with the forest destroyed, a new beginning in this place was definitely out of the question.

The Rainbow Land doctor was still worried because he had been waiting for Paraiso's return for a while. The waiting had already lasted too long, in his opinion. The land at the end of the rainbow must already have perished.

With every passing second when Paraiso did not show up, he became more anxious about the possibility of Paraiso not having made it in time. And this would be a tragedy, as Paraiso was the only one capable of recreating their magical world. Only a real Chief with all the colors of the rainbow in his plumage could produce the necessary energy to generate a new country.

Even if Anna were to show up with the witch book and its embedded magical stone, a recreation would not be possible without Paraiso. Paraiso also needed the building instructions, illustrated in the witch book, to make it happen. Although Paraiso had promised to write down the creation instructions, he had postponed this due to his important beauty sessions, forgetting about it in the process.

To make matters worse, parrots kept bombarding him with questions about Paraiso, which he couldn't answer. This only increased the feeling of despair spreading among all of them.

"The evacuation was a farce," Dr. Schubidou thought in frustration. He now had to admit that he had initially underestimated Paraiso's abilities to lead this magical land. Somehow, it seemed to him that Paraiso had even foreseen the disaster waiting for them in their old home.

A screeching rainbow parrot, who had flown up in front of him, abruptly brought him back to his senses. The parrot had sustained a minor burn on its upper body, some of its feathers now blackened. Dr. Schubidou quickly applied one of his homemade healing creams to alleviate the discomfort.

Three days had passed since Anna's departure from the land at the end of the rainbow. How could she be so late? Had something happened to her? Dr. Schubidou pondered over it, but these thoughts didn't take him any further. It took a lot of strength for him to push aside the thought that Anna might have failed in her endeavor as well. He could not continue this way indefinitely. At some point, he would have to tell the parrot people the truth. Perplexed, he scratched his feathered chin. He knew that it was essential to find a suitable place where his unique species could survive. Then, he could at least offer an end to their misery.

He turned his gaze away from the remnants of the once-proud rainforest to the sky, searching for the ideas he so desperately needed right now.

At first, he perceived only the seemingly endless blue of the sky. But then, a beautiful double rainbow forming on the horizon pushed its way into his field of vision. The vibrant colors of the rainbow contrasted with the clear blue sky, creating a breathtaking sight.

As the rainbow began to shrink, the colors seemed to intensify. Suddenly, it detached itself from the sky and came directly towards him. He could not take his eyes off it. Then, he finally saw what was coming towards him. It was Paraiso, the leader of the rainbow parrots. Thick tears of joy rolled down Dr. Schubidou's cheeks.

"Paraiso is coming!" He shouted enthusiastically, and the other rainbow parrots flocked to give their leader a special welcome. Thunderous applause greeted Paraiso. He was so moved that he even flew an extra round before landing on the still-steaming ground and immediately burning the soles of his feet.

"Why didn't anyone warn me about this!" He then grumpily complained to his subjects.

Dr. Schubidou described to him what had happened. Paraiso immediately grasped the problem. They needed a new home, and quickly. But without the witch book, it was not going to be possible.

All the rainbow parrots were now in South America, in the place where they had lived more than 500 years ago. Paraiso told the others about the last moments of the rainbow world. He had survived only by an incredible amount of luck. The rainbow parrots gathered around him, listening intently to his every word.

Paraiso did not hesitate another moment but immediately met with the council of the wisest rainbow parrots. They were to discuss how best to proceed. The panel decided to stay here for the time being. If the rescue team that was sent out had been successful, they would surely return with the book. By leaving this place too early, they would certainly miss each other.

So they started to build a parrot camp here. Fortunately, there were still a few trees that the fire had not destroyed. The camp was situated in a lush green area, surrounded by towering trees and cascading waterfalls.

The following day, Paraiso woke up. He was in a terrible mood because he had to skip the beauty treatments essential for him. He found a basin formed by some large stones in which to check his appearance in the still water. He looked terrible! Simply terrible. But then, all of a sudden, a large, heavy object fell into the water and splashed him so badly that he looked more like a drenched poodle than a parrot. The rainbow parrots, who had witnessed this event, shrieked with glee.

Paraiso shook his water-logged head. What was that? Then, out of the water emerged a parrot he knew. It was Pinky.

"I know, I know I shouldn't have taken the broom. I should have flown with my own wings, but that young lady talked me into it." Pinky glanced in the direction of the aforementioned young lady, who turned out to be none other than Anna, who had just landed her broom and was laughing out loud.

"I'm sorry, Pinky!" Apologized Anna. "I shouldn't have taken such a tight turn."

"Yeah, yeah, it's okay," Pinky accepted the apology. "Your broom was going too fast for sudden maneuvers."

"Do you have the witch book?" The doctor, bursting with curiosity, asked them.

"Yes, but we don't need it any longer because the light source that caused the climate in Rainbow Land to change has been destroyed," Anna replied.

"That may be true, but the land at the end of the rainbow no longer exists," the doctor explained. "That's why we need your book to create a new one."

"Well, er, there is a slight problem," Anna replied hesitantly. "I have the book but not the magic stone. It vanished after the museum burglary."

Paraiso and Dr. Schubidou stared at her, unable to believe it.

"But it's is not such a big problem as I can just time travel and retrieve the stone before it was stolen," Anna proposed.

"Maybe there is another possibility," Pinky interrupted them. "All we need is a meteorite, right?"

The others nodded.

"Maybe I have one!" Pinky claimed with a grin.

"Come on! This is not the time for jokes," Anna scolded.

"Ok, let me explain. How did Lara and Nina's parents go back in time?"

"They must have had a meteorite," Anna replied.

"Yes, exactly the same meteorite that was part of your ring, Anna. This ring was given to…"

"The parents of Lara and Nina!" Anna cut in. "In that case, we have to contact them and…"

"No, we don't have to," Pinky interrupted. "Lara gave the ring to me so I could save our rainbow land." Pinky held the ring in his claws for everyone to see. Lara had fastened it to his leg just before he went on his mission to retrieve her rainbow clock.

Shivering a little, they put the stone from the ring in its place on the front cover of the book. Then something magical happened. An additional page appeared at the end of the book.

"We have to try it to see if it still works," Paraiso suggested enthusiastically.

Soon, Paraiso was standing on a large rock by the waterfall, wearing Dr. Schubidou's goggles. The other rainbow parrots gathered around him, some sitting just a few meters away from him on the ground. Others found a rock outcrop beside the waterfall. The latter had the best view of the ongoing ceremony.

The last page of the witch book was open.

Without hesitation, Paraiso read the spell, now visible, to restore the rainbow land, his tone tense:

"Create a new world quickly with

many rainbows bright

and a river in the middle of the country

for the people of parrots, please!"

When he read the last sentence of the spell, it started to rain from one big black cloud right above him. Paraiso, a majestic phoenix with fiery feathers, flinched as the cold raindrops pelted his iridescent plumage. Fear gripped him, for he knew that any disruption in the process of creation could have dire consequences.

He glanced at the ancient tome in his talons, hoping for a solution. As if in response, the book began to glow with an ethereal light, and a single word on the page changed before his eyes. The word "sea" had been added to the incantation, subtly altering its meaning and purpose.

"...with a river and a sea in the middle of the land..."

Therefore, Paraiso did not notice the mistake in the spell immediately. He read the entire incantation, now altered from its original form. But as soon as he finished, he recognized the error. Unfortunately, it was already too late for him to make any improvements.

As the other parrots watched, something extraordinary occurred. A magnificent rainbow appeared just above the waterfall, a few meters above Paraiso. Suddenly, all the greenery and animals that had disappeared during the wildfire reappeared. The parrots saw hundreds of smaller birds resembling bats land on nearby rocks. It seemed as if they had come to celebrate the rainbow parrots' creation of a new home at the end of the rainbow.

First was Pinky, and then Paraiso traveled to the newly created land to verify that it had worked. Overjoyed, they returned to announce the news that they had succeeded to all the other rainbow parrots. The birds sang with joy as they, one by one, used their rainbow clocks and the newly formed rainbow to travel to their new home.

Soon, the rainbow parrots had entirely returned to their newly created home. All the magic colors had come back, even the countless rainbows and their hometown, the rainbow village, as if nothing had ever happened. From the perspective of the rainbow parrots, Paraiso's actions had once again made him the most important rainbow parrot in the country. He felt their affection and enjoyed it.

27

A HAPPY END?

The creation of the new Rainbow Land was celebrated extensively, with a holiday specially introduced for this purpose. Lara, Nina, and Anna, along with the entire Rainbow Parrot community, celebrated their joint success as if in a frenzy. But the new land looked different. A small sea had been created, explained by the fact that a different stone than the original one had been inserted in the book cover, leading to this change.

However, for Lara and Nina, there were still a few unresolved issues. "But I don't understand why the clock could send us back in time and spoil the weather for everyone in Rainbow Land if it was broken!" Asked Lara, confused.

"Oh, I don't think the clock was defective, but rather that it wasn't working quite right. The implosion of Rainbow Land must have caused an energy recoil that destroyed the essential components of the clock. This already destroyed clock was then recovered and examined by the military," explained Dr. Schubidou.

"So we were lucky Rainbow Land imploded when it did? Otherwise, the military would have gained knowledge of its existence," Nina reasoned.

"Yes, you could say that!" Nodded the doctor. "No one knows if Rainbow Land would have remained a haven for the Rainbow Parrot people in the future. I guess we'll never know." The doctor's words made everyone except Lara pleased. She was still embarrassed that she had caused the disaster by dropping the clock.

Pinky, noticing Lara's depression, tried to cheer her up. "But there's something good about the whole thing, even if you don't see it right away," he said.

"Really? What?" Asked Lara in surprise.

"Well, they realized the danger posed by the meteorite rock. The whole area is now a restricted military zone. This is the only way to prevent anything else coming into contact with the meteorite surface in the future, leading to new, serious consequences," Pinky explained.

"Tom, the man from the far future, said something about there being information stored in the meteorite rock," Lara said. "But unfortunately, he didn't get to tell us more about it because we were interrupted."

"Yes, that's right," Nina added. "Unfortunately, now we won't know what information the stone had in it."

"I took another close look at the stone on the cover of the witch book and examined it with my latest photometer. With it, I succeeded in getting probably the last secret out of this strange stone," said the doctor.

"Well?" The girls asked eagerly.

"Well, what we knew from previous research was that there was information in the meteorite that could cause those who came in contact with it for an extended period to become power-hungry. However, we did not know why this was. But based on new findings, a new, shocking picture emerges," the doctor said, taking a brief pause.

"Brace yourselves! This meteorite stone contains invaluable information about what triggers climate change and how to counteract it. For all we now know, this was mistakenly delivered to the land at the end of the rainbow by the fusion of Lara's clock with the mountain's meteorite rock, which used the greenish band of light as a means of transportation. There, it caused the cooling effect necessary for combatting manmade climate change," the doctor finished with a dramatic tone.

"Excuse me?" Lara asked in disbelief. "Are you saying that the winter weather was just an accident?"

"Yes, it was exactly that," nodded Dr. Schubidou. "You got it!"

"This means that the hunger for power generated by the meteorite is related to saving the climate because people who want to make a difference in this regard must have the ability to do so, right?" Lara asked for confirmation.

"Yes, that's exactly right," the doctor agreed with her. "I couldn't have put it much better myself."

Pinky interjected, "But how did you know, Lara, that the stone embedded in the ring was the same type of stone as the meteorite? The stone in the ring looked different to the meteorite stone."

"Well, I didn't know at first," Lara replied with a grin. "The stone in the ring had, of course, been processed to look more beautiful than the rest of the meteorite stone. When we were reunited with our parents and our mom handed the ring to me, it happened to slip from her grasp. That was when I noticed that the stone in the ring emitted a greenish light when it came into contact with the floor of the cave. Only then did I know."

Everyone was satisfied with the explanation except for Anna, who continued to scowl.

"What's wrong?" Asked Nina, noticing Anna's expression.

"Nothing. I think I need a break from all the disasters," Anna replied.

"Well, then move in with us. There's plenty of room in the guest room," said Lara, who had overheard the conversation.

"Thank you, that's great!" Anna said enthusiastically, beaming with joy.

"We'd be honored to host such a famous witch," Lara returned.

A few days later, Anna grinned with excitement as she looked around the cozy living room of Lara and Nina's Swedish wooden house. She was moving in with them today, and they had assigned her a place in the comfortably furnished guest room. Not only did living together work out well, but the family's family tree also got a long overdue update. Besides Anna's picture, one could now find a more detailed description of her.

Not long after Anna had settled in, a letter fluttered into the mailbox. It was addressed to Anna and came directly from a far-off country at the rainbow's end, as evidenced by the colorful stamp.

Anna opened the letter in amazement, and her eyes scanned the page as she read it aloud to Lara and Nina.

Dear Anna,

The High Parrot Council has met again and decided that the Witch Book must be returned immediately to the land at the end of the rainbow. The book is dangerous but benefits more than makeup for the possible danger.

I would appreciate it if you could return to your newfound homeland of choice. Without your magical abilities, we probably would not have managed to save our land. The high parrot council has decided that the witch's book must return to a chest in the cave behind the waterfall. Not far from this cave, we have had a new home built for you, from which you can enjoy a beautiful view of the waterfall. In return, we ask you to guard the treasure hidden behind the waterfall.

You have time to think about this step.

With rainbow greetings

Paraiso

After reading the letter aloud, Anna had a strong feeling for the very first time that she was genuinely welcome in the home of the rainbow parrot people.

A thick tear ran down Anna's cheek as she told Lara and Nina about her decision.

"I have enjoyed my stay with you very much. But I think I'm drawn back to the land of rainbow parrots. This wasn't an easy decision to make," she said with a heavy heart.

One day, an envelope containing numerous pictures taken with a cell phone camera and printed out landed in the police mailbox. It was passed to the police officer once

One day, an envelope containing numerous pictures taken with a cell phone camera and printed out landed in the police mailbox. It was passed to the police officer once

tasked with investigating the museum burglary. This policeman opened the envelope, feeling curious but a little apprehensive, took out the letter inside, and began to read:

Hello,

I called your office very early this morning, and they told me that they still haven't found the thief who stole the precious meteorite from the museum - but I have.

The pupils of the policeman reading the letter widened in surprise.

The letter continued: *I want to inform you that my suspicion was correct. The man caught by the surveillance cameras a few days*

The officer stumbled. He was now annoyed that he had not believed Ed and followed up his lead. However, in his eyes, this was because the night watchman had acted like a know-it-all.

He reached across his cluttered desk for his phone. "Quickly! Send a strike team to the following marina..." he announced urgently.

But the police arrived too late. They couldn't find the sailing yacht with the name Sea Breeze, as it had already departed for the Caribbean. Moreover, there was no entry for the sailboat in the register book of the marina.

Gordon had changed the name of his yacht instantly upon arrival and had set sail for his long-awaited destination - the Caribbean. The marina was bustling with activity as other boaters prepared for their own voyages, adding to the confusion and providing cover for Gordon's getaway.

Tom had dropped Gordon off at the base of the mountain range, where they were met by a soldier whose form Tom quickly adopted so as to blend in with the surroundings. Tom was able to leave the restricted zone with Gordon as his supposed prisoner. Afterwards, Tom continued on to the future while Gordon finally arrived back on his luxury boat. With that, he did what he had planned all along. He sailed to the Caribbean and retired there. His time as a thief was over once and for all.

In the weeks that followed, time seemed to blur together for Nina. But one day, her mother handed her the mail with a cheerful smile.

"Nina, there's a letter for you," she said, holding out an envelope.

Nina's heart fluttered as she read the sender's name: it was the Publisher who had initiated the photo contest. With trembling hands, she tore open the envelope and began to read the letter. As she read, her eyes widened, and her pupils grew larger with each passing sentence.

Dear Nina,

Congratulations!!! We are happy to inform you that you have won this year's photo contest.

Nina had to take a seat because she was so overwhelmed. The envelope also contained the picture that Nina had sent to the photo competition. It showed a greenish light that looked like the Northern Lights, but next to it were several rainbows, which was an unusual thing. The shot was unique because Nina had taken it in Rainbow Land, intending to ask Gunnar about the light phenomenon.

On Saturday, overjoyed and full of pride, Nina accepted first prize:

a set of professional camera equipment and had her photograph taken for the daily newspaper.

Lara was glad that the Witch Book had found its final place in Rainbow Land, just as the Clock Monk had wanted from the beginning. Lara now concluded that he had reckoned very well with the fact that such a paradisiacal world could come under threat in the future. With the witch book, the Rainbow Parrots would have had an easier time saving their world. But then, the paths of Lara and Pinky would never have crossed, and the two sisters would never have found out that this magical world even existed. Without this discovery, the story of the Rainbow Parrots would never have been put to paper.

THE END